CW01210799

CLASSIC LITERATURE BOOKS

THE FILM MYSTERY

ARTHUR B. REEVE

Table of Contents

THE FILM MYSTERY

I

A CAMERA CRIME

"Camera!"

Kennedy and I had been hastily summoned from his laboratory in the city by District-Attorney Mackay, and now stood in the luxurious, ornate library in the country home of Emery Phelps, the banker, at Tarrytown.

"Camera!—you know the call when the director is ready to shoot a scene of a picture?—well—at the moment it was given and the first and second camera men began to grind—she crumpled—sank to the floor—unconscious!"

Hot and excited, Mackay endeavored to reenact his case for us with all the histrionic ability of a popular prosecutor before a jury.

"There's where she dropped—they carried her over here to this davenport—sent for Doctor Blake—but he couldn't do a thing for her. She died—just as you see her. Blake thought the matter so serious, so alarming, that he advised an immediate investigation. That's why I called you so urgently."

Before us lay the body of the girl, remarkably beautiful even as she lay motionless in death. Her masses of golden hair, disheveled, added to the soft contours of her features. Her wonderfully large blue-gray eyes with their rare gift for delicate shades of expression were closed, but long curling lashes swept her cheeks still and it was hard to believe that this was anything more than sleep.

It was inconceivable that Stella Lamar, idol of the screen, beloved of millions, could have been taken from the world which worshiped her.

I felt keenly for the district attorney. He was a portly little man of the sort prone to emphasize his own importance and so, true to type, he had been upset completely by a case of genuine magnitude. It was as though visiting royalty had dropped dead within his jurisdiction.

I doubt whether the assassination of a McKinley or a Lincoln could have unsettled him as much, because in such an event he would have had the whole weight of the Federal government behind him. There was no question but that Stella Lamar enjoyed a country-wide popularity known by few of our Presidents. Her sudden death was a national tragedy.

Apparently Mackay had appealed to Kennedy the moment he learned the identity of Stella, the moment he realized there was any question about the circumstances surrounding the affair. Over the telephone the little man had been almost incoherent. He had heard of Kennedy's work and was feverishly anxious to enlist his aid, at any price.

All we knew as we took the train on the New York Central was that Stella was playing a part in a picture to be called "The Black Terror," that the producer was Manton Pictures, Incorporated, and that she had dropped dead suddenly and without warning in the middle of a scene being photographed in the library at the home of Emery Phelps.

I was singularly elated at the thought of accompanying Kennedy on this particular case. It was not that the tragic end of a film star whose work I had learned to love was not horrible to me, but rather because, for once, I thought Kennedy actually confronted a situation where his knowledge of a given angle of life was hardly sufficient for his usual analysis of the facts involved.

"Walter," he had exclaimed, as I burst into the laboratory in response to a hurried message, "here's where I need your help. You know all about moving pictures, so—if you'll phone your city editor and ask him to let you cover a case for the Star we'll just about catch a train at One Hundred and Twenty-fifth Street."

Because the film world had fascinated me always I had made a point of being posted on its people and their activities. I remembered the very first appearance of Stella Lamar back in the days of General Film, when pictures were either Licensed or Independent, when only two companies manufactured worth-while screen dramas, when any subject longer than a reel had to be of rare excellence, such as the art films imported from France for the Licensed program. In those days, Stella rose rapidly to prominence. Her large wistful eyes had set the hearts of many of us to beating at staccato rate.

Then came Lloyd Manton, her present manager, and the first of a new type of business man to enter the picture field. Manton was essentially a promoter. His predecessors had been men carried to success by the growth of the new art. Old Pop Belman, for instance, had been a fifth-rate oculist who rented and sold stereopticons as a side line. With blind luck he had grasped the possibilities of Edison's new invention. Just before the break-up of General Film he had become many times a millionaire and it was then that he had sent a wave of laughter over the entire country by an actual cable to William Shakespeare, address London, asking for all screen rights to the plays written by that gentleman.

Manton represented a secondary phase in film finance. Continent Films, his first corporation, was a stockjobbing concern. Grasping the immense popularity of Stella Lamar, he had coaxed her away from the old studio out in Flatbush where all her early successes had been photographed. With the magic of her name he sold thousands of shares of stock to a public already fed up on the stories of the fortunes to be made in moving pictures. When much of the money so raised had been dissipated, when Continent's quotation on the curb sank to an infinitesimal fraction, then it developed that Stella's contract was with Manton personally. Manton Pictures, Incorporated, was formed to exploit her. The stock of this company was not offered to outside investors.

Stella's popularity had in no way suffered from the business methods of her manager. Manton, at the least, had displayed rare foresight in his estimation of public taste. Except for a few attempts with established stage favorites, photographed generally in screen versions of theatrical classics and backed by affiliations with the producers of the legitimate stage, Continent Films was the first concern to make the five-reel feature. Stella, as a Continent player, was the very first feature star. Under the banner of Manton Pictures, she had never surrendered her position of pre-eminence.

Also, scandal somehow had failed to touch her. Those initiated to the inner gossip of the film world, like myself, were under no illusions. The relations between Stella and Manton were an open secret. Yet the picture fans, in their blind worship, believed her to be as they saw her upon the screen. To them the wide and wistful innocence of her remarkably large eyes could not be anything but genuine. The artlessness of the soft curves of her mouth was proof to them of the reality of an ingenuous and very girlish personality.

Even her divorce had helped rather than harmed her. It seemed irony to me that she should have obtained the decree instead of her husband, and in New York, too, where the only grounds are unfaithfulness. The testimony in the case had been sealed so that no one knew whom she had named as corespondent. At the time, I wondered what pressure had been exerted upon Millard to prevent the filing of a cross suit. Surely he should have been able to substantiate the rumors of her association with Lloyd Manton.

Lawrence Millard, author and playwright and finally scenario writer, had been as much responsible for the success of his wife as Manton, and in a much less spectacular way. It was Millard who had written her first great Continent success, who had developed the peculiar type of story best suited for her, back in the early days of the one reel and General Film.

It is commonly known in picture circles that an actress who screens well, even if she is only a moderately good artist, can be made a star with one or two or three good stories and that, conversely, a star may be ruined by a succession of badly written or badly produced vehicles. Those of us not blinded by an idolatrous worship for the girl condemned her severely for throwing her husband aside at the height of her success. The public displayed their sympathy for her by a burst of renewed interest. The receipts at the box office whenever her films were shown probably delighted both Manton and Stella herself.

I had wondered, as Kennedy and I occupied a seat in the train, and as he left me to my thoughts, whether there could be any connection between the tragedy and the divorce. The decree, I knew, was not yet final. Could it be possible that Millard was unwilling, after all, to surrender her? Could he prefer deliberate murder to granting her her freedom? I was compelled to drop that line of thought, since it offered no explanation of his previous failure to contest her suit or to start counter action.

Then my reflections had strayed away from Kennedy's sphere, the solving of the mystery, to my own, the news value of her death and the events following. The Star, as always, had been only too glad to assign me to any case where Craig Kennedy was concerned; my phone message to the city editor, the first intimation to any New York paper of Stella's death, already had resulted without doubt in scare heads and an extra edition.

The thought of the prominence given the personal affairs of picture players and theatrical folk had disgusted me.

There are stars against whom there is not the slightest breath of gossip, even among the studio scandal-mongers. Any number of girls and men go about their work sanely and seriously, concerned in nothing but their success and the pursuit of normal pleasures. As a matter of fact it had struck me on the train that this was about the first time Craig Kennedy had ever been called in upon a case even remotely connected with the picture field. I knew he would be confronted with a tangled skein of idle talk, from everybody, about everybody, and mostly without justification. I hoped he would not fall into the popular error of assuming all film players bad, all studios schools of immorality. I was glad I was able to accompany him on that account.

The arrival at Tarrytown had ended my reflections, and Kennedy's—whatever they may have been. Mackay himself had met us at the station and with a few words, to cover his nervousness, had whisked us out to the house.

As we approached, Kennedy had taken quick note of the surroundings, the location of the home itself, the arrangement of the grounds. There was a spreading lawn on all four sides, unbroken by plant or bush or tree—sheer prodigality of space, the better to display a rambling but most artistic pile of gray granite. Masking the road and the adjoining grounds was thick, impenetrable shrubbery, a ring of miniature forest land about the estate. There was a garage, set back, and tennis courts, and a practice golf green. In the center of a garden in a far corner a summerhouse was placed so as to reflect itself in the surface of a glistening swimming pool.

As we pulled up under the porte-cochere Emery Phelps, the banker, greeted us. Perhaps it was my imagination, but it seemed to me that there was a repressed animosity in his manner, as though he resented the intrusion of Kennedy and myself, yet felt powerless to prevent it. In contrast to his manner was the cordiality of Lloyd Manton, just inside the door. Manton was childishly eager in his welcome, so much so that I was able to detect a shade of suspicion in Kennedy's face.

The others of the company were clustered in the living room, through which we passed to reach the library. I found small opportunity to study them in the rather dim light. Mackay beckoned to a man standing in a window, presenting him to Kennedy as Doctor Blake. Then we entered the long paneled chamber which had been the scene of the tragedy.

Now I stood, rather awed, with the motionless figure of Stella Lamar before me in her last pitiable close-up. For I have never lost the sense of solemnity on entering the room of a tragedy, in spite of the long association I have had with Kennedy in the scientific detection of crime. Particularly did I have the feeling in this case. The death of a man is tragic, but I know nothing more affecting than the sudden and violent death of a beautiful woman—unless it be that of a child.

I recalled a glimpse of Stella as I had seen her in her most recent release, as the diaphragm opened on her receiving a box of chocolates, sent by her lover, and playfully feeding one of them to her beautiful collie, "Laddie," as he romped about upon a divan and almost smothered her with affection. The vivacity and charm of the scene were in sad contrast with what lay before me.

As I looked more carefully I saw now that her full, well-rounded face was contorted with either pain or fear—perhaps both. Even through the make-up one could see that her face was blotched and swollen. Also, the muscles were contorted; the eyes looked as if they might be bulging under the lids; and there was a bluish tinge to her skin. Evidently death had come quickly, but it had not been painless.

"Even the coroner has not disturbed the body," Mackay hastened to explain to Kennedy. "The players, the camera men, all were sent out of the room the moment Doctor Blake was certain something more than a natural cause lay behind her death. Mr. Phelps telephoned to me, and upon my arrival I ordered the doors and windows closed, posted my deputies to prevent any interference with anything in the room, left my instructions that everyone was to be detained, then got in touch with you as quickly as I could."

Kennedy turned to him. Something in the tone of his voice showed that he meant his compliment. "I'm glad, Mackay, to be called in by some one who knows enough not to destroy evidence; who realizes that perhaps the slightest disarrangement of a rug, for instance, may be the only clue to a murder. It's—it's rare!"

The little district attorney beamed. If he had found it necessary to walk across the floor just then he would have strutted. I smiled because I wanted Kennedy to show again his marvelous skill in tracing a crime to its perpetrator. I was anxious that nothing should be done to hamper him.

II

THE TINY SCRATCH

Kennedy, before his own examination of the body, turned to Doctor Blake. "Tell me just what you found when you arrived," he directed.

The physician, whose practice embraced most of the wealthy families in and around Tarrytown, was an unusually tall, iron-gray-haired man of evident competency. It was very plain that he resented his unavoidable connection with the case.

"She was still alive," he responded, thoughtfully, "although breathing with difficulty. Nearly everyone had clustered about her, so that she was getting little air, and the room was stuffy from the lights they had been using in taking the scene. They told me she dropped unconscious and that they couldn't revive her, but at first it did not occur to me that it might be serious. I thought perhaps the heat—"

"You saw nothing suspicious," interrupted Kennedy, "nothing in the actions or manner of anyone in the room?"

"No, when I first entered I didn't suspect anything out of the way. I had them send everyone into the next room, except Manton and Phelps, and had the doors and windows thrown open to give her air. Then when I examined her I detected what seemed to me to be both a muscular and nervous paralysis, which by that time had proceeded pretty far. As I touched her she opened her eyes, but she was unable to speak. She was breathing with difficulty; her heart action was weakening so rapidly that I had little opportunity to apply restorative measures."

"What do you think caused the death?"

"So far, I can make no satisfactory explanation." The doctor shrugged his shoulders very slightly. "That is why I advised an immediate investigation. I did not care to write a death certificate."

"You have no hypothesis?"

"If she died from any natural organic disorder, the signs were lacking by which I could trace it. Everything indicates the opposite, however. It would be hard for me to say whether the paralysis of respiration or of the heart actually caused her death. If it was due to poison—Well, to me the whole affair is shrouded in mystery. The symptoms indicated nothing I could recognize with any degree of certainty."

Kennedy stooped over, making a superficial examination of the girl. I saw that some faint odor caught his nostrils, for he remained poised a moment, inhaling reflectively, his eyes clouded in thought. Then he went to the windows, raising the shades an additional few inches each, but that did not seem to give him the light he wished.

In the room were the portable arcs used in the making of scenes in an actual interior setting. The connections ran to heavy insulated junction boxes at the ends of two lines of stiff black stage cable. Near the door the circuits were joined and a single lead of the big duplex cord ran out along the polished hardwood floor, carried presumably to the house circuit at a fuse box where sufficient amperage was available. Kennedy's eyes followed out the wires quickly. Then, motioning to me to help, he wheeled one of the heavy stands around and adjusted the hood so that the full strength of the light would be cast upon Stella. The arc in place, he threw the switch, and in the sputtering flood of illumination dropped to his knees, taking a powerful pocket lens from his waistcoat and beginning an inch by inch examination of her skin.

I gained a fresh realization of the beauty of the star as she lay under the dazzling electric glow, and in particular I noticed the small amount of make-up she had used and the natural firmness of her flesh. She was dressed in a modish, informal dinner dress, of embroidered satin, cut fairly low at front and back and with sleeves of some gauzelike material reaching not halfway to her elbow, hardly sleeves at all, in fact.

Kennedy with his glass went over her features with extreme care. I saw that he drew her hair back, and that then he parted it, to examine her scalp, and I wondered what infinitesimal clue might be the object of his search. I had learned, however, never to question him while he was at work.

With his eye glued to his lens he made his way about and around her neck, and down and over her throat and chest so far as it remained unprotected by the silk of her gown. With the aid of Mackay he turned her over to examine her back. Next he returned the body to its former position and began to inspect the arms. Very suddenly something caught his eye on the inside of her right forearm. He grunted with satisfaction, straightened, pulled the switch of the arc, wiped his eyes, which were watering.

"Find anything, Mr. Kennedy?" Doctor Blake seemed to understand, to some extent, the purpose of the examination.

Kennedy did not answer, probably preoccupied with theories which I could see were forming in his mind.

The library was a huge room of greater length than breadth. At one end were wide French windows looking out upon the garden and summer house. The door to the hallway and living room was very broad, with heavy sliding panels and rich portieres of a velours almost the tint of the wood-work. Between the door, situated in the side wall near the opposite end, and the windows, was a magnificent stone fireplace with charred logs testifying to its frequent use. The couch where Stella lay had been drawn back from its normal position before the fire, together with a huge table of carved walnut. The other two walls were an unbroken succession of shelves, reaching to the ceiling and literally packed with books.

Facing the windows and the door, so as to include the fireplace and the wide sweep of the room within range, were two cameras still set up, the legs of their tripods nested, probably left exactly as they were at the moment of Stella's collapse. I touched the handle of one, a Bell & Howell, and saw that it was threaded, that the film had not been disturbed. The lights, staggered and falling away from the camera lines, were arranged to focus their illumination on the action of the scenes. There were four arcs and two small portable banks of Cooper-Hewitts, the latter used to cut the sharp shadows and give a greater evenness to the photography. Also there were diffusers constructed of sheets of white cloth stretched taut on frames. These reflected light upward upon the faces of the actors, softening the lower features, and so valuable in adding to the attractiveness of the women in particular.

All this I had learned from visits to a studio with the Star's photoplay editor. I was anxious to impress my knowledge upon Kennedy. He gave me no opportunity, however, but wheeled upon Mackay suddenly.

"Send in the electrician," he ordered. "Keep everyone else out until I'm ready to examine them."

While the district attorney hurried to the sliding doors, guarded on their farther side by one of the amateur deputies he had impressed into service, Kennedy swung the stand of the arc he had used back into the place unaided. I noticed that Doctor Blake was nervously interested in spite of his professional poise. I certainly was bursting with curiosity to know what Kennedy had found.

The electrician, a wizened veteran of the studios, with a bald head which glistened rather ridiculously, entered as though he expected to be held for the death of the star on the spot.

"I don't know nothin'," he began, before anyone could start to question him. "I was outside when they yelled, honest! I was seeing whether m'lead was getting hot, and I heard 'em call to douse the glim, an'—"

"Put on all your lights"—Kennedy was unusually sharp, although it was plain he held no suspicion of this man, as he added—"just as you had them."

As the electrician went from stand to stand sulkily, there was a sputter from the arcs, almost deafening in the confines of the room, and quite a bit of fine white smoke. But in a moment the corner of the library constituting the set was brilliantly, dazzlingly lighted. To me it was quite like being transported into one of the big studios in the city.

"Is this the largest portion of the room they used?" Kennedy asked.
"Did you have your stands any farther back?"

"This was the biggest lay-out, sir!" replied the man.

"Were all the scenes in which Miss Lamar appeared before her death in this corner of the room?"

"Yes, sir!"

"And this was the way you had the scene lighted when she dropped unconscious?"

"Yes, sir! I pulled m'lights an'—an' they lifted her up and put her right there where she is, sir!"

Kennedy paid no attention to the last; in fact, I doubt whether he heard it. Dropping to hands and knees immediately, he began a search of the floor and carpet as minutely painstaking as the inspection he had given Stella's own person. Instinctively I drew back, to be out of his way, as did Doctor Blake and Mackay. The electrician, I noticed, seemed to grasp now the reason for the summons which undoubtedly had frightened him badly. He gave his attention to his lights, stroking a refractory Cooper-Hewitt tube for all the world as if some minor scene in the story were being photographed. It was hard to realize that it was not another picture scene, but that Craig Kennedy, in my opinion the founder of the scientific school of modern detectives, was searching out in this strange environment the clue to a real murder so mysterious that the very cause of death was as yet undetermined.

I was hoping for a display of the remarkable brilliance Craig had shown in so many of the cases brought to his attention. I half expected to see him rise from the floor with some tiny something in his hand, some object overlooked by everyone else, some tangible evidence which would lead to the immediate apprehension of the perpetrator of the crime. That Stella Lamar had met her death by foul means I did not doubt for an instant, and so I waited feverishly for the conclusion of Kennedy's search.

As it happened, this was not destined to be one of his cases cleared up in a brief few hours of intensive effort. He covered every inch of the floor within the illuminated area; then he turned his attention to the walls and furniture and the rest of the room in somewhat more perfunctory, but no less skillful manner. Fully fifteen minutes elapsed, but I knew from his expression that he had discovered nothing. In a wringing perspiration from the heat of the arcs, but nevertheless glad to have had the intense light at his disposal, he motioned to the electrician to turn them off and to leave the room.

"Find anything, Mr. Kennedy?" queried the physician once more.

Kennedy beckoned all of us to the side of the ill-fated actress. Lifting the right arm, finding the spot which had caused his exclamation before, he handed his pocket lens to Doctor Blake. After a moment a low whistle escaped the lips of the physician.

Next it was my turn. As I stooped over I caught, above the faint scent of imported perfume which she affected, a peculiar putrescent odor. This it was which had caught Kennedy's nostrils. Then through the glass I could detect upon her forearm the tiniest possible scratch ending in an almost invisible puncture, such as might have been made by a very sharp needle or the point of an incredibly fine hypodermic syringe. Drawing back, I glanced again at her face, which I had already noted was blotched and somewhat swollen beneath the make-up. Again I thought that the muscles were contorted, that the eyes were bulging slightly, that there was a bluish tinge to her skin such as in cyanosis or asphyxiation. It may have been imagination, but I was now sure that her expression revealed pain or fear or both.

When I looked at her first I had been unable to forget my impression of years. Before me there had been the once living form of Stella Lamar, whom I had dreamed of meeting and whom I had never viewed in actual life. I had lacked the penetration to see beneath the glamour. But to Kennedy there had been signs of the poisoning at once. Doctor Blake had searched merely for the evidences of the commoner drugs, or the usual diseases such as cause sudden death. I recalled the cyanides. I thought of curare, or woorali, the South American arrow poison with which Kennedy once had dealt. Had Stella received an injection of some new and curious substance?

Mackay glanced up from his inspection of the mark on the arm.

"It's an awfully tiny scratch!" he exclaimed.

Kennedy smiled. "Yet, Mackay, it probably was the cause of her death."

"How?"

"That—that is the problem before us. When we learn just exactly how she scratched herself, or was scratched—" Kennedy paced up and down in front of the fireplace. Then he confronted each of us in turn, suddenly serious. "Not a word of what I have discovered," he warned.

III

TANGLED MOTIVES

"Do you wish to examine the people now?" Mackay asked.

Kennedy hesitated. "First I want to make sure of the evidence concerning her actual death. Can you arrange to have the clothes she has on, and those she brought with her, all of them bundled up and sent in to my laboratory, together with samples of her body fluids as soon as the coroner can supply you?"

Mackay nodded. This pleased him. This seemed to be tangible action, promising tangible results.

Again Kennedy glanced about in thought. I knew that the scratch was worrying him. "Did she change her clothes out here?" he inquired.

The district attorney brightened. "She dressed in a small den just off the living room. I have a man posted and the door closed. Nothing has been disturbed."

He started to lead the way without further word from Kennedy, proud to have been able once more to demonstrate his foresight.

As we left the library, entering the living room, there was an appreciable hush. Here were grouped the others of the party brought out by the picture company, a constrained gathering of folk who had little in common beyond the highly specialized needs of the new art of the screen, an assembly of souls who had been forced to wait during all the time required for the trip of Kennedy and myself out from New York, who were compelled to wait now until he should be ready to examine them.

I picked out the electrician in the semi-gloom and with him his fellow members of the technical staff needed in the taking of the scenes in the library. The camera men I guessed, and a property boy, and an assistant director. The last, at any event, of all those in the huge room, had summoned up sufficient nonchalance to bend his mind to details of his work. I saw that he was thumbing a copy of the scenario, or detailed working manuscript of the story, making notations in some kind of little book, and it was that which enabled me to establish his identity at a glance.

In a different corner were the principals, two men and a girl still in make-up, and with them the director, and Manton and Phelps. Apart from everyone else, in a sort of social ostracism common to the studios, the two five-dollar-a-day extras waited, a butler and a maid, also in make-up. Oddly enough the total number of these material witnesses to the tragedy was just thirteen, and I wondered if they had noticed the fact.

Doctor Blake turned to Kennedy the moment we left the library.

"Do you feel it is necessary for me to remain any longer?" he asked. He was apologetic, yet distinctly impatient. "I have neglected several very important calls as it is."

Kennedy and Mackay both hastened to assure the physician that they appreciated his co-operation and that they would spare him as much notoriety and inconvenience as possible. Then the three of us hurried across and to the little den which had been converted into a dressing room for Stella's use.

Here were all the evidences of femininity, the little touches which a woman can impart to the smallest corner in a few brief moments of occupancy. It was a tiny alcove shut off from the rest of the living room by heavy silk hangings, drawn now and pinned together so as to assure her the privacy she wished. The one window was high and fitted with leaded glass, but it was raised and afforded the maximum of light. Stella's traveling bag sprawled wide open, with many of her effects strewn about in attractive disarray. Her suit, in which she had made the trip to Tarrytown, was thrown carelessly over the back of a chair. Her mirror was fastened up ruthlessly, upon a handsome woven Oriental hanging, with a long hatpin. Powder was spilled upon the couch cover, another Oriental fabric, and her little box of rouge lay face downward on the floor.

As we pulled the curtains aside I caught the perfume which still clung to her clothes in the library beyond. As Mackay sniffed also, Kennedy smiled.

"Coty's Jacqueminot rose," he remarked.

With his usual swift and practiced certainty Kennedy then inspected the extemporized dressing room. He seemed to satisfy himself that no subtle attack had been made upon the girl here, although I doubt that he had held any such supposition seriously in the first place. In my association of several years with Kennedy, following our first intimacy of college days, I had learned that his success as a scientific detective was the result wholly of his thoroughness of method. To watch him had become a never-ending delight, even in the dull preliminary work of a case as baffling as this one. Mackay also seemed content just to enact the role of spectator.

Kennedy thumbed through the delicate intimacies of her traveling bag with the keen, impersonal manner which always distinguished him; then he found her beaded handbag and proceeded to rummage through that. Suddenly he paused as he unfolded a piece of note paper, and we gathered around to read:

MY DEAR STELLA: Have something very important to tell you. Will you lunch Tuesday at the P. G. tearoom? LARRY.

"Tuesday—" murmured Kennedy. "And this is Monday. Who—who is Larry, I wonder?"

I hastened to answer the question for him. It was my first opportunity to display my knowledge of the picture players. "Larry—that's Lawrence, Lawrence Millard!" I exclaimed. Then I went on to tell him of the divorce and the circumstances surrounding Stella's life as I knew it. "It—it looks," I concluded, "as if they might have been on the point of composing their differences, after all."

Kennedy nodded. I could see, however, that he made a mental note of his intention to question the girl's former husband.

All at once another thought struck me and I became eager. It was a possible explanation of the mystery.

"Listen, Craig," I began. "Suppose Millard wanted to make up and she didn't. Suppose that she refused to see him or to meet him. Suppose that in a jealous fit he—"

"No, Walter!" Kennedy headed me off with a smile. "This wasn't an ordinary murder of passion. This was well thought out and well executed. Not one medical examiner in a thousand would have found that tiny scratch. It may be very difficult yet to determine the exact cause of death. This, my dear Jameson"—it was playful irony—"is a scientific crime."

"But Millard—"

"Of course! Anyone may be the culprit. Yet you tell me Millard did not contest her divorce and that it would have been very easy for him to file a counter-suit because everyone knew of her relationship with Manton. That, offhand, shows no ill-will on his part. And now we find this note from him, which at least is friendly in tone—"

I shrugged my shoulders. It was the same blind alley in which my thoughts had strayed upon the train on our way out.

"It's too early to begin to try to fasten the guilt upon anyone," Kennedy added, as we returned to the library through the living room. Then he turned to Mackay. "Have you succeeded in gleaning any facts about the life of Miss Lamar?" he asked. "Anything which might point to a motive, so that I can approach the case from both directions?"

"If you ask me," the little district attorney rejoined, "it's a matter of tangled motives throughout. I—I had no sword to cut the Gordian knot and so"—graciously—"I sent for you."

"What do you mean by tangled motives?" Kennedy ignored the other's compliment.

"Well!" Mackay indicated me. "Mr. Jameson explained about her divorce. No one heard whom she named as corespondent. That's an unknown woman in the case, although it may not mean anything at all. Then there's Lloyd Manton and all the talk about his affair with Miss Lamar. Some one told one of my men that Manton's wife has left him on that account."

"Did you question Manton?"

"No, I thought I ought to leave all that to you. I was afraid I might put them on their guard."

"Good!" Kennedy was pleased. "Did you learn anything else?"

"This deputy of mine obtained all these things by gossiping with the girl who plays the maid, and so they may not be reliable. But among the players it is reported that Werner, the director, was having an affair with Stella also, and that Merle Shirley, the 'heavy' man, was seen with her a great deal recently, and that Jack Gordon, the leading man, who was engaged to marry her as soon as her decree was final, was jealous as a consequence, and that Miss Loring, playing the vampire In the story and engaged to Shirley, was even more bitter against the deceased than Gordon, Miss Lamar's fiance.

"That made eight people with possible motives for the crime. When I got that far I gave it up. In fact"—Mackay lowered his voice, suddenly—"I don't like the attitude of Emery Phelps. This is his house, you know, and he is the financial backer of Manton Pictures, yet there seems to be an undercurrent of friction between Manton and himself. I—I wanted him to show me some detail of the arrangement of things in the library, but he wouldn't come into the room. He said he didn't want to look at Miss Lamar. There—there was something—and, I don't know. If he is concerned in any way—that would make nine."

"You think Miss Lamar and Phelps—"

Mackay shook his head. "I don't know."

Kennedy turned to me, expression really serious. "Is this the way they carry on in the picture world, Walter?" he asked. "Is this the usual thing or—or an exception?"

I flushed. "It's very much an exception," I insisted. "The film people are just like other people, some good and some bad. Probably three-quarters of all this is gossip."

"I hope so." He straightened. "The only thing to do is to go after them one at a time and disentangle all the conflicting threads. It looks as though there will be any number of possible false leads and so we must be careful and deliberate. I think I'll question each in turn—here."

He walked over to the fireplace, stopping for just a moment to glance at the body of Stella. Then he pulled the blinds down halfway, so that the room seemed somber and gruesome. He drew a chair so that the different individuals as he examined them, would be unable to lose sight of the dead woman. His arrangements completed, he faced the district attorney.

"Manton first," he directed.

In an instant I caught the psychology of it—the now darkened library, the beautiful body still lying on the davenport, the quiet and quick arrival of ourselves. If anything could be extracted from these people, surely it would be betrayed under these surroundings.

IV

THE FATAL SCRIPT

I had no real opportunity to study Manton when he greeted us upon our arrival, and at that time neither Kennedy nor I possessed even a passing realization of the problem before us. Now I felt that I was ready to grasp at any possible motive for the crime. I was prepared to suspect any or all of the nine people enumerated by Mackay, so far as I could speak for myself, and at the very least I was certain that this was one of the most baffling cases ever brought to Craig's attention.

Yet I was sure he would solve it. I waited most impatiently for the outcome of his examination of Lloyd Manton.

The producer-promoter was a well-set-up man just approaching middle age. About him was a certain impression of great physical strength, of bulk without flabbiness, and in particular I noticed the formation of his head, the square broad development which indicated his intellectual power, and I found, too, a fascinating quality about his eyes, deeply placed and of a warm dark gray-brown, which seemed to hold a fundamental sincerity which, I imagined, made the man almost irresistible in a business deal.

His weakness, so far as I could ascertain it, was revealed by his mouth and chin, and by a certain nervousness of his hands, hands where a square, practical palm was belied by the slight tapering of his fingers, the mark of the dreamer. His mouth was unquestionably sensuous, with the lips full and now and then revealing out of the studied practiced calm of his face an almost imperceptible twitching, as though to betray a flash of emotion, or fear. His chin was feminine, softening his expression and showing that his feelings would overbalance the cool calculation denoted by his eyes and the rather heavy level brows above.

As he entered the room, taking the chair indicated by Kennedy, he seemed perfectly cool and his glance, as it strayed to the lifeless form of Stella, revealed his iron self-control. The little signs which I have mentioned, which betrayed the real man beneath, were only disclosed to me little by little as Kennedy's questioning progressed.

"Tell me just what happened?" Kennedy began.

"Well—" Manton responded quickly enough, but then he stopped and proceeded as though he chose each word with care, as if he framed each sentence so that there would be no misunderstanding, no chance of wrong impression; all of which pleased Kennedy.

"In the scene we were taking," he went on, "Stella was crouched down on the floor, bending over her father, who had just been murdered. She was sobbing. All at once the lights were to spring up. The young hero was to dash through the set and she was to see him and scream out in terror. The first part went all right. But when the lights flashed on, instead of looking up and screaming, Stella sort of crumpled and collapsed on top of Werner, who was playing the father. I yelled to stop the cameras and rushed in. We picked her up and put her on the couch. Some one sent for the doctor, but she died without saying a word. I—I haven't the slightest idea what happened. At first I thought it was heart trouble."

"Did she have heart trouble?"

"No, that is—not that I ever heard."

Kennedy hesitated. "Why were you taking these scenes out here?"

It was on the tip of my tongue to answer for Manton. I knew that at one time many fine interiors were actually taken in houses, to save expense. I was sorry that Kennedy should draw any conclusion from a fact which I thought was too well known to require explanation. Manton's answer, however, proved a distinct surprise to me.

"Mr. Phelps asked us to use his library in this picture."

"Wouldn't it have been easier and cheaper in the long run to reproduce it in the studio?"

Manton glanced up at Kennedy, echoing my thought. Had Kennedy, after all, some knowledge of motion pictures stored away with his vast fund of general and unusual information?

"Yes," replied the producer. "It would save the trip out here, the loss of time, the inconvenience—why, in an actual dollars and cents comparison, with overhead and everything taken into account, the building of a set like this is nothing nowadays."

"Do you know Mr. Phelps's reason?"

Manton shrugged his shoulders. "Just a whim, and we had to humor it."

"Mr. Phelps is interested in the company?"

"Yes. He recently bought up all the stock except my own. He is in absolute control, financially."

"What is the story you are making? I mean, I want to understand just exactly what happened in the scenes you were photographing today. It is essential that I learn how everyone was supposed to act and how they did act. I must find out every trivial little detail. Do you follow me?"

Manton's mouth set suddenly, showing that it possessed a latent quality of firmness. He glanced about the room, then rose, went to the farther end of the long table, and returned with a thick sheaf of manuscript bound at the side in stiff board covers. "This is the scenario, the script of the detailed action," he explained.

As Kennedy took the binder, Manton opened it and turned past several sheets of tabulation and lists, the index to the sets and exterior locations, the characters and extras, the changes of clothes, and other technical detail. "The scenes we are taking here," he went on, "are the opening scenes of the story. We left them until now because it meant the long trip out to Tarrytown and because it would take us away from the studio while they were putting up the largest two sets, a banquet and a ballroom which need the entire floor space of the studio." He turned over two or three pages, pointing. "We had taken up to scene thirteen; from scenes one to thirteen just as you have them in order there. It—it was in the unlucky thirteenth that she"—was it my imagination or did he tremble, for just an instant, violently?—"that she died."

Kennedy started to read the script. I hurried to his side, glancing over his shoulder.

THE BLACK TERROR
FEATURING STELLA LAMAH
SCENE 1

LOCATION.—Remsen library. This is a modern, luxurious library set with a long table in the center of the room, books around the walls, French windows leading from the rear, and an entrance through a hallway to the right through a pair of portieres. Note: E. P. wishes us to use his library at Tarrytown.

ACTION.—Open diaphragm slowly on darkened set as a spot of light is being played on the walls and French windows in the rear. As the diaphragm opens slowly the light vanishes, leaving the scene dark at times and then brightened until, as the diaphragm opens full, we discover that the light is that of a burglar's flash light, traveling over the walls of the library. When the diaphragm is fully opened we discover also a faint line of light streaming through the almost closed portieres leading to the hallway outside. This ray of light, striking along the floor, pauses by the library table, just disclosing the edge of it but not revealing anything else in the room. The spotlight in the hands of a shadowy figure roves across the wall and to the portieres. As it pauses there the portieres move and the fingers of a girl are seen on the edge of the silk. A bare and beautiful arm is thrust through the portieres almost to the shoulder, and it begins to move the portieres aside, reaching upward to pull the curtains apart at the rings.

SCENE 2

LOCATION.—Remsen library. Close foreground of portieres.

ACTION.—Our heroine parts the portieres and stands revealed in the spotlight's glare. She is in dinner gown and about her throat is a peculiar locket of flashing jewels. She cries out and backs away, closing the portieres. The spotlight retreats from the curtains, leaving them dark.

SCENE 3

LOCATION.—Hallway, Remsen house. Close foreground of portieres leading to library. This hallway is lighted.

ACTION.—The girl holding the portieres shut screams for help.

SCENE 4

LOCATION.—Foot of stairway, Remsen house.

ACTION.—The butler and maid are discovered talking. They hear the girl's scream and start running.

SCENE 5

LOCATION.—Hallway, Remsen house. Close foreground of portieres.

ACTION.—The girl hears help coming and glances off to indicate that she sees the butler and the maid. She continues to cling to the closed curtains.

SCENE 6

LOCATION.—Remsen library. Full shot.

ACTION.—The unknown drops the spotlight to the floor and we first see his legs crossing the rays of light on the floor. Then the spotlight rolls, revealing the body of an elderly man of the American millionaire type, lying crumpled against the table. Finally it rolls a little farther and stops, directing its rays into the fireplace.

SCENE 7

LOCATION.—Remsen hallway, outside library.

ACTION.—The girl indicates determined resolve. She throws apart the portieres with a quick motion of her arms and dashes inside. The portieres close after her. The butler and maid come on running and looking about.

SCENE 8

LOCATION.—Remsen library. Full shot.

ACTION.—The spotlight is showing into the fireplace when the girl crosses quickly into its rays. She stoops into the light, revealing her face and picking up the spotlight. She flashes it about the room, pausing as it strikes the French windows and reveals the murderer making his escape out on a balcony which is revealed in the background. When the rays of light reach the murderer he deliberately turns.

SCENE 9

LOCATION.—Remsen library. Close foreground of French windows.

ACTION.—The intruder, now in the close foreground, pauses as he is about to shut the window and blinks deliberately into the rays of light, then laughs and closes the French windows.

SCENE 10

LOCATION.—Hallway, Remsen home. Close foreground of portieres to library.

ACTION.—The butler and maid look around hopelessly. A young man, the exact counterpart of the man who in the previous scene looked into the spotlight at the French windows, comes up to the butler and demands to know what has happened. The butler explains hurriedly that he heard his mistress cry out for help. The young man steps to the portieres and pauses.

SCENE 11

LOCATION.—Remsen library. Full shot.

ACTION.—The girl, using the spotlight, flashes it about the room and down on the floor, seeing for the first time the body of the American millionaire.

SCENE 12

LOCATION.—Exterior Remsen house. Night tint.

ACTION.—The murderer scrambles down a column from the upper porch and leaps to the ground, darting across the lawn out of the picture.

SCENE 13

LOCATION.—Remsen library. Full shot.

ACTION.—The spotlight on the floor reveals the girl sobbing over the body of the millionaire and trying to revive him. She screams and cries out. The portieres are parted and from the lighted hallway we see the young man, the butler, and the maid, who enter. The young man switches on the lights and the room is revealed. The three cry out in horror. The young man, glancing about, leaps toward the partly opened French windows, drawing a revolver. As the girl sees him she screams again and denotes terror.

Finishing the thirteenth scene, Kennedy closed the covers and handed the script to me. Then he confronted Manton once more.

"What became of the locket about the girl's neck? In the manuscript Miss Lamar is supposed to have a peculiar pendant at her throat. There was none."

"Oh yes!" The promoter remained a moment in thought. "The doctor took it off and gave it to Bernie, the prop. boy, who's helping the electrician."

"Is he outside?"

"Yes."

"Now try to remember, Mr. Manton." Kennedy leaned over very seriously. "Just who approached closely to Miss Lamar in the making of that thirteenth scene? Who was near enough to have inflicted a wound, or to have subjected her, suppose we say, to the fumes of some subtle poison?"

"You think that—" Manton started to question Kennedy, but was given no encouragement. "Gordon, the leading man, passed through the scene," he replied, after a pause, "but did not go very near her. Werner was playing the dead millionaire at her feet."

"Who is Werner?"

"He's my director. Because it was such a small part, he played it himself. He's only in the two or three scenes in the beginning and I was here to be at the camera."

While Kennedy was questioning Manton I had been glancing through the script of the picture. My own connection with the movies had consisted largely of three attempts to sell stories of my own to the producers. Needless to remark I had not succeeded, in that regard falling in the class with some hundreds of thousands of my fellow citizens. For everybody thinks he has at least one motion picture in him. And so, though I had managed to visit studios and meet a few of the players, this was my very first shot at a manuscript actually in production. I took advantage of Kennedy's momentary preoccupation to turn to Manton.

"Who wrote this script, Mr. Manton?" I asked.

"Millard! Lawrence Millard."

"Millard?" Kennedy and I exclaimed, simultaneously.

"Why, yes! Millard is still under contract and he's the only man who ever could write scripts for Stella. We—we tried others and they all flivved."

"Is Millard here?"

Manton burst into laughter, somehow out of place in the room where we still were in the company of death. "An author on the lot at the filming of his picture, to bother the director and to change everything? Out! When the scenario's done he's through. He's lucky to get his name on the screen. It's not the story but the direction which counts, except that you've got to have a good idea to start with, and a halfway decent script to make your lay-outs from. Anyhow—" He sobered a bit, perhaps realizing that he was going counter to the tendency to have the author on the lot. "Millard and Stella weren't on speaking terms. She divorced him, you know."

"Do you know much about the personal affairs of Miss Lamar?"

"Well"—Manton's eyes sought the floor for a moment—"Like everyone else in pictures, Stella was the victim of a great deal of gossip. That's the experience of any girl who rises to a position of prominence and—"

"How were the relations between Miss Lamar and yourself?" interrupted Kennedy.

"What do you mean by that?" Manton flushed quickly.

"You have had no trouble, no disagreements recently?"

"No, indeed. Everything has been very friendly between us—in a strictly business way, of course—and I don't believe I've had an unpleasant word with her since I first formed Manton Pictures to make her a star."

"You know nothing of her difficulties with her husband?"

"Naturally not. I seldom saw her except at the studio, unless it was some necessary affair such as a screen ball here, or perhaps in Boston or Philadelphia or some near-by city where I would take her for effect—"

Kennedy turned to Mackay. "Will you arrange to keep the people I have yet to question separate from the ones I have examined already?"

As the district attorney nodded, Kennedy dismissed Manton rather shortly; then turned again to Mackay as the promoter drew out of earshot.

"Bring in Bernie, the property-boy, before anyone can tell him to hide or destroy that locket."

V

AN EMOTIONAL MAZE

Bernie proved to be as stupid a youth as any I had ever seen. He possessed frightened semi-liquid eyes and overshot ears and hair which might have been red beneath its accumulation of dust. Without doubt the boy had been coached by the electrician, because he began to affirm his innocence in similar fashion the moment he entered the door.

"I don't know nothin', honest I don't," he pleaded. "I was out in the hall, I was, and I didn't come in at all until the doc. came."

"I suppose you were anxious to see if the cable was becoming hot," Kennedy suggested, gravely.

"That's it, sir! We was lookin' at it because it was on the varnish and the butler he says—"

"Where's the locket?" interrupted Kennedy. "The one Miss Lamar wore in the scenes."

"Oh!" in disdain, "that thing!" With some effort Bernie fished it from the capacious depths of a pocket, disentangling the sharp corners from the torn and ragged lining of his coat.

I glanced at it as Kennedy turned it over and over in his hands, and saw that it was a palpable stage prop, with glass jewels of the cheapest sort. Concealing his disappointment, Kennedy dropped it into his own pocket, confronting the frightened Bernie once more.

"Do you know anything about Miss Lamar's death?"

"No! I don't know nothing, honest!"

"All right!" Kennedy turned to Mackay. "Werner, the director."

Of Stanley Werner I had heard a great deal, through interviews, character studies, and other press stuff in the photoplay journals and the Sunday newspaper film sections. Now I found him to be a high-strung individual, so extremely nervous that it seemed impossible for him to remain in one position in his chair or for him to keep his hands motionless for a single instant. Although he was of moderate build, with a fair suggestion of flesh, there were yet the marks of the artist and of the creative temperament in the fine sloping contours of his head and in his remarkably long fingers, which tapered to nails manicured immaculately. Kennedy seemed to pay particular attention to his eyes, which were dark, soft, and amazingly restless.

"Who was in the cast, Mr. Werner? What were they playing and just exactly what was each doing at the time of Miss Lamar's collapse?"

"Well"—Werner's eyes shifted to mine, then to Mackay's, and there was a subtle lack of ease in his manner which I was hardly prepared to classify as yet—"Stella Lamar was playing the part of Stella Remsen, the heroine, and—uh, I see your associate has the script—"

He paused, glancing at me again. When Kennedy said nothing, Werner went on, growing more and more nervous. "Jack Gordon plays Jack Daring, the hero—the handsome young chap who runs down the steps and encounters the butler and the maid in the hall just outside the library—"

"Wasn't it his face in the French windows of the library at the same time?" Kennedy asked. "Wasn't he the murderer of the father, also?"

"No!" Werner smiled slightly, and there was an instant's flash of the man's personality, winning and, it seemed to me, calculated to inspire confidence. "That is the mystery; it is a mystery plot. While the parts are played by Jack in both cases now, we explain in a subtitle a little later that the criminal himself, the 'Black Terror,' is a master of scientific impersonation, and that he changes the faces of his emissaries by means of plastic surgery and such scientific things, so that they look like the characters against whom he wishes to throw suspicion. So while Jack plays the part it is really an accomplice of the 'Black Terror' who kills old Remsen."

Kennedy turned to me. "A new idea in the application of science to crime!" he remarked, dryly. "Just suppose it were practicable!"

"The 'Black Terror'" Werner continued, "is played by Merle Shirley. You've heard of him, the greatest villain ever known to the films? Then there's Marilyn Loring, the vampire, another good trouper, too. She plays Zelda, old Remsen's ward, and it's a question whether Zelda or Stella will be the Remsen heir. Marilyn herself is an awfully nice girl, but, oh, how the fans hate her!" The director chuckled. "No Millard story is ever complete without a vamp and Marilyn's been eating them up. She's been with Manton Pictures for nearly a year."

"You played the millionaire yourself?"

"Yes, I did old Remsen."

I realized suddenly, for the first time, that Werner was still in the evening clothes he had donned for the part. On his face were streaks in the little make-up that remained after his frequent mopping of his features with his handkerchief. Too, his collar was melted. I could imagine his discomfort.

"Did you have any business with Stella?" Kennedy asked, using the stage term for the minor bits of action in the playing of a scene. "Did you move at all while she was going through her part?"

"No, Mr. Kennedy, I was 'dead man' in all the scenes."

"Show me how you lay, if you will."

Obligingly, Werner stretched out on the carpet, duplicating his positions even to the exact manner in which he had placed his hands and arms. Rather to my own distaste, Kennedy impressed me to represent, I am sure in clumsy fashion, the various positions of Stella Lamar. Most painstakingly Kennedy worked back from the thirteenth scene to the first, referring to the script and coaxing details of memory from the mind of Werner.

I grasped Kennedy's purpose almost at once. He was endeavoring to reproduce the action which had been photographed, so as to determine just how the poison had been administered. Of course he made no reference to the tiny scratch and Mackay and I were careful to give no hint of it to Werner. The director, however, seemed most willing to assist us. I certainly felt no suspicion of him now. As for Kennedy, his face was unrevealing.

"When the film in the camera is developed—" I suggested to Kennedy, suddenly.

He silenced me with a gesture. "I haven't overlooked that, but the scenes will be from one angle only and in a darkened set. I can determine more this way."

Somewhat crestfallen, I continued my impersonation of the slain star not altogether willingly. Soon Kennedy had completed his reconstruction of the action.

"Who else entered the scene besides Gordon?" he asked.

"The butler and the maid, after the lights were flashed on."

"I'll question the camera men," he announced. "Who are they?"

"Harry Watkins is the head photographer," Werner explained. "He's a crackerjack, too! One of the best lighting experts in the country. Al Penny's grinding the other box."

"Let's have Watkins first." Kennedy nodded to Mackay to escort the director from the room.

Neither Watkins nor Penny were able to add anything to the facts which Kennedy had gleaned from Manton and Werner. When he had finished his patient examination of the junior camera man he recalled Watkins and had both, under his eyes, close and seal the film cartridges which contained the photographic record of the thirteen scenes. Dismissing the men, he handed the two black boxes to Mackay.

"Can you arrange to have these developed and printed, quickly, but in some way so neither negative nor positive will be out of your sight at any time?"

Mackay nodded. "I know the owner of a laboratory in Yonkers."

"Good! Now let's have the leading man."

Jack Gordon immediately impressed me very unfavorably. There was something about him for which I could find no word but "sleek." Learning much from my long association with Kennedy I observed at once that he had removed the make-up from his face and that he had on a clean white collar. Since the linen worn before the camera is dyed a faint tint to prevent the halation caused by pure white, it was a sure sign to me that he had spruced up a bit. I knew that he was engaged to Stella. Here in this room she lay dead, under the most mysterious circumstances. There was little question, in fact, that she had been murdered. How could he, really loving her, think of such things as the make-up left on his face, or his clothes?

I had to admit that he was a handsome individual. Perhaps slightly less than average in height, and very slender, he had the close-knit build of an athlete. The contour of his head and the perfect regularity of rather large features made him an ideal type for the screen at any angle; in close-ups and foregrounds as well as full shots. In actual life there were little things covered by make-up in his work, such as the cold gray tint of his eyes and the lines of dissipation about his mouth.

Kennedy questioned him first about his movements in the different scenes, then asked him if he had seen or noticed anything suspicious during the taking of any of them or in the intervals between.

"I had several changes, Mr. Kennedy," he replied. "Part of the time I was Jack Daring, my regular role, but I was also the emissary who looked like Daring. I went out each time because I make up the emissary to look hard. Werner wanted to fool the people a little bit, but he didn't want them to be positive the emissary was Daring, as would happen if both make-ups were the same."

"Did you have any opportunity to talk to Miss Lamar?"

"None at all. Werner was pushing us to the limit."

"Did she seem her usual self at the start of the scene?"

"No, she seemed a little out of sorts. But"—Gordon hesitated—"something had been troubling her all day. She hardly would talk to me in the car on the way out at all. It didn't strike me that she acted any different when she went in to take the scene."

"You were engaged to her?"

"Yes." Gordon's eyes caught the body on the davenport before him. He glanced away hastily, taking his lower lip between his teeth.

"Had you been having any trouble?"

"No—that is, nothing to amount to anything."

"But you had a quarrel or a misunderstanding."

His face flushed slowly. "She was to obtain her final decree early next week. I wanted her to marry me then at once. She refused. When I reproached her for not considering my wishes she pretended to be cool and began an elaborate flirtation with Merle Shirley."

"You say she only pretended to be cool?"

For a few moments Gordon hesitated. Then apparently his vanity loosened his tongue. He wished it to be understood that he had held the love of Stella to the last.

"Last night," he volunteered, "we made everything up and she was as affectionate as she ever had been. This morning she was cool, but I could tell it was pretense and so I let her alone."

"There has been no real trouble between you?"

The leading man met Kennedy's gaze squarely. "Not a bit!"

Kennedy turned to Mackay. "Mr. Shirley," he ordered.

By a miscalculation on the part of the little district attorney the heavy man entered the room a moment before Gordon left. They came face to face just within the portieres. There was no mistaking the hostility, the open hate, between the two men. Both Kennedy and I caught the glances.

Then Merle Shirley approached the fireplace, taking the chair indicated by Kennedy.

"I wasn't in any of the opening scenes," he explained. "I remained out in the car until I got wind of the excitement. By that time Stella was dead."

"Do you know anything of a quarrel between Miss Lamar and Gordon?"

Shirley rose, clenching his fists. For several moments he stood gazing down at the star with an expression on his face which I could not analyze. The pause gave me an opportunity to study him, however, and I noticed that while he had heavier features than Gordon, and was a larger man in every way, ideally endowed for heavy parts, there was yet a certain boyish freshness clinging to him in subtle fashion. He wore his clothes in a loose sort of way which suggested the West and the open, in contrast to Gordon's metropolitan sophistication and immaculate tailoring. He was every inch the man, and a splendid actor—I knew. Yet there was the touch of youth about him. He seemed incapable of a crime such as this, unless it was in anger, or as the result of some deep-running hidden passion.

Now, whether he was angry or in the clutch of a broad disgust, I could not tell. Perhaps it was both. Very suddenly he wheeled upon Kennedy. His voice became low and vibrant with feeling. Here was none of the steeled self-control of Manton, the deceptive outer mask which Werner used to cover his thoughts, the nonchalant, cold frankness of Gordon.

"Mr. Kennedy," the actor exclaimed, "I've been a fool, a fool!"

"How do you mean?"

"I mean that I allowed Stella to flatter my vanity and lead me into a flirtation which meant nothing at all to her. God!"

"You are responsible for the trouble between Miss Lamar and Gordon, then?"

"Never!" Shirley indicated the body of the star with a quick, passionate sweep of his hand. Now I could not tell whether he was acting or in earnest. "She's responsible!" he exclaimed. "She's responsible for everything!"

"Her death—"

"No!" Shirley sobered suddenly, as if he had forgotten the mystery altogether. "I don't know anything at all about that, nor have I any idea unless—" But he checked himself rather than voice an empty suspicion.

"Just what do you mean, then?" Kennedy was sharp, impatient.

"She made a fool of me, and—and I was engaged to Marilyn Loring—"

"Were engaged? The engagement—"

"Marilyn broke it off last night and wouldn't listen to me, even though I came to my senses and saw what a fool I had been."

"Was"—Kennedy framed his question carefully—"was your infatuation for Miss Lamar of long duration?"

"Just a few weeks. I—I took her out to dinner and to the theater and—and that was all."

"I see!" Kennedy walked away, nodding to Mackay.

"Will you have Miss Loring next?" asked the district attorney.

Kennedy nodded.

Marilyn Loring was a surprise to me. Stella Lamar both on the screen and in real life was a beauty. In the films Marilyn was a beauty also, apparently of a cold, unfeeling type, but in the flesh she was disclosed as a person utterly different from all my preconceived notions. In the first place, she was not particularly attractive except when she smiled. Her coloring, hair frankly and naturally red, skin slightly mottled and pale, produced in photography the black hair and marble, white skin which distinguished her. But as I studied her, as she was now, before she had put on any make-up and while she was still dressed in a simple summer gown of organdie, she looked as though she might have stepped into the room from the main street of some mid-Western town. In repose she was shy, diffident in appearance. When she smiled, naturally, without holding the hard lines of her vampire roles, there was the slight suggestion of a dimple, and she was essentially girlish. When a trace of emotion or feeling came into her face the woman was evident. She might have been seventeen or thirty-seven.

To my surprise, Kennedy made no effort to elicit further information concerning the personal animosities of these people. Perhaps he felt it too much of an emotional maze to be straightened out in this preliminary investigation.

When he found Marilyn had watched the taking of the scenes he compared her account with those which he had already obtained. Then he dismissed her.

In rapid succession, for he was impatient now to follow up other methods of investigation, he called in and examined the remaining possible witnesses of the tragedy. These were the two extra players—the butler and the maid, the assistant director, Phelps's house servants, and Emery Phelps himself. For some unknown reason he left the owner of the house to the very last.

"Why did you wish these scenes photographed out here?" he asked.

"Because I wanted to see my library in pictures."

"Were you watching the taking of the scenes?"

"Yes!"

"Will you describe just what happened?"

Phelps flushed. He was irritated and in no mood to humor us any more than necessary. A man of perhaps forty, with the portly flabbiness which often accompanies success in the financial markets, he was accustomed to obtaining rather than yielding obedience. A bachelor, he had built this house as a show place merely, according to the gossip among newspaper men, seldom living in it.

"Haven't about a dozen people described it for you already?" he asked, distinctly petulant.

Kennedy smiled. "Did you notice anything particularly out of the way, anything which might be a clue to the manner in which Miss Lamar met her death?"

Phelps's attitude became frankly malicious. "If I had, or if any of us had, we wouldn't have found it necessary to send for Prof. Craig Kennedy, or"—turning to me—"the representative of the New York Star."

Kennedy, undisturbed, walked to the side of Mackay. "I'll leave Mr. Phelps and his house in your care," he remarked, in a low voice.

Mackay grinned. I saw that the district attorney had little love for the owner of this particular estate in Tarrytown.

Kennedy led the way into the living room. Immediately the various people he had questioned clustered up with varying degrees of anxiety. Had the mystery been solved?

He gave them no satisfaction, but singled out Manton, who seemed eager to get away.

"Where is Millard? I would like to talk to him."

"I'll try to get him for you. Suppose—" Manton looked at his watch. "I should be in at the studio," he explained. "Everything is at a standstill, probably, and—

and so, suppose you and Mr. Jameson ride in with me in my car. Millard might be there."

Kennedy brightened. "Good!" Then he looked back to catch the eye of Mackay. "Let everyone go now," he directed. "Don't forget to send me the samples of the body fluids and"—as an afterthought—"you'd better keep a watch on the house."

VI

THE FIRST CLUE

Manton's car was a high-powered, expensive limousine, fitted inside with every luxury of which the mind of even a prima donna could conceive, painted a vivid yellow that must have made it an object of attention even on its familiar routes. It was quite characteristic of its owner, for Manton, as we learned, missed no chance to advertise himself.

In the back with us was Werner, while the rest of the company were left to return to the city in the two studio cars which had brought them out in the morning. The director, however, seemed buried with his reflections. He took no part in the conversation; paid no attention to us upon the entire trip.

Manton's mind seemed to dwell rather upon the problems brought up by the death of Stella than upon the tragedy itself. The Star's photoplay editor once had remarked to me that the promoter was 90 per cent "bull," and 10 per cent efficiency. I found that it was an unfair estimation. With all his self-advertisement and almost obnoxious personality, Manton was a more than capable executive in a business where efficiency and method are rare.

"This has been a hoodoo picture from the start," he exclaimed, suddenly. "We have been jinxed with a vengeance. Some one has held the Indian sign on us for sure."

Kennedy, I noticed, listened, studying the man cautiously from the corners of his eyes, but making no effort to draw him out.

"First there were changes to be made in the script, and for those Millard took his own sweet time. Then we were handed a lot of negative which had been fogged in the perforator, a thing that doesn't happen once in a thousand years. But it caught us just as we sent the company down to Delaware Water Gap. A whole ten days' work went into the developer at once. Neither of the camera men caught the fog in their tests because it came in the middle of the rolls. Everything had to be done over again.

"And accidents! We carefully registered the principal accomplice of the 'Black Terror,' a little hunchback with a face to send chills down your back. After we had him in about half the scenes of a sequence of action he was taken sick and died of influenza. First we waited a few days; then we had to take all that stuff over again.

"Our payroll on this picture is staggering. Stella's three thousand a week is cheap for her, the old contract, but it's a lot of money to throw away. Two weeks when she was under the weather cost us six thousand dollars salary and there was half a week we couldn't do any work without her. Gordon and Shirley and Marilyn Loring draw down seventeen hundred a week between them. The director's salary is only two hundred short of that. All told 'The Black Terror' is costing us a hundred thousand dollars over our original estimate.

"And now"—it seemed to me that Manton literally groaned—"with Stella Lamar dead—excuse me looking at it this way, but, after all, it is business and I'm the executive at the head of the company—now we must find a new star, Lord knows where, and we must retake every scene in which Stella appeared. It—it's enough to bankrupt Manton Pictures for once and all."

"Can't you change the story about some way, so you won't lose the value of her work?" asked Kennedy.

"Impossible! We've announced the release and we've got to go ahead.
Fortunately, some of the biggest sets are not taken yet."

The car pulled up with a flourish before the Manton studio, which was an immense affair of reinforced concrete in the upper Bronx. Then, in response to our horn, a great wide double door swung open admitting us through the building to a large courtyard around which the various departments were built.

Here, there was little indication that the principal star of the company had just met her death under mysterious and suspicious circumstances. Perhaps, had I been familiar with the ordinary bustle of the establishment, I might have detected a difference. Indeed, it did strike me that there were little knots of people here and there discussing the tragedy, but everything was overshadowed by the aquatic scene being filmed in the courtyard for some other Manton picture. The cramped space about the concrete tank was alive with people, a mob of extras and stage hands and various employees, a sight which held Kennedy and me for some little time. I was glad when Manton led the way through a long hall to the comparative quiet of the office building. In the reception room there was a decided hush.

"Is Millard here?" he asked of the boy seated at the information desk.

"No, sir," was the respectful reply. "He was here this morning and for a while yesterday."

"You see!" Manton confronted Kennedy grimly. "This is only one of the things with which we have to contend in this business. I give Millard an office but he's a law unto himself. It's the artistic temperament. If I interfere, then he says he cannot write and he doesn't produce any manuscript. Ordinarily he cannot be bothered to work at the studio. But"—philosophically—"I know where to get him as a general thing. He does most of his writing in his rooms downtown; says there's more inspiration in the confusion of Broadway than in the wilds of the Bronx. I'll phone him."

We followed the promoter up the stairs to the second and top floor. Here a corridor gave access to the various executive offices. Its windows at frequent intervals looked down upon the courtyard and the present confusion.

Werner, who had preceded us into the building, now came up. As Manton bustled into his own office to use the telephone the director turned to Kennedy, indicating the next doorway.

"This is my place," he explained. "It connects with Manton, on one side, through his reception room. You see, in addition to directing Stella Lamar I have been in general charge of production and most of the casting is up to me."

Kennedy entered after Werner, interested, and I followed. The door through to the reception room stood open and beyond was the one to Manton's quarters. I could see the promoter at his desk, receiver at his ear, an impatient expression upon his face. In the reception room a rather pretty girl, young and of a shallow-pated type I thought, was busy at a clattering typewriter. She rose and closed the door upon Manton, so as not to disturb him.

"The next office on this side is Millard's," volunteered Werner. "He's the only scenario writer dignified with quarters in this building."

"Manton has other writers, hasn't he?" Kennedy asked.

"Yes, the scenario department is on the third floor across the court, above the laboratory and cutting rooms."

"Who else is in the building here?"

"There are six rooms on this floor," Werner replied. "Manton, the waiting room, myself, Millard, and the two other directors. Below is the general reception room, the cashier, the bookkeepers and stenographers."

As Manton probably was having trouble obtaining his connection, and as Kennedy continued to question Werner concerning the general arrangement of the different floors in the different buildings about the quadrangle, all uninteresting to me, I determined to look about a bit on my own hook. I was still anxious to be of genuine assistance to Kennedy, for once, through my greater knowledge of the film world.

Strolling out into the corridor, I went to the door of Millard's room. To my disappointment, it was locked. Continuing down the hall, I stole a glance into each of the two directors' quarters but saw nothing to awaken my suspicion or justify my intrusion. Beyond, I discovered a washroom, and, aware suddenly of the immense amount of dust I had acquired in the ride in from Tarrytown, I entered to freshen my hands and face at the least. It was a stroke of luck, a fortunate impulse.

The amount of money to be made in the movies had resulted, in the case of Manton, in luxurious equipment for all the various departments of his establishment. I had noticed the offices, furnished with a richness worthy of a bank or some great downtown institution. Now, in the lavatory, immaculate with its white tile and modern appointments, I saw a shelf literally stacked, in this day of paper, with linen towels of the finest quality.

As I drew the water, hot instantly, my eye caught, half in and half out of the wire basket beneath the stand, one of the towels covered with peculiar yellow spots. Immediately my suspicions were awakened. I picked it up gingerly. At close range I saw that the spots were only chrome yellow make-up, but there were also spots of a different nature. I did not stop to think of the unlikeliness of the discovery of a real clue under these circumstances, analyzed afterward by Kennedy. I folded the towel hastily and hurried to rejoin him, to show it to him.

I found him with Werner, waiting for the results of Manton's efforts to locate Millard. Almost at the moment I rejoined the two a boy came to summon Werner to one of the sets out on the stage itself. Kennedy and I were alone. I showed him the towel.

At first he laughed, "You'll never make a detective, Walter," he remarked. "This is only simple coloring matter-Chinese yellow, to be exact. And will you tell me, too"—he became ironical—"how do you expect to find clues of this sort here for a murder committed in Tarrytown when all the people present were held out there and examined, when we are the first to arrive back here?

"Yellow, you know, photographs white. Chinese yellow is used largely in studios in place of white in make-up because it does not cause halation, which, to the picture people, is the bane of their existence. White is too glaring, reflects rays that blur the photography sometimes.

"If you will notice, the next time you see them shooting a scene, you will find the actors' faces tinged with yellow. Even tablecloths and napkins and 'white' dresses are frequently colored a pale yellow, although pale blue has the actinic qualities of white for this purpose, and is now perhaps more frequently used than yellow."

I was properly chastened. In fact, though I did not say much, I almost determined to let him conduct his case himself.

Kennedy saw my crestfallen expression and understood. He was about to say something encouraging, as he handed back the towel, when his eye fell on the other end of it, which, indeed, I myself had noticed.

He sobered instantly and studied the other spots. Indeed, I had not examined them closely myself. They were the very faint stains of some other yellow substance, a liquid which had dried and did not rub off as the make-up, and there were also some small round drops of dark red, almost hidden in the fancy red scrollwork of the lettering on the towel, "Manton Pictures, Inc." The latter had escaped me altogether.

"Blood!" Kennedy exclaimed. Then, "Look here!" The marks of the pale yellow liquid trailed into a slender trace of blood. "It looks as if some one had cleaned a needle on it," he muttered, "and in a hurry."

I remembered his previous remark. The murder had been in Tarrytown. We had just arrived here.

"Would anyone have time to do it?" I asked.

"Whoever used the towel did so in a hurry," he reiterated, seriously. "It may have been some one afraid to leave any sort of clue out there at Phelps's house. There were too many watchers about. It might have seemed better to have run the risk of a search. With no sign of a wound on Miss Lamar's person, it was pretty certain that neither Mackay nor I would attempt to frisk everyone. It was not as though we were looking for a revolver, if she were shot, or a knife, if she had been stabbed. And"—he could not resist another dig at me—"and that we should look in a washroom here for a towel was, well, an idea that wouldn't occur to anyone but the most amateur and blundering sort of sleuth. It's beginner's luck, Walter, beginner's luck."

I ignored the uncomplimentary part of his remarks. "Who could have been in the washroom just before me?" I asked.

Suddenly he hurried through the waiting room to the door to Manton's office, opening it without ceremony. Manton was gone. We exchanged glances. I remembered that Werner had preceded us upstairs. "It means Werner or Manton himself," I whispered, so the girl just behind us would not hear.

Kennedy strode out to the hall, and to a window overlooking the court. After a moment he pointed. I recognized both the cars used to transport the company to the home of Emery Phelps. There was no sign that either had just arrived, for even the chauffeurs were out of sight, perhaps melted into the crowd about the tank in the corner.

"They must have arrived immediately behind us," Kennedy remarked. "We wasted several valuable minutes looking at that water stuff ourselves."

At that moment Werner's voice rose from the reception room below. It was probable that he would be up to rejoin us again. I remembered that he had not been at all at ease while Kennedy questioned him in Tarrytown; that here at the studio he had been palpably anxious to remain close at our heels. I felt a surge of suspicion within me.

"Listen, Craig," I muttered, in low tones. "Manton had no opportunity to steal down the hall after the girl closed the door, and—"

"Why not!" he interrupted, contradicting me. "We had our backs to the door while we were talking with Werner."

"Well, anyhow, it narrows down to Manton and Werner because that is the washroom for these offices—"

"'Sh!" Kennedy stopped me as Werner mounted the stairs. He turned to the director with assumed nonchalance. "How long have the other cars been here?" he asked. "I thought we came pretty fast."

Werner smiled. "I guess those boys had enough of Tarrytown. They rolled into the yard, both of them, while you and Mr. Jameson and Manton were stopping to watch the people in the water."

"I see!" Kennedy gave me a side glance. "Where are the dressing rooms?" he inquired. It was a random shot.

Werner pointed to the end of the hall, toward the washroom. "In the next building, on this floor—that is, the principals'. It's a rotten arrangement," he added. "They come through sometimes and use our lavatory, because it's a little more fancy and because it saves a trip down a flight of stairs. Believe me, it gets old Manton on his ear."

VII

ENID FAYE

Behind Werner was the assistant director, to whom I had given little attention at the time of the examination of the various people in the Phelps library. Even now he impressed me as one of those rare, unobtrusive types of individuals who seem, in spite of the possession of genuine ability and often a great deal of efficiency, to lack, nevertheless, any outstanding personal characteristics. As a class they are human machines, to be neither liked nor disliked, never intruding and yet always on hand when needed.

"This is Carey Drexel, my assistant," Werner stated, forgetting that Kennedy had questioned him at Tarrytown, and so knew him. "There are a few people I simply must see and I'm tied up, therefore, for perhaps half an hour; and Manton's downstairs still trying to locate Millard for you. But Carey's at your disposal, Mr. Kennedy, to show you the arrangement of the studio and to cooperate with you in any way if you think there's any possible chance of finding anything to bear upon Stella's death here."

If Werner was the man who had used the towel, I could see that he was an actor and a cool villain. Of course no one could know, yet, that we had discovered it, but the very nonchalance with which it had been thrown into the basket was a mark of the nerve of the guilty man. It was more than carelessness. Nothing about the crime had been haphazard.

Kennedy thanked Werner and asked to be shown the studio floor used in the making of "The Black Terror." Carey led the way, explaining that there were actually two studios, one at each end of the quadrangle, connected on both sides by the other buildings; offices and dressing rooms and the costume and property departments at the side facing the street; technical laboratories and all the detail of film manufacture in a four-story structure to the rear. Most of Werner's own picture was being made in the so-called big studio, reached through the dressing rooms from the end of the corridor where we stood.

I had been in film plants before, but when we entered the huge glass-roofed inclosure beyond the long hallway of dressing rooms I was impressed by the fact that here was a place of genuine magnitude, with more life and bustle than anything I had ever imagined. The glass had, however, been painted over, because of late years dark stages, with the even quality of artificial light, had come into vogue in the Manton studios in place of stages lighted by the uneven and undependable sunlight.

The two big sets mentioned by Manton, a banquet hall and a ballroom, were being erected simultaneously. Carpenters were at work sawing and hammering. Werner's technical director was shouting at a group of stage hands putting a massive mirror in position at the end of the banquet hall, a clever device to give the room the appearance of at least double its actual length. In one corner several electricians and a camera man were experimenting with a strange-looking bank of lights. In the ballroom set, where the flats or walls were all in place, an unexcited paperhanger was busy with the paraphernalia of his craft, somehow looking out of his element in this reign of pandemonium.

It seemed hard indeed to believe that any sort of order or system lay behind this heterogeneous activity, and the incident which took Carey Drexel away from us only added to the wonder in my mind, a wonder that anything tangible and definite could be accomplished.

"Oh, Carey!" Another assistant director, or perhaps he was only a property boy, rushed up frantically the moment he saw Drexel. "Miss Miller's on a rampage because the grand piano you promised to get for her isn't at her apartment yet, and Bessie Terry's in tears because she left her parrot here overnight, as you suggested, and some one taught the bird to swear." The intruder, a youth of perhaps eighteen, was in deadly earnest. "For the love of Mike, Carey," he went on, "tell me how to unteach that screeching thing of Bessie's, or we won't get a scene today."

Carey Drexel looked at Kennedy helplessly.

With all these troubles, how could he pilot us about? Later we learned that this was nothing new, once one gets on the inside of picture making. Props., or properties, particularly the living ones, cause almost as much disturbance as the temperamental notions of the actors and actresses. Sometimes it is a question which may become the most ridiculous.

Kennedy seemed to be satisfied with his preliminary visit to this studio floor.

"We can get back to Manton's office alone," he told Drexel. "We will just keep on circling the quadrangle."

Relieved, the assistant director pointed to the door of the manufacturing building, as the four-story structure in the rear was called. Then he bustled off with the other youth, quite unruffled himself.

When we passed through the heavy steel fire door we found ourselves in another long hallway of fire-brick and reinforced-concrete construction. Unquestionably there was no danger of a serious conflagration in any part of Manton's plant, despite the high inflammability of the film itself, of the flimsy stage sets, of practically everything used in picture manufacture.

Immediately we entered this building I detected a peculiar odor, at which I sniffed eagerly. I was reminded of the burnt-almond odor of the cyanides. Was this another clue?

I turned to Kennedy but he smiled, anticipating me.

"Banana oil, Walter," he explained, with rather a superior manner. "I imagine it's used a great deal in this industry. Anyway"—a chuckle—"don't expect chance to deliver clues to you in wholesale quantities. You have done very well for today."

A sudden whirring noise, from an open door down the hall, attracted us, and we paused. This, I guessed, was a cutting room. There were a number of steel tables, with high steel chairs. At the walls were cabinets of the same material. Each table had two winding arrangements, a handle at the operator's right hand and one at his left, so that he could wind or unwind film from one reel to another, passing it forward or backward in front of his eyes.

There were girls at the tables except nearest the hall. Here a man stopped now and then to glance at the ribbon of film, or to cut out a section, dropping the discarded piece into a fireproof can and splicing the two ends of the main strip together again with liquid film cement from a small bottle. He looked up as he sensed our presence.

"Isn't it hell?" he remarked, in friendly fashion. "I've got to cut all of Stella Lamar out of 'The Black Terror,' so they can duplicate her scenes with another star, and meanwhile we had half the negative matched and marked for colors and spliced in rolls, all ready for the printer."

Without waiting for an answer from us, or expecting one, he gave one of his reels a vicious spin, producing the whirring noise; then grasping both reels between his fingers and bringing them to an abrupt stop, so that I wondered he did not burn himself from the friction, he located the next piece to be eliminated.

We followed the hall into the smaller studio and there found a comedy company at work. Without stopping to watch the players, ghastly under the light from the Cooper-Hewitts and Kliegel arcs, we found a precarious way back of the set around and under stage braces, to the covered bridge leading once more to the corridor outside Manton's office.

Now the girl was absent from her place in the little waiting room. Manton's door stood open. Without ceremony Kennedy led the way in and dropped down at the side of the promoter's huge mahogany desk.

"I'm tired, Walter," he said. "Furthermore, I think this picture world of yours is a bedlam. We face a hard task."

"How do you propose to go about things?" I asked.

"I'm afraid this is a case which will have to be approached entirely through psychological reactions. You and I will have to become familiar with the studio and home life of all the long list of possible suspects. I shall analyze the body fluids of the deceased and learn the cause of death, and I will find out what it is on the towel, but"—sighing—"there are so many different ramifications, so many—"

Suddenly his eye caught the corner of a piece of paper slid under the glass of Manton's desk. He pulled it out; then handed it to me.

MEMORANDUM FOR MR. MANTON

Have learned Enid Faye is out of Pentangle and can be engaged for about twelve hundred if you act quickly. Why not cancel Lamar contract after "Black Terror," if she continues up-stage?

WERNER.

"I caught the name Lamar," Kennedy explained. Then an expression of gratification crept into his face. "Miss Lamar was 'up-stage'?" he mused. "That's a theatrical word for cussedness, isn't it?"

I paid little attention. The name of Enid Faye had attracted my own interest. This was the little dare-devil who had breezed into the Pacific Coast film colony and had swept everything before her. Not only had she displayed amazing nerve for her sex and size, but she had been pretty and beautifully formed, had been as much at home in a ballroom as in an Annette Kellermann bathing suit. In less than six months she had learned to act and had been brought to the Eastern studios of Pentangle. Now it was possible that she would be captured by Manton, would be blazoned all over the country by that gentleman, would become another star of his making.

"Let's go, Walter!" Kennedy, impatient, rose. I noticed that he folded the little note, slipping it into his pocket.

Out in the hall voices came to us from Werner's office. After some little hesitation Kennedy opened the door unceremoniously. At the table, littered with blue prints and drawings and colored plates of famous home interiors, was the director. With him was Manton. Seated facing them, in rare good humor, was a fascinating little lady.

The promoter rose. "Professor Kennedy, I want you to meet Miss Enid Faye, one of our real comers. And Mr. Jameson, Enid, of the New York Star."

She acknowledged the introduction to Kennedy gracefully. Then she turned, rising, and rushed to me most effusively, leading me to a leather-covered couch and pulling me to a seat beside her.

"Mr. Jameson," she purred. "I just love newspaper men; I think they're perfectly wonderful always. Tell me, do you like little Enid?"

I nodded, confused and unhappy, and as red as a schoolboy.

"That's fine," she went on, in the best modulated and most wonderful voice I thought I had ever heard. "I like you and I know we're going to be the best of friends. Tell me, what's your first name?"

"Now, Enid," reproved Manton, in fatherly tones, "you'll have plenty of time to vamp your publicity later. For the present, please listen to me. We're talking business."

"Shoot every hair of this old gray head!" she directed, pertly.

She did not move away, however, I could feel the warmth of her, could catch the delicacy of the perfume she used. I noted the play of her slender fingers, the trimness of her ankle, the piquancy of a nose revealed to me in profile—and nothing else.

"This is your chance, Enid," Manton continued, earnestly and rather eagerly. "You know the film will be the most talked about one this year. We've got the Merritt papers lined up and that's the best advertising in the world. Everyone will know you took Stella's place, and—well, you'll step right in."

She studied the tips of her boots, stretching boyish limbs straight in front of her, then smoothing the soft folds of her skirt.

"Talk money to me, Mr. Man!" she exclaimed. "Talk the shekels, the golden shekels."

"We're broke," he protested. "A thousand—"

She shook her head.

Werner broke in, suddenly anxious. "Don't pass up the chance, Enid," he pleaded. "What can Pentangle do for you? And I've always wanted to direct you again—"

"I'll make it twelve hundred," Manton interrupted, "if you'll make the contract personally with me. Then if Manton Pictures—"

"All right!" She jumped to her feet, extending a hand straight forward to each, the right to Manton, the left to Werner. "You're on!"

I thought that I was forgotten. A wave of jealousy swept over me. After all, she simply wanted me to write her up. In a daze I heard Manton.

"You're a wise little girl, Enid," he told her. "Play the game right with me and you'll climb high. The sky's the limit, now. I'll make you—make you big!"

With a full, warm smile she swung around to me and I knew I was not being slighted, after all.

"That's what Longfellow said, isn't it, Mr. Jameson?"

"What?" My heart began to beat like a trip hammer.

"Excelsior! Excelsior! It packs them in!"

She laughed so infectiously that we all joined in. Then Manton turned to Kennedy.

"I've located Millard for you. He's to meet us at my apartment at seven. It's six-thirty now. And you, Enid"—facing her—"if you'll come, too, there's another man I want you to meet, and Larry, of course, will be there—"

Enid studied Kennedy. He was hesitating as though not sure whether to accompany Manton or not. I never did learn what other course of action had occurred to him.

But I did notice that the little star, with her pert, upturned face, seemed more anxious to have Kennedy go along than she was to meet the mysterious individual mentioned without name by Manton. For an instant she was on the point of addressing him, flippantly, no doubt. Then, I think she was rather awed at Craig's reputation.

All at once she shrugged her shoulders and turned to me, plucking my sleeve, her expression brightening irresistibly. "You'll come, too"—dimpling—"Jamie!"

VIII

LAWRENCE MILLARD

It struck me on the trip to Manton's apartment that the film people were wholly unfeeling, were even uninterested in the death of Stella Lamar except where it interfered with their business arrangements. Werner excused himself and did not accompany us, on the score of the complete realignment of production necessary to place Enid in Stella's part. It seemed to me that he felt a certain relish in the problem, that he was almost glad of the circumstances which brought Enid to him. His last words to Manton were, to be sure to have Millard recast the action of the scenes wherever possible, so as to give Enid the better chance to display her own personality.

I marveled as I realized that the remains of Stella Lamar were scarcely cold before these people were figuring on the star to take her place.

As Manton talked, the thought crossed my mind that such a man needed no publicity manager. I dismissed the idea that he might be capable even of murder for publicity. But at least it was an insight into some methods of the game.

As our car mounted to the Concourse and turned Manhattanward I was distinctly unhappy. Manton monopolized Enid completely, insisting upon talking over everything under the sun, from the wardrobe she would need in Stella's part and the best sort of personal advertising campaign for her, to the first available evening when she could go to dinner with him.

She sat in the rear seat, between Kennedy and the promoter, which did not add to my sense of comfort. The only consoling feature from my viewpoint was that I was admirably placed to study her, and that Manton held her so engrossed that I had every opportunity to do so unnoticed. Because she had overwhelmed me so completely I did nothing of the kind. I knew we were riding with the most beautiful woman in New York, but I did not know the color of her hair or eyes, or even the sort of hat or dress she wore. In short I was movie-struck.

We stopped at last at a huge, ornate apartment house on Riverside Drive and Manton led the way through the wide Renaissance entrance and the luxurious marble hall to the elevator. His quarters, on the top floor, facing the river, were almost exotic in the lavishness and barbaric splendor of their furnishings. My first impression as we entered the place was that Manton had purposely planned the dim lights of rich amber and the clinging Oriental fragrance hovering about everything so as to produce an alluring and enticing atmosphere. The chairs and wide upholstered window seats, the soft, yielding divans in at least two corners, with their miniature mountains of tiny pillows, all were comfortable with the comfort one associates with lotus eating and that homeward journey soon to be forgotten. There was the smoke of incense, unmistakably. On a taboret were cigarettes and cigars and through heavy curtains I caught a glimpse of a sideboard and decanters, filled and set out very frankly.

A Japanese butler, whom Manton called Huroki, took our hats and retreated with a certain emanating effluvium of subtlety such as I had known only once before, when the Oriental attendant left me on the occasion of my only visit to an opium den in Chinatown.

A moment later Millard, who had been waiting, rose to greet us.

I would have guessed him to be an author, I believe, had I met him at random anywhere in the city. He affected all the professional marks and mannerisms, and yet he did so gracefully. I noticed, in the little hall where Huroki placed our headgear, a single-jointed Malacca stick, a dark-colored and soft-brimmed felt hat, and a battered brief-case. That was Millard, unquestionably. The man himself was tall and loose-limbed, heavy with an appearance of slenderness. His face was handsome, rather intellectual in spite of rather than because of large horn-rimmed glasses. His mouth and chin showed strength and determination, which was a surprise to me. In fact, in no way did he seem to reveal the artist. Lawrence Millard was a commercial writer, a dreamer never.

First he greeted Enid, taking both of her hands in his. In this one brief moment all my own little romance went glimmering, for I could not blind myself to the softening of his expression, the welcoming light in hers, the long interval in which their fingers remained interlaced.

And then another thought came to me, hastened, fed and fattened upon my jealousy. The sealed testimony in the case of Millard vs. Millard! Could Enid, by any chance, be concerned in that?

The next moment I dismissed the thought, or at least I thought I did so. I tried to picture Enid's work on the Coast, to remember the short time she had been in the East. It was possible Millard had known her before she went to Los Angeles, but unlikely.

Millard next turned to Kennedy.

"I just learned of the tragedy a short while ago, Professor," he exclaimed. "It is terrible, and so amazingly sudden, too! It—it has upset me completely. Tell me, have you found anything? Have you discovered any possible clue? Is there anything at all I can do to help?"

"I would like to ask a few questions," Kennedy explained.

"By all means!"

He extended a hand to me and I found it damp and flabby, as though he were more concerned than his manner betrayed. He faced Kennedy again, however, immediately.

"Stella and I didn't make a go of our married life at all," he went on, frankly enough. "I was very sorry, too, because I was genuinely fond of her."

"How recently have you seen her?"

"Stella? Not for over a month—perhaps longer than that."

Manton took Enid by the arm. It was evidently her first visit to the apartment and he was anxious to show her his various treasures.

Millard, Kennedy, and I found a corner affording a view out over the Hudson. After Kennedy had described, briefly, the circumstances of Stella's death, at Millard's insistence, he produced the note he had found in her handbag. The author recognized it at once, without reading it.

"Yes, I wrote that!" Then just a trace of emotion crept into his voice.

"I was too late," he murmured.

"What was it you wanted to say?" Kennedy inquired.

Millard's glance traveled to Manton and Enid, a troubled something in his expression. I could see that the promoter was making the most of his tete-a-tete with the girl, but she seemed perfectly at ease and quite capable of handling the man, and I, certainly, was more disturbed at the interest of Millard.

"I thought there was something about the business I ought to tell Stella," he answered, finally. "Manton Pictures is pretty shaky."

"Oh! Then Manton wasn't talking for effect when he told Miss Faye that the company was broke?"

"No, indeed! In fact, didn't Enid make her agreement with Manton personally? That's what I advised her to do."

Kennedy nodded. "But is Manton himself financially sound?"

Millard laughed. "Lloyd Manton always has a dozen things up his sleeve. He may have a million or he may owe a million." In the author's voice was no respect for his employer. A touch of malice crept into his tone. "Manton will make money for anyone who can make money for him," he added, "that is, provided he has to do it."

Kennedy and I exchanged glances. This was close to an assertion of downright dishonesty. At that moment Huroki stole in on padded feet, as noiseless as a wraith.

"Yes, Huroki?" His master turned, inquiringly.

"Mr. Leigh," was the butler's announcement.

"Show him in," said Manton; then he hurried over to us. "Courtlandt Leigh, the banker, you know."

I imagine I showed my surprise, for Kennedy smiled as he caught my face. Leigh was a bigger man than Phelps, of the highest standing in downtown financial circles. If Manton had interested Courtlandt Leigh in moving pictures he was a wizard indeed.

It seemed to me that the banker was hardly in the apartment before he saw Enid, and from that moment the girl engrossed him to the exclusion of everything else. For Enid, I will say that she was a wonder. She seemed to grasp the man's instant infatuation and immediately she set about to complete the conquest, all without permitting him so much as to touch her.

"You'll excuse us?" remarked Manton, easily, as he drew Phelps and Enid away.

"See!" exclaimed Millard, in a low voice, frowning now as he watched the girl. "Manton's clever! I've never known him unable to raise money, and that's why I wanted Enid to have her contract with him personally. If Manton Pictures blows up he'd put her in some other company."

"He has more than one?" This seemed to puzzle Kennedy.

"He's been interested in any number on the side," Millard explained. "Now he's formed another, but it's a secret so far. You've heard of Fortune Features, perhaps?"

Kennedy looked at me, but I shook my head.

"What is 'Fortune Features'?" Kennedy asked the question of Millard.

"Just another company in which Manton has an interest," he replied, casually. "That was why I said I advised that Enid make her contract personally with Manton. If Manton Pictures goes up, then he will have to swing her into Fortune Features—the other Manton enterprise, don't you see?" He paused, then added: "By the way, don't say anything outside about that. It isn't generally known—and as soon as anyone does hear it, everybody in the film game will hear it. You don't know how gossip travels in this business."

Kennedy asked a few personal questions about Stella, but Millard's answers indicated that he had not contemplated or even hoped for a reconciliation, that his interest in his former wife had become thoroughly platonic. Just now, however, he seemed unable to keep Manton out of his mind.

"Oh, Manton's clever!" he said, confidentially to Kennedy, as he watched the promoter deftly maneuvering Leigh and Enid into a position side by side.

And indeed, as Millard talked, I began to get some inkling of how really clever was the game which Manton played.

"Why," continued Millard, warming up to his story—for, to him, above all, a good story was something that had to be told, whatever might result from it—"I have known him to pay a visit some afternoon to Wall Street—go down there to beard the old lions in their den. He always used to show up about the closing time of the market.

"I've known him to get into the office of some one like Leigh or Phelps. Then he'll begin to talk about his brilliant prospects in the company he happens to be promoting at the time. If you listen to Manton you're lost. I know it—I've listened," he added, whimsically.

"Well," he continued, "the banker will begin to get restless after a bit—not at Manton, but at not getting away. 'My car is outside,' Manton will say. 'Let me drive you uptown.' Of course, there's nothing else for the banker to do but to accept, and when he gets into Manton's car he's glad he did. I don't know anyone who picks out such luxurious things as he does. Why, that man could walk right out along Automobile Row, broke, and some one would GIVE him a car."

"How does he do it?" I put the question to him.

"How does a fish swim?" said Millard, smiling. "He's clever, I tell you. Once he has the banker in the car, perhaps they stop for a few moments at a club. At any rate, Manton usually contrives it so that, as they approach his apartment, he has his talk all worked up to the point where the banker is genuinely interested. You know there's almost nothing people will talk to you longer about than moving pictures.

"Well, on one pretext or another, Manton usually persuades the banker to step up here for a moment. Poor simp! It's all over with him then. I'll never forget how impressed Phelps was with this place the first time. There, now, watch this fellow, Leigh. He thinks this looks like a million dollars. We're all here, playing Manton's game. We're his menagerie—he's Barnum. I tell you, Leigh's lost, lost!"

I did not know quite what to make of Millard's cynicism. Was he trying to be witty at Manton's expense? I noticed that he did not smile himself. Although he was talking to us, his attention was not really on us. He was still watching Enid.

"Then, along would happen Stella, as if by chance."

Millard paused bitterly, as though he did not quite relish the telling it, but felt that Kennedy would pry it out of him or some one else finally, and he might as well have it over with frankly.

"Yes," he said, thoughtfully, "but it all wasn't really Manton's fault, after all. Stella liked the Bohemian sort of life too much—and Manton does the Bohemian up here wonderfully. It was too much for Stella. Then, when Phelps came along and was roped in, she fell for him. It was good-by, poor Millard! I wasn't rapid enough for that crowd."

I almost began to sympathize with Millard in the association into which, for his living's sake, his art had forced him. I realized, too, that really the banker, the wise one from Wall Street, was the sucker.

Indeed, as Millard told it, I could easily account for the temptation of Stella. To a degree, I suppose, it was really her fault, for she ought to have known the game, shown more sense than to be taken in by the thing. I wondered at the continued relations of Millard with Manton, under the circumstances. However, I reflected, if Stella had chosen to play the little fool, why should Millard have allowed that to ruin his own chances?

What interested me now was that Millard did not seem to relish the attentions which the banker was paying to Enid. Was Manton framing up the same sort of game again on Leigh?

However, when Enid shot a quick glance at Millard in an aside of the conversation, accompanied by a merry wink, I saw that Millard, though still doubtful, was much more at ease.

Evidently there was a tacit understanding between the two.

Kennedy glanced over at me. Bit by bit the checkered history of Stella Lamar's life was coming to light.

I began to see more clearly. Deserting Millard and fascinated by Manton and his game, she had been used to interest Phelps in the company. In turn she had been dazzled by the glitter of the Phelps gold. She had not proved loyal even to the producer and promoter.

Perhaps, I reflected, that was why Millard was so apparently complacent. One could not, under the circumstances, have expected him to display wild emotion. His attitude had been that of one who thought, "She almost broke me; let her break some one else."

That, however, was not his attitude toward Enid now. Indeed, he seemed genuinely concerned that she should not follow in the same steps.

Later, I learned that was not all of the history of Stella. Fifteen hundred dollars a week of her own money, besides lavish presents, had been too much for her. Even Phelps's money had had no over-burdening attraction for her. The world—at least that part of it which spends money on Broadway, had been open to her.

Jack Daring had charmed her for a while—hence the engagement. Of Shirley, I did not even know. Perhaps the masterful crime roles he played might have promised some new thrill, with the possibility that they expressed something latent in his life. At any rate, she had dilettanted about him, to the amazement and dismay of Marilyn. That we knew.

The dinner hour was approaching, and, in spite of the urgent invitation of Manton, Leigh was forced to excuse himself to keep a previous appointment. I felt, though, that he would have broken it if only Enid had added her urging. But she did not, much to the relief of Millard. Manton took it in good part. Perhaps he was wise enough to reflect that many other afternoons were in the lap of the future.

"What is Manton up to?" Kennedy spoke to Millard. "Is it off with the old and on with the new? Is Phelps to be cast aside like a squeezed-out lemon, and Leigh taken on for a new citrus fruit?"

Millard smiled. He said nothing, but the knowing glance was confirmation enough that in his opinion Kennedy had expressed the state of affairs correctly.

Millard hastened to the side of Enid at once and we learned then that they had a theater engagement together and that Millard had the tickets in his pocket. Once more I realized it was no new or recent acquaintanceship between these two. Again I wondered what woman had been named in Stella Lamar's divorce suit, and again dismissed the thought that it could be Enid.

Kennedy took his hat and handed me mine. "We must eat, Walter, as well as the rest of them," he remarked, when Manton led the way to the door.

I was loath to leave and I suppose I showed it. The truth was that little Enid Faye had captivated me. It was hard to tear myself away.

In the entrance I hesitated, wondering whether I should say good-by to her. She seemed engrossed with Millard.

A second time she took me clean off my feet. While I stood there, foolishly, she left Millard and rushed up, extending her little hand and allowing it to rest for a moment clasped in mine.

"We didn't have a single opportunity to get acquainted, Mr. Jameson," she complained, real regret in the soft cadences of her voice. "Won't you phone me sometime? My name's in the book, or I'll be at the studio—"

I was tongue-tied. My glance, shifting from hers because I was suddenly afraid of myself, encountered the gaze of Millard from behind. Now I detected the unmistakable fire of jealousy in the eyes of the author. I presume I was never built to be a heavy lover. Up and down my spine went a shiver of fear. I dropped Enid's hand and turned away abruptly.

IX

WHITE-LIGHT SHADOWS

"What do you think of it?" I asked Kennedy, when we were half through our meal at a tiny restaurant on upper Broadway.

"We're still fumbling in the dark," he replied.

"There's the towel—"

"Yes, and almost any one on Mackay's list of nine suspects could have placed it in that washroom."

"Well—" I was determined to draw him out. My own impressions, I must confess, were gloriously muddled. "Manton heads the list," I suggested. "Everyone says she was mixed up with him."

"Manton may have philandered with her; undoubtedly he takes a personal interest in all his stars." Kennedy, I saw, remembered the promoter's close attentions to Enid Faye. "Nevertheless, Walter, he is first and foremost and all the time the man of business. His heart is in his dollars and Millard even suggests that he is none too scrupulous."

"If he had an affair with Stella," I rejoined, "and she became up-stage—the note you found suggested trouble, you know—then Manton in a burst of passion—"

"No!" Kennedy stopped me. "Don't forget that this was a cold-blooded, calculated crime. I'm not eliminating Manton yet, but until we find some tangible evidence of trouble between Stella and himself we can hardly assume he would kill the girl who's made him perhaps a million dollars. Every motive in Manton's case is a motive against the crime."

"That eliminates Phelps, then, too. He nearly owned the company."

"Yes, unless something happened to outweigh financial considerations in his mind also."

"But, good heavens! Kennedy," I protested. "If you go on that way you'll not eliminate anyone."

"I can't yet," he explained, patiently. "It's just as I said. We're fishing in the dark, absolutely. So far we haven't a single basic fact on which to build any structure of hypothesis. We must go on fishing. I expect you to dig up all the facts about these people; every odd bit of gossip or rumor or anything else. I'll bring my science to play, but there's nothing I can do except analyze Stella's stomach contents and the spots on the towel; that is, until we've got a much more tangible lead than any which have developed so far."

"Is there anything I can do to-night?"

"Yes!" He looked at his watch. "There are two men who were very close to Miss Lamar. Jack Gordon was engaged to her, Merle Shirley seemed to have been mixed up with her seriously. All the picture people have night haunts. See what you can find about these two men."

"But I don't know where to find them offhand, and—"

"Both belong to the Goats Club, probably. Try that as a start."

I nodded and began to hurry my dessert. But I could not resist questioning him.

"You think they are the most likely suspects?"

"No, but they were intimately associated with Miss Lamar in her daily life and they are the two we have learned the least about."

"Oh!" I was disappointed. Then I rallied to the attack for a final time. "Who is the most likely one. Just satisfy my curiosity, Craig."

He took a folded note from his pocket, opening it. It was the memorandum from Manton's desk which I had mentioned. In a flash I understood.

"Werner!" I exclaimed. "They said he was mixed up with her, too. He was the first back and out of the car and he had time to clean a needle on the towel, had a better opportunity than anyone else. More"—I began to get excited—"he was lying on the floor close to her in the scene and could have jabbed her with a needle very easily, and—and he was extremely nervous when you questioned him, the most nervous of all, and—and, finally, he had a motive, he wanted to get Enid Faye with Manton Pictures, as this note shows."

"Very good, Walter." Kennedy's eyes were dancing in amusement. "It is true that Werner had the best motive, so far as we know now, but it's a fantastic one. Men don't commit cold-blooded murder just to create a vacancy for a movie star. If Werner was going to kill Miss Lamar he never would have written this note about Miss Faye."

"Unless to divert suspicion," I suggested.

He shook his head. "The whole thing's too bizarre."

"Werner was close to her in the dark. All the other things point to him, don't they?"

"It's too bad everyone wasn't searched, at that," Kennedy admitted. "Nevertheless, at the time I realized that Werner had had the best opportunity for the actual performance of the crime and I watched him very closely and made him go through every movement just so I could study him. I believe he's innocent—at least as far as I've gone in the case."

I determined to stick to my opinion. "I believe it's Werner," I insisted.

"By the time you've dug up all the gossip about Gordon and Shirley you won't be so sure, Walter."

I was, however. Kennedy was not as familiar with the picture world as I. I had heard of too many actual happenings more strange and bizarre and wildly fantastic than anything conceivable in other walks of life. People in the film game, as they call it, live highly seasoned lives in which everything is exaggerated. The mere desire to make a place for Enid might not have actuated Werner, granting he was the guilty man. Nevertheless it could easily have contributed. And it struck me suddenly, an additional argument, that Werner, of all of them, was the most familiar with the script. He had been able to cast himself for the part of old Remsen. There was not a detail which he could not have arranged very skillfully.

At the Goats Club I was lucky to discover a member whom I knew well enough to take into my confidence by stating my errand. He was one of the Star's former special writers and an older classman of the college which had graduated Kennedy and myself.

"Merle Shirley is not a member here," he said. "As a matter of fact, I've only just heard the name. But Jack Gordon's a Goat, worse luck. That fellow's a bad actor—in real life—and a disgrace to us."

"Tell me all you know about him?" I asked.

"Well, to give you an example, he was in here just about a week ago. I was sitting in the grill, eating an after-theater supper, when I heard the most terrible racket. He and Emery Phelps, the banker, you know, were having an honest-to-goodness fight right out in the lobby. It took three of the men to separate them."

"What was it all about."

"Well, Gordon owes money right and left, not a few hundred or some little personal debts like that, but thousands and thousands of dollars. I got it from some of the other men here that he has been speculating on the curb downtown, losing consistently. More than that, he's engaged to Stella Lamar—you knew that?—and he's been blowing money on her. Then they tell me his professional work is suffering, that his recent screen appearances are terrible; the result of late hours and worry, I suppose."

"The fight with Phelps was over money?"

"Of course! I figure that he kept drawing against his salary at the studio until the film company shut down on him. Then probably he began to borrow from Phelps, who's Manton's backer now, until the banker shut down on him also. At any rate, Phelps had begun to dun him and it led to the fight."

"That's all you know about Gordon?"

"Lord! Isn't it enough?"

I walked out of the club and toward Broadway, reflecting upon this information. Could Gordon's debts have any bearing upon the case? All at once one possibility struck me. He had been borrowing from Phelps. Perhaps he had borrowed from Stella also. Perhaps that was the cause of their quarrel. Perhaps she had threatened to make trouble—it was a slender motive, but worth bringing to the attention of Kennedy.

My immediate problem, however, was to obtain some information about Merle Shirley. At first I thought I would make the rounds of some of the better-known cafes, but that seemed a hopeless task. Suddenly I remembered Belle Balcom, formerly with the Star. I recollected a previous case of Kennedy's where she and I had been great rivals in the quest of news. I recalled a trip we had made to Greenwich Village together. Belle knew more people about town than any other newspaper woman. Now, for some months, she had been connected with Screenings, a leading cinema "fan" magazine, and would unquestionably be posted upon the photoplayers.

Luckily, I caught her at home.

"Bless your soul," she told me over the phone, in delight, "I've just been aching for some one to take me out to-night. We'll go to the Midnight Fads and if Shirley isn't there the head waiter will tell you all I don't remember. It was a glorious fight."

She wouldn't say any more over the phone, but I was hugely curious. Had there been another encounter with fists? And who had been involved?

When she met me finally, at the Subway station, and when we obtained an out-of-the-way table at the Fads, she explained. It seemed that Shirley had met Stella there a number of times and that Gordon, at last, had got wind of it. Gordon first had come up himself, quietly, pleading with Stella. She had been in a high humor and had refused even to listen to him. Then he had become insulting. At that Shirley knocked him down.

The head waiter, a witness of the affair, ordered Gordon put out, but did not request Shirley or Stella to leave, because the other man had been the aggressor without any question. After more than an hour Gordon returned, quietly and unobtrusively, with another girl. From Belle's description I knew it was Marilyn Loring. Taking another table, Marilyn had stared at Shirley reproachfully while Gordon had glared at Stella.

Shirley put up with this for just about so long. As Belle described it, his face gradually became more and more red and he controlled himself with increasing difficulty. Stella, seeing the coming of the storm, tried to get him to go. He refused. She threatened to leave him. He paid no attention. All at once he boiled over and with great strides walked over to Gordon and mauled him all over the place. The leading man had no chance whatever in the hands of the irate Westerner. Several waiters, attempting to intervene, were flung aside. Only when Shirley began to cool off were they able to eject the two men. Both Stella and Marilyn had left, separately, before that. Neither of the men or women had been at the Fads since, or at least the head waiter, called over by Belle, so informed us.

Unable to obtain any other facts of interest, I returned finally to the apartment shared by Kennedy and myself. First he listened to my account, plainly interested. Then, when I had concluded, he rose and faced me rather gravely.

"It's getting more and more complicated, Walter," he exclaimed. "After you left I remembered that there was one point of investigation I had failed to cover—Miss Lamar's home here in the city. I got our old friend, First-Deputy O'Connor, on the wire and learned that at the request of Mackay, from Tarrytown, they had sent a man up to the place and that just an hour or less before I called they had located and were holding her colored maid. I hurried down to headquarters and questioned the girl."

"Yes?" To me it sounded promising.

"The negress didn't know a thing so far as the crime is concerned," Kennedy went on, "but I gained quite an insight into the private life of the star."

"You mean—"

"I mean I know the men who went to Miss Lamar's apartment, although beyond the fact of her receiving them I can tell nothing, for she sent the maid home at night; there were no maid's quarters."

"Their visits may have been perfectly innocent?"

"Of course! We can only draw conclusions."

"Who were the various callers?"

"Jack Gordon—"

"Her fiance!"

"Merle Shirley—"

"Shirley admitted it when you questioned him."

"Manton—"

"Everyone knows that!"

"Werner—" A side glance at me.

I said nothing. My expression spoke for me.

"And Emery Phelps!"

At that I did show surprise. Although Mackay had hinted at something of the kind, I, for one, had not considered the banker seriously.

"Good heavens! Kennedy," I exploded. "She was mixed up with just about every man connected with the company."

"Exactly!" As usual, he seemed calm and unconcerned.

I could regard the case only with increasing amazement—the bitter, conflicting emotions of Manton and Phelps, of Daring, Shirley, and Millard. With them all Stella had been the pretty trouble maker.

"How do you suppose they could all remain in the same company?" I showed my surprise at the situation.

Kennedy pondered a moment, then replied:

"A moment's reflection ought to give you one answer. I think, Walter, they were either under contract or they had their money in the company. They couldn't break."

"I suppose so. What I wonder is, was Marilyn as jealous of Stella as her screen character would make her in a story? She's the only one we don't hear much about."

Kennedy did not seem, at least at present, to give this phase of it anything like the weight he credited to the frenzied financial relations the case was uncovering.

It was true, as I learned later, that Manton was at that very moment doing perhaps as much as anyone else ever did to discredit the picture game in Wall Street.

X

CHEMICAL RESEARCH

The following morning I found Kennedy up ahead of me, and I felt certain that he had gone to the laboratory. Sure enough, I found him at work in the midst of the innumerable scientific devices which he had gathered during years of crime detection of every sort.

As usual, he was surrounded by a perfect litter of test tubes, beakers, reagents, microscopes, slides, and culture tubes. He had cut out the curious spots from the towel I had discovered and was studying them to determine their nature. From the mass of paraphernalia I knew he was neglecting no possibility which might lead to the hidden truth or produce a clue to the crime.

"Have you learned anything yet?" I asked.

"Those brownish spots were blood, of course," was his reply as he stopped a moment in his work. "In the blood I discovered some other substance, though I can't seem to identify it yet. It will take time. I thought it might be a drug or poison, but it doesn't seem to be—at least nothing one might ordinarily expect."

"How about the other spots, not the Chinese yellow?"

"Another problem I haven't solved. I dissolved enough of them so that I have plenty of material to study if I don't waste it. But so far I haven't been able to identify the substance with anything I know. There's a lot more work of elimination, Walter, before we're on the road to the solution of this case. Whatever stained the towel was very unusual. As near as I can make out the spots are of some protein composition. But it's not exactly a poison, although many proteins may be extremely poisonous and extremely difficult to identify because they are of organic nature."

I was disappointed. It seemed to me that he had made comparatively little progress so far.

"There's one thing," he added. "Samples of the body fluids of the victim have been sent down by the coroner at Tarrytown and I have analyzed them. While I haven't decided what it was that killed Stella Lamar, I am at least convinced that it has something to do with these towel spots. They are not exactly the same—in fact, I should say they were complementary, or, perhaps better, antithetical."

"The mark wasn't made by the needle which scratched her, then?"

"That's what I thought at first, that the point used had been wiped off on the towel. Then I decided that the spots had nothing to do with the case at all. Now I believe there is some connection, after all."

"I—I don't understand it," I protested.

"It's very baffling," he agreed, absent-mindedly.

"If the towel wasn't used to clean the fatal needle," I went on, "then it may have been used before they went out instead of afterward."

"Exactly. As a matter of fact, if I had not been so confused yesterday by all the details of the case, by the many people involved, I would have noticed at a glance that the blood spots on the towel could not come from some one using it to wipe the needle. And any hypothesis that it had been used out in Tarrytown was ridiculous, because Miss Lamar was only scratched faintly and lost no blood. If I had been a little more clever I might have been altogether too clever. I might possibly have thrown the towel away, because there certainly was no logical reason for connecting it with the crime."

"Just when do you suppose Stella was pricked?" I asked.

"That's a vital consideration. Just now I do not know the poison and so cannot tell how quickly it acted." He began to put aside his various paraphernalia. "Suppose we go at this thing by a process of deduction rather than from the end of scientific analysis." He sat on a corner of the bench. "What do we find?" he began.

"While I've been working here with the test tubes and the microscope I've been trying to reconstruct what must have happened, trying to trace out every action of Stella Lamar as nearly as it is possible for us to do so. I don't think we need to go back of their arrival at the house, for the present. They seem to have been there a long while before the taking of the particular scene, since there were twelve other scenes preceding and since it requires time to put up the electric lights and make the connections, as well as to set the cameras, take tests, rearrange the furniture, and all the rest of it.

"They arrived at the house in two automobiles; with the exception of Phelps, who was there already, and Manton, who came in his own limousine. That means that Miss Lamar had company on the trip out, the principals probably riding with each other in one car. At the house they were all more or less together. There were people about constantly and it would seem as if there was small opportunity for anyone to inflict the scratch which caused her death. I don't mean that it would have been impossible to prick her. I mean that she would have felt the jab of the point. In all likelihood she would have cried out and glanced around. Take a needle yourself, sometime, Walter, and try to duplicate the scratch on your own arm in such a way that you would not be aware of it.

"So you see I'm counting upon some sort of exclamation from Miss Lamar. If she were inoculated with the poison with other folks about, it is sure some one would have remembered a cry, a questioning glance, a quick grasp of the forearm—for the nerves are very sensitive in the skin there—"

"No one did recall anything of the kind," I interrupted.

"It is from that fact that I hope to deduce something. Now let's follow her, figuratively, to her little dressing room. This was a part of the living room where the rest waited. It is not a certainty, but yet rather a sure guess, that if she had received a scratch behind those thin silk curtains her cry would have been heard. What is even more plausible is that she would have hurried out, or at least put her head out, to see who had pricked her.

"I made a very careful examination of that little alcove with the idea that some artifice might have been used. It occurred to me that a poisoned point could have been inserted in her belongings in some way so that she would have brought about her own death, directly. To have caught herself on a needle point in her bag, for instance, would not have impressed her to the point of making a disturbance. She might have checked her exclamation, in that case, because she would be blaming herself.

"But I found nothing in her things, nor did I discover anything in the library. It seems to me, therefore, that we must look for a direct human agency."

A thought struck me and I hastened to suggest it. "Could some device have been arranged in her clothes, Craig; something like the poison rings of the Middle Ages, a tiny metal thing to spring open and expose its point when pressed against her in the action of the scenes?"

"That occurred to me at the time. That's why I asked Mackay to send all her clothes down here, every stitch and rag of them. I've gone over everything already this morning. Not only have I examined the various materials for stains, but I've tested each hook and eye and button and pin. I've been very careful to cover that possibility."

"You think, then, she was scratched deliberately by some one during the taking of the scenes?"

"If you've followed my line of reasoning you will see that we are driven to that assumption. Perhaps later I will make tests on a given number of girls of Stella's general age and type and temperament to show that they will cry out at the unexpected prick of a fine needle. It's illogical to expect that a cry from Miss Lamar, even an exclamation, would have passed unnoticed except during the excitement of actual picture taking."

Another inspiration came to me, but I was almost afraid to voice it. It seemed a daring theory. "Could death have resulted from poison administered in some other fashion, by something she had eaten, for instance?" I ventured. "Couldn't the scratch be coincidental?"

Kennedy shook his head. "There's the value of our chemical analysis and scientific tests. Her stomach contents showed nothing except as they might have been affected by her weakened condition. From Doctor Blake's report—and he found no ordinary symptoms, remember—and from my own observation, too, I can easily prove in court that she was killed by the mark which was so small that it escaped the physician altogether."

I turned away. Once more Kennedy's reasoning seemed to be leading into a maze of considerations beyond me. How could the deductive method produce results in a case as mysterious as this?

"Having determined that Miss Lamar received the inoculation during the making of one of the scenes, as nearly as we can do so," Kennedy went on, "suppose we take the scenes in order, one at a time, from the last photographed to the first, analyzing each in turn. Remember that we seek a situation where there is not only an opportunity to jab her with a needle, but one in which an outcry would be muffled or inaudible."

I now saw that Kennedy had brought in the bound script of the story, "The Black Terror," and I wondered again, as I had often before, at his marvelous capacity for attention to detail.

"'The spotlight on the floor reveals the girl sobbing over the body of the millionaire,'" he read, aloud, musingly. "H'mm! 'She screams and cries out.' Then the others rush in."

For several moments Kennedy paced the floor of the laboratory, the manuscript open in his hands.

"We rehearsed that, with Werner; and we questioned everyone, too. And remember! Miss Lamar, instead of crying out as she was supposed to do, just crumpled up silently. So"—thumbing over a page—"we work back to scene twelve. She—she was not in that at all. Scene eleven—"

Slowly, carefully, Kennedy went through each scene to the beginning. "Certainly a dramatic opening for a mystery picture," he remarked, suddenly, as though his mind had wandered from his problem to other things. "We must admit that Millard can handle a moving-picture scenario most beautifully."

Whether it was professional jealousy or the thought of Enid, rather than the memory of my own poor attempts at screen writing, I certainly was in no mood to agree with Kennedy, for all that I knew he was correct.

"Here!" He thrust the binder in my hands. "Read that first scene," he directed. "Meanwhile I am going to phone Mackay to make sure he has had the house guarded and to make double sure no one goes near the library. We're going out to Tarrytown again, Walter, and in the biggest kind of hurry."

"What's the idea, Craig?" Kennedy's occasional bursts of mysteriousness, characteristic of him and often necessary when his theories were only half formed and too chaotic for explanations, always piqued me.

He did not seem to hear. Already he was at the telephone, manipulating the receiver hook impatiently. "What a dummy I am!" he exclaimed, with genuine feeling. "What—what an awful dummy!"

Knowing I would get nothing out of him just yet, I turned to the scene, reading as he told me. At first I could not see where the detail concerned Stella Lamar in any way. Then I came to the description of her introductory entrance, the initial view of her in the film. The lines of typewriting suddenly stood out before me in all their suggestive clearness.

> The spotlight in the hands of a shadowy figure roves across the wall and to the portieres. As it pauses there the portieres move and the fingers of a girl are seen on the edge of the silk. A bare and beautiful arm is thrust through almost to the shoulder and it begins to move the portieres aside, reaching upward to pull the curtains apart at the rings.

"You think there's something about the portieres—" I began.

Then I saw that Kennedy had his connection, that something disturbed him, that some intelligence from the other end had caught him by surprise.

"You say you were just trying to get me, Mackay? You've something to tell me and you want me to come right out—you have summoned Phelps and he's on his way from the city also—?"

"What happened?" I asked, as Kennedy hung up.

"I don't know, Walter. Mackay said he didn't want to talk over the phone and that we had just time to catch the express."

"But—"

"Hurry!" He glanced about as if wondering whether any of his scientific instruments would help him.

XI

FORESTALLED

On the train Kennedy left me, to look through the other cars, having the idea that Phelps might be aboard also. But there were no signs of the banker. We would reach Tarrytown first unless he had chosen to motor out.

Mackay was waiting at the station to meet us and to take us to the house. The little district attorney was obviously excited.

"Was the place guarded well last night?" asked Kennedy, almost before we had shaken hands.

"Yes—that is, I thought it was. That's what I want to tell you. After you left with Manton and Werner the rest of the company packed up and pulled out in the two studio cars. I was a little in doubt what to do about Phelps, but he settled it himself by announcing that he was going to town. The coroner came and issued the permit to remove the body and that was taken away. I think the house and the presence of the dead girl and all the rest of it got on Phelps's nerves, because he was irritable and impatient, unwilling to wait for his own car, until finally I drove him to the station myself."

"Was anyone, any of those on our list of possible suspects at least, alone in the room—or in the house?"

"Not while I was there," Mackay replied. "I took good care of that. Then, when everyone was gone and while Phelps was waiting for me, I detailed two of my deputies to stay on guard—one inside and one outside—for the night. I thought it sufficient precaution, since you had made your preliminary examination."

"And—" Kennedy nodded, seeking to hurry the explanation.

"And yet," added Mackay, "some one entered the house last night in spite of us."

Kennedy fairly swore under his breath. He seemed to blame himself for some omission in his investigation the previous afternoon.

"How did it happen?" I asked, rather excitedly.

"It was about three o'clock, the guards tell me. The man inside was dozing in a chair before the living-room fireplace. He was placed so he could command a view of the doorway to the library as well as the stairs and reception hall. All at once he was awakened by a shot and a cry from outside. He jumped up and ran toward the library. As he did so the portieres bellied in toward him, as if in stiff sudden draught, or as if some one had darted into their folds quickly, then out. With no hesitation he drew his own weapon, rushing the curtains. There was no one secreted about them. Then, with the revolver in one hand, he switched on the lights. The room was empty. But one pair of French windows at the farther end were wide open and it was that which had caused the current of air. He ran over and found the lock had been forced. It was not even an artistic job of jimmying."

"What about the deputy posted outside?" prompted Kennedy.

"That's the strange part of it. He was alert enough, but it's a big house to watch. He swears that the first thing he knew of any trouble was the sharp metallic click which he realized later was the sound made by the intruder in forcing the catch of the French window. It was pretty loud out in the quiet of a Tarrytown night.

"He started around from the rear and then the next thing he caught was the outline of a shadowy slinking figure as a man dropped out of the library. He called. The intruder broke into a run, darting across the open space of lawn and crashing through the shrubbery without any further effort at concealment. My man called again and began to chase the stranger, finally firing and missing. In the shrubbery a sharp branch whipped him under the chin just as he obtained a clear view of the outlined figure of his quarry and as he raised his weapon to shoot again. The revolver was knocked from his hand and he was thrown back, falling to the ground and momentarily stunned. Whoever broke into the library got away, of course."

"What did the intruder look like?" There was an eagerness in Kennedy's manner. I grasped that the case was beginning to clarify itself in his mind.

Mackay shook his head. "There was no moon, you know, and everything happened swiftly.

"But was he tall or short or slender or stout—the deputy must have got some vague idea of him at least."

"It was one of my amateur deputies," Mackay admitted, reluctantly. "He thought the man was hatless, but couldn't even be sure of that."

"Were there footprints, or fingerprints—"

"No, Mr. Kennedy, we're out of luck again. When he jumped out he fell to his hands and knees in a garden bed. The foot marks were ruined because his feet slid and simply made two irregular gashes. The marks of his hands indicated to me, anyhow, that he wore heavy gloves, rubber probably."

"Any disturbance in the library?"

"Not that I could notice. That's why I phoned you at once. I'm hoping you'll discover something."

"Well—" Kennedy sighed. "It was a wonderful opportunity to get to the bottom of this."

"I haven't told you all yet, Mr. Kennedy," Mackay went on. "There was a second man, and—"

"A second man?" Kennedy straightened, distinctly surprised. "I would swear this whole thing was a one-man job."

"They weren't together," the district attorney explained. "That's why I didn't mention them both at once. But my deputy says that when he was thrown by the lash of the branch he was unable to move for a few seconds, on account of the nerve shock I suppose, and that while he was motionless, squatted in a sort of sitting position with hands braced behind him, just as he fell, he was aware of a second stranger concealed in the shrubbery.

"The second fellow was watching the first, without the question of a doubt. While the deputy slowly rose to his feet this other chap started to follow the man who had broken into the house. But at that moment there was the sudden sound of a self-starter in a car, then the purr of a motor and the clatter of gears. Number one spun off in the darkness of the road as pretty as you please. Number two grunted, in plain disgust.

"By this time my deputy had his wind. His revolver was gone, but he jumped the second stranger with little enough hesitation and they battled royally for several minutes in the dark. Unfortunately, it was an unequal match. The intruder apparently was a stocky man, built with the strength of a battleship. He got away also, without leaving anything behind him to serve for identification."

"You have no more description than of the first man?"

"Unfortunately not. Medium height, a little inclined to be stocky, strong as a longshoreman—that's all."

"Are you sure your deputy isn't romancing?"

"Positively! He's the son of one of our best families here, a sportsman and an athlete. I knew he loved a lark, or a chance for adventure, and so I impressed him and a companion as deputies when I met them on the street on my way up to Phelps's house just after the tragedy."

Kennedy lapsed into thought. Who could the self-constituted watcher have been? Who was interested in this case other than the proper authorities? Apparently some one knew more than Mackay, more than Kennedy. Whoever it was had made no effort to communicate with any of us. This was a new angle to the mystery, a mystery which became deeper as we progressed.

At the house Kennedy first made a careful tour of the exterior, but found nothing. Mackay had doubled his guards and had sent Phelps's servants away so that there could be no interference.

Once inside, I noticed that Kennedy seemed indisposed to make another minute search of the library. He went over the frame of the French window with his lens carefully, for fingerprints. Finding nothing, he went back directly to the portieres.

For several moments he stood regarding them in thought. Then he began a most painstaking inspection of the cloth with the pocket glass, beginning at the library side.

I remembered that first scene in the manuscript which Kennedy had insisted I read. I recalled the suspicion which had flashed to me before the message from Mackay had disturbed both Kennedy's thoughts and mine. Stella Lamar had thrust her bare arm through this curtain. A needle, cleverly concealed in the folds, might easily have inflicted the fatal scratch. It was for a trace of the poison point that Kennedy searched. Of that I was sure, knowing his methods.

I glanced up and down the heavy hanging silk, looking for the glint of fine sharp steel as Kennedy had done before starting his inspection with the glass. The color of the silk, a beautiful heavy velour, was a strange dark tint very close to the grained black-brown of the woodwork. Both the thickness of the material and its dull shade made the portieres serve ideally for the purpose assumed now both by Kennedy and myself. A tiny needle might remain secreted within their folds for days. Nothing, certainly, caught my naked eye.

At last a little exclamation from Kennedy showed us that he had discovered something. I moved closer, as did Mackay.

"It's lucky none of us toyed with these curtains yesterday," he remarked, with a slight smile of gratification. "There might have been more than one lying where Stella Lamar lies at the present moment."

With wholesome respect neither Mackay nor myself touched the silk as Kennedy pointed. There were two small holes, almost microscopic, in the close-woven material. About the one there was the slightest discoloration. Not a fraction of an inch away I saw two infinitesimal spots of a dark brownish-red tinge.

"What does it mean?" I asked, although I could guess.

"The dark spots are blood, the discoloration the poison from the needle."

"And the needle?"

He shrugged his shoulders. "That's where our very scientific culprit has forestalled me, Walter! The needle was in these curtains all day yesterday. Unfortunately, I did not study the manuscript, did not attach any importance to Miss Lamar's scene at the portieres."

"The man who broke in last night—"

"Removed the needle, but"—almost amused—"not the traces of it. You see, Walter, after all, the scientific detective cannot be forestalled even by the most scientific criminal. There is nothing in the world which does not leave its unmistakable mark behind, provided you can read it. The hole in the cloth serves me quite as well as the needle itself."

Very suddenly a voice from behind us interrupted.

"Find something?"

I turned, startled, to see Emery Phelps. There was a distinct eagerness in the banker's expression.

"Yes!" Kennedy faced him, undisturbed, apparently not surprised. His scrutiny of Phelps's face was frank and searching. "Yes," he repeated, "bit by bit the guilty man is revealing himself to us."

XII

EMERY PHELPS

"There—there is something the matter with the curtains?" Phelps suggested.

Kennedy pointed to the two holes and the spots. "Miss Lamar met her death from poison introduced into her system through a tiny scratch from a prepared needle."

"Yes?" Phelps was calm now, and cool. I wondered if it were pretense on his part. "What have these little marks to do with that?"

"Don't you see?" rejoined Kennedy. "If some one had come here before the scene in the picture was played; had thrust a small needle, perhaps a hollow needle from a hypodermic syringe, through the heavy thickness of this silk—thrust it in here, the point sticking out here—well, there would be two holes left where the threads were forced apart, like this!" Kennedy took his stickpin, demonstrating.

"How could that cause Stella's death?" Phelps, at first quite upset apparently by Kennedy's discovery, now was lapsing again into his hostile mood. His question was cynical.

"Try to recall Miss Lamar's actions," Kennedy went on, patiently. "What was she supposed to do in the very first scene? 'The portieres move and the fingers of a girl are seen on the edge of the silk. A bare and beautiful arm is thrust through almost to the shoulder and it begins to move the portieres aside, reaching upward to pull the curtains apart at the rings.'"

"Do you mean to tell me—" Phelps's eyes were very wide as he paused, grasping the scheme and yet disbelieving—unless it all were a bit of fine acting—"do you mean to tell me it is possible to calculate a thing like that? How would anyone know where her arm would be?"

"It is simpler than it sounds, Mr. Phelps." Kennedy was suddenly harsh. "There is only one natural movement of an arm in that case. The culprit was undoubtedly familiar with Miss Lamar's height and with her manner of working. It is a bit of action which has to be repeated in both the long shot and close-up scenes. Jameson here can tell you how many times a scene is rehearsed. There probably were a dozen sure chances of the needle striking the girl's bare flesh. You will see from the position of the holes that it was arranged point downward and slightly turned in, and on a particular fold of the curtain, too; showing that some one placed it there only after a nice bit of calculation. Furthermore, it was high enough so that there was little chance of anyone being pricked except the star, whose death was intended."

Phelps either seemed convinced, or else he felt it inadvisable to irritate Kennedy by a further pretense of skepticism.

A point occurred to me, however. "Listen, Craig!" I spoke in a low voice. "Remember all the emphasis you placed upon the fact that she would cry out. She was not supposed to cry out in that first scene."

"No, Walter, but if you'll read the second, the close-up, you'll see that the script actually calls for a cry. Now suppose she makes an exclamation in the first instead. Nobody would think anything of it. They would assume that she had played her action a little in advance, perhaps.

"And then consider this, too! Miss Lamar, receiving the scratch, would cry out unquestionably. But she has been before the camera for years and she is trained in the idea that film must not be wasted uselessly. She would not interrupt her action for a little scratch because in these circumstances any little startled movement would fit in with the action. By the time the scene was over she would have forgotten the incident. It would mean very little to her in the preoccupation of bringing the mythical Stella Remsen into flesh-and-blood existence. The poison, however, would be putting in its deadly work."

"Wouldn't it act before the thirteenth scene—" I began.

"Not necessarily. As a matter of fact, an actress, in the excitement of her work, might resist the effects for a much longer period than some one who realizes he is sick. Some day I'm going to write a book on that. I'm going to collect hundreds of examples of people who keep plugging along because they refuse to admit anything's the matter with them. It's like Napoleon's courier who didn't drop until he'd delivered his message and made his last precise military salute."

One other thought struck me. "The blood spots on the curtain cannot be Miss Lamar's if, as you say, the scratch brought no blood."

"How about the nocturnal visitor who removed the needle in the dark? Can't you imagine him pricking himself beautifully in his hurry."

"Good heavens!" I felt the chills travel up and down my spine. "There may be another fatality, then!" I exclaimed.

Kennedy was noncommittal. "It would be too bad for justice to be cheated in that fashion," he remarked.

Phelps meanwhile had been listening to us impatiently. Finally he turned to Mackay.

"Was that all you called me out here for? Did you just want to show me the pinholes in those portieres?"

"Not exactly," Mackay replied, eyeing him sharply. "Some one forced his way into this library last night. My guard saw him, and also saw a second man who remained out in the shrubbery and seemed to be watching the first. One shot was fired, but both men got away. An automobile was waiting, perhaps two of them."

"How does this concern me?" Phelps's voice rose in anger. He strode into the library and over to the French windows, inspecting the damage to the fine woodwork with steadily rising color. Then he hurried back to the side of Mackay.

"It's up to you, District-Attorney Mackay," he said, with a great show of his ill feeling. "You practically forced me out of my own house. You sent my servants away. You put your own guards in charge, young, inexperienced deputies who don't know enough to come in when it's wet. Now you have me make this trip out here in business hours just to show me where a needle has been stuck in a curtain and where a pair of imported window sashes have been ruined."

Mackay was unruffled. "It is necessary, Mr. Phelps, that you look over this room and see that nothing else has been disturbed; that there is no further damage. Moreover, I thought you might be interested, might wish to help us determine the identity of the intruder."

"If there's any way I can really help you to do that"—sarcastically—"I'll be delighted."

"Were you here the night before the murder?" Mackay asked.

"You know I seldom spend the night in Tarrytown. I have quarters in New York, at the club, and recently I have been spending all my time in New York, on account of the situation in the picture business."

"You were not here the night before the murder, then?"

"No!"

"But you were out here yesterday before the actors arrived, before Manton or any of his technical staff and crew came?"

"I was out very early, to make sure the servants had the house ready." Phelps was red now. "Are you insinuating anything, Mackay?"

The little district attorney was demonstrating a certain quality of dogged perseverance. "Some one put the needle in the curtain before the company arrived. You probably were in the house at the time; or at the least your servants were. Whoever did was the one who murdered Stella Lamar."

"And also," rejoined Phelps, tartly, "was the intruder who broke in here last night and ruined my window sash. If you had had better guards you might have caught him, too!"

"Are you sure of your servants? Are they reliable—"

"I never anticipated a murder and so I didn't question them as to their poisoning proclivities when I engaged them. But you know where they are and you can examine them. If I were you, Mackay—"

"Gentlemen!" Kennedy hastened to stop the colloquy before it became an out-and-out quarrel. Then he faced the banker.

"Mr. Phelps," Kennedy's voice was soft, coaxing, "I don't think Mr. Mackay quite understands. It would be a great service to me if you would give the house a quick general inspection. You are familiar with the things here, enough to state whether they have been disturbed to any appreciable degree. You see, we do not know the interior arrangements as they were before this unfortunate happening."

With rather ill grace Phelps stalked up the steps, acceding to Kennedy's request, but disdaining to answer.

Kennedy turned to Mackay as the banker disappeared out of earshot. "That's just to cool him off a bit. I have everything I came to get right here." Producing a pair of pocket scissors, he cut the pierced and spotted bit of silk from the portieres, ruthlessly. It was necessary vandalism.

"What was the poison, Mr. Kennedy?" Mackay asked, in a low voice.

"I think that it was closely allied to the cyanide groups in its rapacious activity."

"But you haven't identified it yet?"

"No. So far I haven't the slightest idea of its true nature. It seems to have a powerful affinity for important nerve centers of respiration and muscular co-ordination, as well as possessing a tendency to disorganize the blood. I should say that it produces death by respiratory paralysis and convulsions. To my mind it is an exact, though perhaps less active, counterpart of hydrocyanic acid. But that is not what it is or I would have been able to prove it before this."

Mackay nodded, listening in silence.

"You'll say nothing of this?" Kennedy added.

"I'll be silent, of course."

Heavy footsteps from the rear marked the return of Phelps, who had covered the upper floors, descending by the back stairs so as to have a look at the kitchen.

"Everything seems to be all right," he remarked, half graciously.

Kennedy led the way to the front porch. There he seemed more interested in the weather than in the case, for he studied the sky intently. Glancing up, I saw that the morning was still gray and cloudy, with no promise that the sun would be able to struggle through the overhanging moisture.

"I don't think we'll go back to the city—that is, all the way in," he remarked, speaking for both of us. "I want to go to the Manton studio first. This is no day for exteriors and so they'll probably be working there." He smiled at Phelps. "I want to see if any of our possible suspects look as though they had been engaging in nocturnal journeys."

Phelps had been rubbing his eyes. He dropped his hand so quickly that I wanted to smile; then to cover his confusion he promptly offered to drive us in. Mackay at the same time volunteered his car.

Kennedy accepted the latter offer. As he thanked the banker I wondered if any suspicion of that individual lurked in the back of his mind. Phelps certainly had made a very bad impression upon me with his antagonistic attitude, with his readiness to transform every question into a personal affront.

"Just one other thing, Mr. Phelps," exclaimed Kennedy, as we were about to descend to Mackay's car. "Why did you wish the scenes in 'The Black Terror' actually taken in your library?"

Kennedy had asked the question before. Had he forgotten? I glanced at the banker and read the same thought in his expression.

"I—I'm proud of my library and I wanted to see it in pictures," he replied, after some hesitation and with a little rancor.

"Not to save money?"

"It would be no appreciable saving."

"I see." Kennedy was tantalizingly deliberate. "How long have you held the controlling interest in Manton Pictures, Mr. Phelps?"

"Uh"—in surprise—"nearly a year."

"You could have had your library photographed at any time, then, simply by stating your request as you did in this case. In that year there have been pictures which would have served the purpose as well as this; better, in fact, because in this picture the library seems to be dark almost altogether. In other stories there probably were infinitely better chances for the exhibition of the room. Why did you wait for 'The Black Terror'?"

As a clear understanding of Kennedy's question and all it entailed filtered into the mind of Phelps he became so red and flushed with anger that I felt sure he was going to explode on the spot.

"Because I didn't think of it before," he sputtered.

"You said the situation in the picture business made it necessary for you to stay in town. Is there any trouble between Manton and yourself?"

"Not a bit!"

"Was Stella Lamar making any trouble, of a business nature, such as threatening to quit Manton Pictures?"

"No!" Phelps' eyes now were narrowed to slits.

"Are you sure?"

With a great effort Phelps achieved a degree of self-control. He forced a smile. His remark, presumed to be a pleasantry, I knew masked the true state of his feelings.

"As sure, Mr. Kennedy," he rejoined, awed by Kennedy's reputation even in the full flood of his anger, "as sure as I am that I'd like to throw you down these steps!"

XIII

MARILYN LORING

The magic of Manton's name admitted us to the studio courtyard, and at once I was struck by the change since the day before. Now the tank was a dry, empty, shallow depression of concrete. The scenery, all the paraphernalia assembled for the taking of water stuff, was gone. Except for the parked automobiles in one corner and a few loitering figures here and there the big quadrangle seemed absolutely deserted.

In the general reception room Kennedy asked for Millard, but was told he had not been out since the previous day. That was to be expected. But Manton, it developed, was away also. He had telephoned in that he would be detained until late afternoon on important business. I know that I, for one, wondered if it were connected with Fortune Features.

"It's just as well," Kennedy remarked, after convincing the boy at the desk it was Manton's wish that we have the run of the place. "My real object in coming was to watch the cast at work."

We found our way to the small studio, called so in comparison with the larger one where the huge ballroom and banquet sets were being built. In reality it possessed a tremendous floor space. Now all the other companies had been forced to make room for "The Black Terror" on account of the emergency created by the death of Stella Lamar, and there were any number of sets put up hastily for the retakes of the scenes in which Stella had appeared. The effect of the whole upon a strange beholder was weird. It was as though a cyclone had swept through a town and had gathered up and deposited slices and corners and sections of rooms and hallways and upper chambers, each complete with furniture and ornaments, curtains, rugs, and hangings. Except for the artistic harmony of things within the narrow lines of the camera's view, nothing in this great armory-like place had any apparent relation to anything else. Some of the sets were lighted, with actors and technical crews at work. Others were dark, standing ready for use. Still others were in varying states of construction or demolition. Rising above every other impression was the noise. It was pandemonium.

We saw Werner at work in a distant corner and strolled over. The director was bustling about feverishly. I do not doubt that the grim necessity of preparing the picture for a release date which was already announced had resulted in this haste, without even a day of idleness in respect for the memory of the dead star, yet it seemed cold-blooded and mercenary to me. I thought that success was not deserved by an enterprise so callous of human life, so unappreciative of human effort.

Most of the cast were standing about, waiting. The scenes were being taken in a small room, fitted as an office or private den, but furnished luxuriously. Later I learned it was in the home of the millionaire, Remsen, close off the library for which the actual room in Phelps's home was photographed.

Shirley and Gordon, I noticed, kept as far apart as possible. It was quite intentional and I again caught belligerent glances between them. On the other hand, both Enid and Marilyn Loring were calm and self-possessed. Yet between these two I caught a coolness, a sort of armed truce, in which each felt it would be a sign of weakness to admit consciously even the near presence of the other.

Werner was irascible, swearing roundly at the slightest provocation, raging up and down at every little error.

"Come now," he shouted, as we approached, "let's get this scene now—number one twenty-six. Loring—Gordon! Shake a leg—here, I'll read it again. 'Daring enters. He is scarcely seated at the desk, examining papers, when Zelda enters in a filmy negligee. Daring looks up amazed and Zelda pretends great agitation. Daring is not unkind to her. He tells her he has not discovered the will as yet. Spoken title: "I am sure that I can find a will and that you are provided for." Continuing scene, Daring speaks the above. Zelda thanks him and undulates toward the door with the well-known swaying walk of the vampire. Daring turns to his papers and does not watch her further. She looks over her shoulder, then exits, registering that she will get him yet.'" Werner dropped his copy of the script. "Understand?" he barked. "Make it fast now. We shouldn't do this over, but you were lousy before, both of you!" Gordon extinguished a cigarette and entered the set with a scowl. Marilyn rose and slipped out of a dressing gown spotted with make-up and dark from its long service in the studios. Underneath the wrapper the finest of silken draperies clung to her, infinitely more intimate here in actuality and in the bright studio lights than it would be upon the screen. I noticed the slim trimness of her figure—could not help myself, in fact. And I saw also that she shrank back just the least little bit before stepping to her place at the door. It was modesty, a genuine girlish diffidence. In a moment I revised my conception of her. Before, I had not been able to decide whether Marilyn Loring was a woman with a gift for looking young, or a flapper with the baffling sophistication affected these days by so many of them. Now I knew somehow that she was just all girl, probably in her early twenties. The brief instant of shyness had betrayed her.

In the scene she changed. Marilyn Loring was an actress. The moment she caught the click of the camera's turn there was a hardness about her mouth, a faint dishonest touch to the play of her eye, a shameless boldness to her movements concealed without concealment. In the flash of a second she was Marilyn no longer, but Zelda, the ward of old Remsen, an unscrupulous and willing ally of the "Black Terror."

Werner damned the amount of footage used in the scene, then turned to the next, with Enid and Gordon, in the same set, one of the necessary retakes for which the room had been put up again.

Enid had not noticed me and I somehow failed to shake off the feeling of fear that the glance of Millard had given me. Faint heart I was, and the answer was that I had yet to win the fair lady. To excuse myself I pretended she was different under the lights. It was really true that, as Zelda Remsen, Enid was not the fascinating creature I had met in Werner's office. There was too much Mascaro on her lashes, too great an amount of red and blue and even bright yellow in her make-up. In striking contrast was the little coloring used by Stella Lamar, or even Marilyn Loring.

Enid's scene was a close-up in which the beginning of the love interest in the story was shown. I noticed that as the cameras turned upon the action the girl inch by inch shifted her position, almost imperceptibly, until she was practically facing the lens. The consequence was that Gordon, playing the lover, was forced to move also in order to follow her face, and so was brought with his back toward the camera. It was the pleasant little film trick known as "taking the picture away" from a fellow actor. Enid was a "lens hog."

The moment the scene was over Gordon rushed to Werner to protest. The director, irritated and in a hurry, gave him small satisfaction. Both players were called back under the lights for the next "take." As Werner's back was turned Enid favored Gordon with a mischievous, malicious glance. The leading man possessed very few friends, from what I had heard. The new star evidently did not propose to become one of them.

"Let's pay our respects, socially," suggested Kennedy, at my elbow.

I followed his glance and saw that Marilyn was seated alone, away from the others, apparently forlorn. As we approached she drew her dressing robe about her, smiling. With the smile her face lighted. It was in the rare moments, just as her smile broke and spread, that she was pretty, strikingly so.

"Professor Kennedy," she exclaimed. "And Mr. Jameson, too! Sit down and watch our new star."

"What do you think of her?" Kennedy asked.

"Enid?" Marilyn's expression became quizzical. "I think she's a clever girl."

"You mean something by that, don't you?" prompted Kennedy.

She sobered. "No! Honestly!" For an instant she studied him with a directness of gaze which I would have found disconcerting. "Don't tell me"—she teased, again allowing the flash of a smile to illuminate her features—"don't tell me the renowned and celebrated Professor Kennedy suspects Enid Faye of murdering poor Stella to get her position."

Kennedy laughed, turning to me. "There's the woman," he remarked. "We may deduce and analyze and catalogue all the facts of science, but"—he spread his palms wide, expressly—"it is as nothing against a woman's intuition." Facing Marilyn again, he became frank. "You caught my thought exactly, although it was not as bad as all that. I simply wondered if Miss Faye might not have had something to do with the case."

"Why?" I realized now that this Miss Loring, in addition to considerable skill as an actress, in addition to rare beauty on the screen, possessed a brain and the power to use it. She followed Kennedy with greater ease than I, who knew him.

"Why?" she repeated.

"Perhaps it's the intuition of the male," he began, hesitatingly.

She shook her head. "A man's intuition is not dependable. You see, a woman gets her intuition first and fits her facts to it, while a man takes a fact and then has an intuitive burst of inspiration as a result. The woman puts her facts last and so is not thrown out when they're wrong, as they usually are. But the man—I think, Professor Kennedy, that you have some facts about Enid stored away and that that's why you put a double meaning in my remark. Am I right?"

He smiled. "I surrender, Miss Loring. You are right."

"What is the little fact? Perhaps I can help you."

"Miss Faye and Lawrence Millard seem to be old friends."

"Oh! Maybe you wonder at the contents of the sealed testimony in the case of Millard VS. Millard?"

Kennedy nodded.

"Do you want to know what I think?" she asked.

"Please."

"Well, I've worked with Stella nearly a year. It's my opinion she divorced Millard because he asked her to do so."

"No, no!" I balked at that, interrupting. "He could have obtained the divorce himself if he had wanted it. Stella Lamar and Manton—"

"That's talk!" she rejoined, with a show of feeling. "That's the thing I hate about pictures. It's always talk, talk, talk! I'm not saying Stella and old Papa Lloyd, as we used to call him, never were mixed up with each other, but it's one thing to repeat a bit of gossip and quite another thing to prove it. I'm not one to help give currency to any rumor of immoral relationship until I'm pretty dog-gone sure it's true."

"You think Miss Lamar wasn't as bad as painted?" asked Kennedy.

"I'm sure of it, Mr. Kennedy. I've known Stella and I've known others of her type. Fundamentally they're the kindest, truest, biggest-hearted people on earth. When Stella and I shared a dressing room I often caught her giving away this or that—frequently things she needed herself. I've known her to draw against her salary to lend money to some actor or actress whom she well knew would never repay her. Stella's biggest fault was an overbalancing quality of sympathy. If she ever did get mixed up with anyone you may bet it was because that person played upon her feelings."

"Have you any theory as to who killed her?" It was a direct question.

"No!" The answer was quick, but then an amazing thing happened. Marilyn suddenly colored, a flush which gathered up around her eyes above the make-up and made me think of a country girl. She started to say something else and then bit her tongue. Her confusion was surprising, due, probably, to the unexpectedness of Kennedy's query.

Kennedy seemed to wish to spare her. Undoubtedly her prompt negative had been the truth. Some afterthought had robbed her of her self-control. "Tell me why you said Miss Faye was a clever girl," he directed.

"Just because she puts her ambition above everything else and works hard and honestly and sincerely, and will get there. That's what people call being clever."

"I see."

Werner's voice, roaring through a megaphone, announced an interval for lunch. Marilyn rose, laughing now, but still in a high color, conscious perhaps that she had revealed some strong undercurrent of feeling.

"If you'll escort me to my dressing room," she said, coaxingly, "and wait until I slip into a skirt and waist, I'll initiate both of you to McCann's across the street. We all eat there, players, stage hands, chauffeurs—all but the stars, who have machines to take them elsewhere."

Kennedy glanced at me. "Delighted!" said I.

"We haven't much time," she went on, leading the way. "Werner's on a rampage to-day."

"He isn't usually that way?"

"It's Stella's death, I guess." She opened one of the steel fire doors. "He's always that way, though, when he's been out the night before."

I flashed a look at Kennedy. Could Werner have been at Tarrytown?

In the long hallway of dressing rooms Marilyn stopped, grasping the knob of her door. "It'll only take me—" she began.

Then her face went white as the concrete of the floor, and that was immaculate. An expression which might have been fear, or horror, or hate—or all three, spread over her features, transforming her.

Following the direction of her stare, I saw Shirley down the hall, just as he stopped at his own door. He caught her glance suddenly, and his own face went red. I thought that his hands trembled.

Marilyn wheeled about, lips pressed tightly together. Throwing open the door, she dashed into her room, slamming it with a bang which echoed and re-echoed up and down the little hall. She had forgotten our presence altogether.

XIV

ANOTHER CLUE

Kennedy looked at me quizzically. "I guess we'd better not wait for Miss Loring to initiate us to McCann's," he remarked.

We found our way to the courtyard, and were headed for the gate when a young man in chauffeur's cap and uniform intercepted us. I had noticed him start forward from one of the cars parked in the inclosure, but did not recognize him.

"May I speak to you a moment, Professor Kennedy—alone?"

"Mr. Jameson here is associated with me, is assisting me in this case, if it is something concerning the death of Miss Lamar."

"It is, sir. I saw you out at Tarrytown yesterday. McGroarty is my name and I drove one of the cars the company went in. They were pointing you out to me, and I'd read about you, and just now I says to myself there's something I ought to tell you."

"That's right." Kennedy lighted a cigar, offering one to the chauffeur. "I'm not supernatural and often I'm able to solve a mystery only with the help of all those who, like myself, want justice done."

"Yes, sir! That's my way of looking at it. Well"—McGroarty blew a cloud of smoke, appreciatively—"I do a good bit of driving for these people, and this morning it was cloudy and dull, no good for exteriors, but yet sort of so it might clear at any moment, and so I was ordered. I brought my car and left it standing here in the yard while I went over to McCann's—the lunch room, you know—for a cup of coffee. When I came back"—again the cigar—"there still was nothing doing, and so I thought—you know how it is—I thought I'd clean up the back of the old boat, to kill time, not saying it wasn't needed. So I took out the cocoa mat to beat it and what do I find on the floor—between the mat and the rear seat it was, I guess—but this."

He handed Kennedy some small object which glinted in the light. Looking closely, I saw that it was a peculiarly shaped little glass tube.

"An ampulla," Kennedy explained. "It's the technical name the doctors have for such a container."

"It must have been between the mat and the rear seat," the chauffeur repeated. Then he discovered that his cigar was out. He struck a match.

Kennedy turned the bit of glass over and over in his hand, examining it carefully. I felt rather fearful, wondering if it might not contain some trace of the deadly poison which had so quickly killed Stella Lamar. I even half expected to see Kennedy find some infinitesimal jagged edge or point which could have inflicted the fatal scratch. Then I realized that McGroarty had handled the thing with impunity, perhaps had carried it about half a day.

Kennedy took his scarf pin. On the outside of the little tube there was no trace of a label or marking of any sort. All about, on the inside, however, the glass was spotted with dried light-yellow incrustations, resembling crystals and at first apt to escape even the sharpest scrutiny. With the pin Kennedy scaled off one of these and put it under his pocket lens. But he came to no conclusion. Rather puzzled and nettled, he dropped the tiny bit of substance back into the tube, then replaced his pin in his scarf, and stowed this latest bit of possible evidence in his pocket carefully.

"How do you suppose it got in the car?" he asked.

"Some one must have dropped it and it must have rolled in that space by the edge of the mat," replied the chauffeur. "There was just room for it, too! I never would have noticed it without taking up the mat."

"It couldn't be broken, by being trampled on?"

"Nope! Not a chance!"

"How long could it have been there?"

"Two or three or four days—since I cleaned up last."

I remembered the cleverness shown by the guilty person in placing the needle in the curtain. It seemed unlikely that this could be an accident. "Isn't it possible," I suggested, "that this is a plant; that the tube was put there deliberately, to throw us off the track?"

"It's quite likely," he admitted. "On the other hand, Walter, the very smartest criminal will do some foolish little thing, enough to ruin the most careful plans and preparations." He turned to McGroarty. "Who rode in your car yesterday?"

"Mine's the principals' car," boasted McGroarty. "Going out I had Miss Lamar, Miss Loring, Mr. Gordon, Mr. Shirley, and Mr. Werner. Coming back Mr. Werner was with you, and Miss Lamar—well, there was only Miss Loring and Mr. Gordon and Mr. Shirley."

"Did you notice how they acted?"

"They never says a word to each other on all the trip back, but I didn't think it strange after what happened, although usually they're always joking and laughing."

"You brought the three to the studio here?"

"Yes. They had to get out of make-up."

"Did you leave the car then?"

"No, I hit it right for the garage."

"Were you away from the car at Tarrytown?"

"Sure! That was a long wait. Peters, Manton's chauffeur, and I found a couple of horseshoes and we were throwing them most of the time."

"How long was the machine alone here in the yard this morning?"

"A couple of hours, maybe. I knew the old boiler was safe enough, and that if they wanted me they'd look over in McCann's."

"Well," Kennedy extended his hand, "I thank you, and I won't forget you, McGroarty."

As soon as the chauffeur was out of earshot I faced Kennedy rather eagerly, to forestall him if he had arrived at the same conclusion as myself.

"See! It's just as I thought yesterday!"

"How's that, Walter?"

"Werner! He rode out in that machine, but not back. In Manton's car he was worried all the time. He probably knew he had dropped the tube. Then he hurried up ahead of us and wiped the needle—" I stopped, lamely.

Kennedy smiled. "See, you're jumping at conclusions too fast. You remember now that we decided that the towel has nothing directly to do with the poison. In a way you cannot assume that this ampulla has, either, although I myself feel sure on that point. But in any case no one is eliminated. It is true Werner did not return in the same automobile. It is also true that he had little opportunity to drop it while others were in the car with him. When McGroarty was away from the car anyone could have lost it, or—as you suggested a moment ago—planted it there deliberately to divert suspicion."

I felt the beginnings of a headache from all these confused threads of the mystery. "Can't—Isn't there anyone we can say is innocent, at least, even if we cannot begin to fasten the guilt upon somebody?" I pleaded.

Kennedy shook his head. "At this stage the one is as hard as the other. I consider myself lucky to have collected as much material as I have for the analysis of the poison." He tapped his pocket significantly.

"Yoo-hoo!" A frankly shrill call in a feminine voice interrupted. We both turned, to see Marilyn Loring hastening toward us.

"Did you think I was going to forget you?" she asked, almost reproachfully and much out of breath. "Let's hurry," she added. "This is roast beef day."

We started toward the gate once more, Marilyn between us, vivacious and rather charming. I noticed that she made no reference to the incident in the hallway, the precipitate manner in which she left us and the very evident confusion of Merle Shirley. Kennedy, too, seemed disposed to drop the matter, although it was obviously significant. For some reason his mind was elsewhere, so that the girl was thrown upon my hands.

It struck me that, after all, she was attractive. At this moment I found her distinctly good-looking.

"Why do you 'vamp'?" I asked, innocently. "You don't seem to me, if you'll pardon the personal remark, at all that type."

She laughed. "It's all the fault of the public. They insist that I vamp. I want to play girly-girly parts, but the public won't stand for it; they won't come to see the picture. They tell the exhibitor, and he tells the producer, and back I am at the vamping again. Isn't it funny?" She paused a moment. "Take Gordon. Doesn't it make you laugh, what the public think he is—clean-cut, hero, and all that sort of thing? Little do they know!"

All at once Kennedy stopped abruptly. We were close to the entrance, just where a smart little speedster of light blue lined with white was parked at the edge of the narrow sidewalk. The sun, after a morning of uncertainty, had just struck through the haze, and it illuminated Marilyn's face and hair most delightfully as we both turned, somewhat in surprise.

"I know you'll never forgive me, Miss Loring," Kennedy began, "but the fact is that just before you came out we stumbled into a new bit of evidence in the case and I believe that Jameson and I will have to hurry in to the laboratory. Much as I would like to lunch with you, and perhaps chat some more during scene-taking this afternoon—"

It seemed to me that her eyes widened a bit. Certainly there was a perceptible change in her face. It was interest, but it was also certainly more than that. I felt that she would have liked to penetrate the mask of Kennedy's expression, perhaps learn just what facts and theories rested in his mind.

"Is it—" Suddenly she smiled, realizing that Kennedy would reveal only the little which suited his purpose. "Is it something you can tell me?" she finished.

He shook his head. His answer was tantalizing, his glance searching and without concealment. "Only another detail concerning the chemical analysis of the poison."

"I see!" If she knew of the ampulla the answer would have been intelligible to her. As it was, her face betrayed nothing. "I guess I'll hurry on over alone, then," she added. She extended a hand to each of us. Her grasp was warm and friendly and frank. "So long, and—and good luck, for Stella's sake!"

"Hello, folks!"

The dancing bantering voice from behind us, with silvery cadence to its laughter, could belong to no one but Enid Faye. I grasped that it was her car which Kennedy leaned upon. I gasped a bit as I saw her directly at my side, her dainty chamois motoring coat brushing my sleeve, the sun which grew in strength every moment casting mottled shadows upon her face through the transparent brim of her bobbing hat, in mocking answer to the mirth in her eyes.

For an instant she gazed after the retreating Marilyn.

"Good-by, Marilyn! DEAR," she called, mega-phoning her hands.

The other girl made no response. Laughing, Enid slipped a hand under my arm, the firm pressure of her fingers thrilling me. She addressed Kennedy, however.

"Do you want a ride in to the city, both of you?"

Kennedy brightened. "That would be fine! How far are you going?"

"The Burrage. I have a luncheon engagement. That's Forty-fourth."

"Can you drop us off at the university?"

"Surely! Climb in. It's a tight fit, three in the seat, but fun.

And"—facing me—"I want Jamie between us, next to me!"

As we rolled out of the studio inclosure she leaned forward on the wheel to question Kennedy.

"What did Marilyn Loring want? You seemed in deep confab!"

"She volunteered to initiate us to McCann's, across the street."

"Oh!" She skidded about a corner skillfully. "And—"

"Well, we bumped into an additional piece of evidence and I thought

Jameson and I ought to hurry in to my laboratory instead."

"I bet"—Enid giggled, readjusting her hat in the breeze—"I bet she wanted to know what you'd found, right away. Didn't she?"

"Yes!" Kennedy's face was noncommittal, "Why do you say that?"

"Because she came into my room, just as we were getting ready for work this morning. Perhaps I'm wrong, but from the way she kept asking me questions about everyone from Manton down I got the idea she was quizzing me, to see how much I knew. Of course this is only my first day, but it seems to me that Marilyn is talking a great deal, without saying very much. I've come to the conclusion she knows a good deal more than she is telling anyone, and that she'd like to find out just how much everyone else knows."

Kennedy nodded almost absent-mindedly, without responding further.

"Well"—Enid speeded up a bit—"not to change connections on the switchboard, I think I'm going to like it with Manton Pictures."

"Will they do justice to your work," Kennedy inquired, "putting you in a partially finished picture in this way?"

"That's where I'm in luck, real bang-up luck. Werner has directed me before and knows just exactly how to handle me."

"What about the story? That was built for Stella, wasn't it?"

"Yes, but they're changing it here and there to fit me. Larry knows my work, too! That's luck again for little Enid."

"How long have you known Millard?" In a flash I realized Kennedy's cleverness. This was the fact he had wished to unearth. The question was as natural as could be. He had led up to it deliberately. I was sure of that.

"Four, nearly five years," she replied, unsuspiciously. Then suddenly she bit her lip, although her expression was well masked. "That is," she added, somewhat lamely—"that is, in a casual way, like nearly everyone knows nearly everyone else in the film game."

"Oh!" murmured Kennedy, lapsing into silence.

XV

I BECOME A DETECTIVE

Important as it was to watch Enid and Marilyn, Werner and the rest, Kennedy decided that it was now much more important to hold to his expressed purpose of returning to the laboratory with our trophies of the day's crime hunt.

"For people to whom emotion ought to be an old story in their everyday stage life, I must say they feel and show plenty of it in real life," I remarked, as Enid set us down and drove off. "It does not seem to pall."

"I don't know why the movie people buy stories," remarked Craig, quaintly. "They don't need to do it—they live them."

When we were settled in the laboratory once more Kennedy plunged with renewed vigor into the investigation he had dropped in the morning in order to make the hurried trip to the Phelps home in Tarrytown.

I had hoped he would talk further of the probabilities of the connection of the various people with the crime, but he had no comment even upon the admission of Enid that she had known Millard for a period long antedating the trouble with Stella Lamar.

It seemed that, after all, he was quite excited at the discovery of the ampulla and was anxious to begin the analysis of its scale-like contents. I was not sure, but it struck me that this might be the same substance which had spotted the towel or the portieres. If that were so, the finding of it in this form had given him a new and tangible clue to its nature, accounting for his eagerness.

I watched his elaborate and thorough preparations, wishing I could be of assistance, but knowing the limitations of my own chemical and bacteriological knowledge. I grasped, however, that he was concentrating his study upon the spots he had cut from the portieres, in particular the stain where the point of the needle had been, and upon the incrustations on the inner surface of the tube. He made solutions of both of these and for some little time experimented with chemical reactions. Then he had recourse to several weighty technical books. Though bursting with curiosity, I dared not question him, nor distract him in any way.

Finally he turned to a cage where he kept on hand, always, a few of those useful martyrs to science, guinea pigs. Taking one of the little animals and segregating him from the others, he prepared to inoculate him with a tiny bit of the solution made from the stain on the piece cut from the portiere.

At that I knew it would be a long and tiresome analysis. It seemed a waste of time to wait idly for Kennedy to reach his conclusions, so I cast about in my mind for some sort of inquiry of my own which I could conduct meanwhile, perhaps collecting additional facts about those we were watching at the studio.

Somehow I could not wholly lose my suspicions of the director, Werner; especially now as I marshaled the evidence against him. First of all he was the only person absolutely in control of the movements of Stella Lamar. If she did not bring up her arm against the curtains in a manner calculated to press the needle against her flesh it certainly would not seem out of the way for him to ask her to do it over again, or even for him to direct changes in her position. This he could do either in rehearsal or in retakes after the scene had actually been photographed. It was not proof, I knew. Practically all of them were familiar with the action of the scene, could guess how Werner would handle it. The point was that the director, next to Millard, was the most thoroughly conversant with the scenes in the script, had to figure out everything down to the very location and angles of the camera.

Another matter, of course, was the placing of the needle in the silk. For that purpose some one had to go to Tarrytown ahead of the others, or at least had to precede the others into the living room. Offhand I was compelled to admit that this was easiest for Phelps—Phelps, the man who had insisted that the scene be taken in his library. At the same time, I knew it was quite possible for the director to have entered ahead of anyone else, possible for him to have issued orders to his people which would keep them out of the way for the brief moment he needed.

A third consideration was the finding of the ampulla in McGroarty's car. Stella, Marilyn, Jack Gordon, Merle Shirley, and Werner had ridden out together. Werner had not returned. While this fact did not indicate definitely that he might have dropped it, coupled with the other considerations it pointed the suspicion of guilt at the director.

Then there was the finding of the towel in the washroom of the office building at the studio. While Kennedy now said it was not used to wipe the needle, while we now knew that the needle remained in the portieres from the morning of Stella's death until late that night, yet Kennedy affirmed the connection of the towel with the crime in some subtle way. It was true that members of the cast sometimes used the washroom, yet it was evident that Manton, Millard, and Werner, who had rooms on the floor, were the more apt to be concerned in the attempt to dispose of it. Against Manton I could see no real grounds for suspicion. In a general way we had been compelled to eliminate Millard early in our investigation. Again I was brought, in this analysis of the mystery, to Werner.

One other point remained—the identity of the nocturnal visitor to Tarrytown. In connection with that I remembered the remark of Marilyn. Werner was acting as he always acted when he was out late the night before, she had said. While my theories offered no explanation of the second man, the watcher, I saw—with an inner feeling of triumph—that everything again pointed to the director.

I determined not to tell my conclusion to Kennedy, yet. I did not want to distract him. Besides, I felt he would disagree.

"What do you think of this, Craig?" I suggested. "Suppose I start out while you're busy and try to dig up some more facts about these people?"

"Excellent!" was his reply. "I can't say how much longer my analysis will keep me. By all means do so, Walter. I shall be here, or, if not, I'll leave a note so you can find me."

Accordingly, I took up my search, determined to go slowly and carefully, not to be misled by any promising but fallacious clues. I knew that Werner would be working at the studio, from all we had heard in the morning. I determined upon a visit to his apartment in his absence.

From the telephone book I discovered that he lived at the Whistler Studios, not far from Central Park on the middle West Side—a new building, I remembered, inhabited almost entirely by artists and writers. As I hurried down on the Subway, then turned and walked east toward the Park, I racked my brain for an excuse to get in. Entering the lower reception hall, I learned from the boy that the director had a suite on the top floor, high enough to look over the roofs of the adjoining buildings directly into the wide expanse of green and road, of pond and trees beyond.

"Mr. Werner isn't in, though," the boy added, doubtfully, without ringing the apartment.

"I know it," I rejoined, hastily. "I told him I'd meet him here this afternoon, however." On a chance I went on, with a knowing smile, "I guess it was pretty late when he came in last night?"

"I'll say so," grinned the youth, friendly all of a sudden. He had interpreted the remark as I intended he should. He believed that Werner and I had been out together. "I remember," he volunteered, "because I had to do an extra shift of duty last night, worse luck. It must have been after four o'clock. I was almost asleep when I heard the taxi at the door."

"I wonder what company he got the taxi from?" I remarked, casually. "I tried to get one uptown—" I paused. I didn't want to get into a maze of falsehood from which I would be unable to extricate myself.

"I don't know," he replied. "It looked like one of the Maroon taxis, from up at the Central Park Hotel on the next block, but I'm not sure."

"I think I won't go upstairs yet," I said, finally. "There's another call I ought to make. If Mr. Werner comes in, tell him I'll be back."

I knew very well that Werner would not return, but I thought that the bluff might pave the way for getting upstairs and into the apartment a little later. Meanwhile I had another errand. The boy nodded a good-by as I passed out through the grilled iron doors to the street. Less than five minutes afterward I was at the booth of the Maroon Taxi Company, at the side of the main entrance of the Central Park Hotel.

Here the starter proved to be a loquacious individual, and I caught him, fortunately, in the slowest part of the afternoon. Removing a pipe and pushing a battered cap to the back of a bald head, he pulled out the sheets of the previous day. Before me were recorded all the calls for taxicab service, with the names of drivers, addresses of calls, and destinations. Although the quarters in the booth were cramped and close and made villainous by the reek of the man's pipe, I began to scan the lists eagerly.

It had been a busy night even down to the small hours of the morning and I had quite a job. As I came nearer and nearer to the end my hopes ebbed, however. When I was through I had failed to identify a single call that might have been Werner's. Several fares had been driven to and from the Grand Central Station, probably the means by which he made the trip to Tarrytown. In each case the record had shown the Central Park Hotel in the other column, not the Whistler Studios. I was forced to give up this clue, and it hurt. I was not built for a detective, I guess, for I almost quit then and there, prepared to return to the laboratory and Kennedy.

But I remembered my first intention and made my way back to the Whistler Studios. Anyhow, I reflected, Werner would hardly have summoned a car from a place so near his home had he wished to keep his trip a secret. It was more important for me to gain access to his quarters. There it was quite possible I might find something valuable. I wondered if I would be justified in breaking in, or if I would succeed if I attempted it.

Things proved easier than I expected. My first visit unquestionably had prepared the way. The hallboy took me up in the elevator himself without telephoning, took me to Werner's door, rang the bell, and spoke to the colored valet who opened it. As I grasped the presence of the servant in the little suite I was glad I had not tried my hand at forcing an entrance. I had quite anticipated an empty apartment.

The darky, pleasant voiced, polite, and well trained, bowed me into a little den and proceeded to lay out a large box of cigarettes on the table beside me, as well as a humidor well filled with cigars of good quality. I took one of the latter, accepting a light and glancing about.

Certainly this was in contrast with Manton's apartment. There was nothing garish, ornate, or spectacular here. Richly, lavishly furnished, everything was in perfect taste, revealing the hand of an artist. It might have been a bit bizarre, reflecting the nervous temperament of its owner. Even the servant showed the touch of his master, hovering about to make sure I was comfortable, even to bringing a stack of the latest magazines. I hope he didn't sense my thoughts, for I cursed him inwardly. I wanted to be alone. Ordinarily I would have enjoyed this, but now I had become a detective, and it was necessary to rummage about, and quickly.

The sudden ringing of the telephone took the valet out into the tiny hall of the suite and gave me the opportunity I wished.

Phelps apparently was calling up to leave some message for Werner, which I could not get, as the valet took it. What, I wondered, was Phelps telephoning here for? Why not at the studio? It looked strange.

I lost no time in speculation over that, however. The moment I was left to myself I jumped up and rushed to a writing desk, a carved antique which had caught my eye upon my entrance, which I had studied from my place in the easy chair. It was unlocked, and I opened it without compunction. With an alert ear, to warn me the moment the colored boy hung up, I first gazed rather helplessly at a huge pile of literary litter. Clearly there was no time to go through all of that.

I gave the papers a cursory inspection, without disturbing them, hoping to catch some name or something which might prove to be a random clue, but I was less lucky than Kennedy had been in his casual look at Manton's desk the afternoon before. Still able to hear the valet at the telephone, I reached down and opened the top drawer of the desk. Here perhaps I might be more fortunate. One glance and my heart gave a startled leap.

There in a compartment of the drawer I saw a hypodermic needle—in fact, two of them—and a bottle. On the desk was a fountain pen ink dropper, a new one which had never been used. I reached over, pressed its little bulb, uncorked the bottle, inserted the glass point, sucked up some of the contents, placed the bulb right side up in my waistcoat pocket, and recorked the bottle. Next I took and pocketed one of the two needles, both of which were alike as far as I could see.

Then I heard a good-by in the hall. I closed drawer and desk hastily.

As I caught the click of the receiver of the telephone on its hook I was halfway across the floor. Before the colored boy could enter again I was back in my chair, my head literally in a whirl.

What a stroke of good fortune! I had no expectation of proving Werner to be the guilty man by so simple a method as this, however. If he were the slayer of the star he would be too clever to leave anything so incriminating about. I have always quarreled with Poe's theory in The Purloined Letter, believing that the obvious is no place to hide anything outside of fiction. What I conceived, rather, was that Werner really was a dope fiend. The nature of the drug Kennedy would tell me very easily, from the sample. Establishing Werner's possession of the needles was another point in my chain of presumptions, showing that he was familiar with their use; and added to that was the psychological effect upon him of the habit, a habit responsible in many other cases for murders as skillfully carried out as that of Stella Lamar, often, too, without the slightest shred of real motive.

I recalled Werner's habitually nervous manner and was sure now that the needles actually were used by him. Was it due to the high pressure of his profession? Had that constant high tension forced him to find relief in the most violent relaxation?

Elated, I was tempted at first to crowd my luck. I wondered if I could not discover another ampulla such as the chauffeur, McGroarty, had picked up in his car. When Werner's servant, almost apologetically, explained that the telephone message was from a near-by shop and that he would have to leave me for a matter of ten or fifteen minutes, I assured him that it was all right and that I would occupy myself with a magazine. The moment he was out the door I sprang to action and began a minute search of every nook and cranny of the rooms.

But gradually a sense of growing fear and trepidation took hold of me. Suppose, after all, Werner should return home unexpectedly? The colored boy did not seem surprised that I should wait, a slight indication that it was possible. Further, I could never tell when the darky might not return himself, breaking in upon me without warning and discovering me. At the best I was not a skillful investigator. I did not know just where to look for hidden evidences of poison, nor was I able to work fast, for fear of leaving too tangible marks of my actions behind me. A great perspiration stood out on my forehead. Gradually a trembling took hold of my limbs and communicated itself to my fingers.

After all, it was essential that Werner be kept in ignorance of my suspicions, granting they were correct. It would be fatal if I should frighten him inadvertently, so that he would take to flight. Realizing my foolhardiness, I returned to my chair at last, picking up a magazine at random. I did so not a moment too soon. A slight sound caught my ear and I looked up to see the valet already halfway into the room. His tread was so soft I never would have heard him.

"I don't think I'll wait any longer," I remarked, rising and stretching slightly, as though I had been seated all the time. "I'll ring up a little later; perhaps come back after I get in touch with Mr. Werner."

"Who shall I say was here, sah?" the boy asked, with just a trace of darky dialect.

Above all I didn't want to alarm Werner. I could not repeat the explanation I had allowed the attendant downstairs to assume from my remark, that I was a friend who had been out with the director the night before. I should have to take a chance that Werner's servant and the hallboy would not compare notes, and that the latter would say nothing to the director upon his arrival.

"I'm an old friend from the Coast," I explained, with a show of taking the negro into my confidence. "I wanted to surprise him and so"—I slipped a half dollar into a willing palm—"if you'll say nothing until I've seen him—"

He beamed. "Yes, sah! You jus' count on George, sah!"

Downstairs I wondered if I could seal the tongue of the youth who had accommodated me before. Then I discovered that he had gone off duty. It would be extremely unlikely that he would be about until the following day. I smiled and hastened out to the street.

Once in the open air again, I realized the full extent of the risk I had taken. All at once it struck me that no amount of explanation from either Kennedy or myself would serve to mollify Werner if he were innocent and learned of my visit. I doubted, in this moment of afterthought, that I would escape censure from Kennedy, who surely would not want his case jeopardized by precipitate actions upon my part. I began to run, to get away from the Whistler Studios as fast as possible.

Then I saw I had grown panicky and I checked myself. But I hurried to the Subway and up to the university again, and to the laboratory, eager to compare notes with Kennedy.

"If I were Alphonse Dupin," he remarked, calmly, grasping my excitement, "I would deduce that you have discovered something. I would also deduce that you believe it important and that you have no intention of withholding the information from me, whatever it is."

"Correct," I answered, grinning in spite of myself.

Then I handed him the needle, telling him in a few brief words of my visit to Werner's apartment, of the hallboy's confirmation of a nocturnal trip of some sort, of my search of the desk and some other parts of the suite. "I fixed it so that he won't hear of my visit, at least for some time. He won't suspect who it was, in any case."

Kennedy examined the hypodermic.

"Not like the one used," he murmured.

"I thought that," I explained. "It simply indicates he is a dope fiend and is familiar with the use of a needle. Here!" I produced the ink filler which I had used to bring a sample of the contents of the bottle. "This seems to be what he uses. What is it?"

Kennedy sniffed, then looked closely at the liquid through the glass of the tube. "It's a coca preparation," he explained. "If Werner uses this, he's unquestionably a regular drug addict."

"Well," I paused, triumphantly, "the case against the chief director of Manton Pictures grows stronger all the time."

"Not necessarily," contradicted Kennedy, perhaps to draw me out.

"He's familiar with hypodermic syringes," I repeated.

"Which doesn't prove that no one else would use one."

"Anyhow, he was out until four A.M. last night and some one broke into Phelps's house to—"

"You can't establish the fact that he went out there. There are plenty of other places he could have been until four in the morning."

"But I can assume—"

"If you are going to assume anything, Walter, why not assume he was the second man, the man who watched the actual intruder?"

I turned away, despairing of my ability to convince Kennedy. As a matter of fact I had forgotten the other prowler at Tarrytown.

Then I noticed that the one guinea pig in the separate cage was dead. In an instant I was all curiosity to know the results of Kennedy's investigations.

"Did you make any progress?" I asked.

"Yes!" Now I noticed for the first time that he was in fine humor. "I had quite finished the first stage of my analysis when you came in."

"Then what was it? What was the poison that killed Stella Lamar?" I glanced at the stiff, prone figure of the little animal.

Kennedy cleared his throat. "Well," he replied, "I began the study with the discovery I made, which I told you, that strange proteins were present." He picked up the ampulla and regarded it thoughtfully. Then he fingered the bit of silk cut from the portieres. "It is a poison more deadly, more subtle, than any ever concocted by man, Walter."

"Yes?" I was painfully eager.

"It is snake venom!"

XVI

ENID ASSISTS

"A poison more subtle than any concocted by man!" repeated Kennedy.

It was a startling declaration and left me quite speechless for the moment.

"We know next to nothing of the composition of the protein bodies in the snake venoms which have such terrific and quick physiological effects on man," Kennedy went on. "They have been studied, it is true, and studied a great deal, but we cannot say that there are any adequate tests by which the presence of these proteins can be recognized.

"However, everything points to the conclusion now that it was snake venom, and my physiological tests on the guinea pig seem to confirm it. I see no reason now to doubt that it was snake venom. The fact of the matter is that the snake venoms are about the safest of poisons for the criminal to use, for the reason of the difficulty they give in any chemical analysis. That is only another proof of the diabolical cleverness of our guilty person, whoever it may be.

"Later I'll identify the particular kind of venom used. Just now I feel it is more important to discover the actual motive for the crime. In the morning I have a plan which may save me further work here in the laboratory, but for to-night I feel I have earned a rest and"—a smile—"I shall rest by searching out the motives of these temperamental movie folk a little more." As he spoke he slipped out of his acid-stained smock.

"What do you mean?" As often, he rather baffled me.

"It's nearly dinner time and we're going out together, Walter, down to Jacques'."

"Why Jacques'?"

"Because I phoned your friend Belle Balcom and she informed me that that was the place where we would be apt to find the elite of the film world dining."

I acquiesced, of course. We hurried to the apartment first for a few necessary changes and preparations, then we started for the Times Square section in a taxi.

"I never heard of the use of snake venom before," I remarked, settling back in the cushions—"that is, deliberately, by a criminal, to poison anyone."

"There are cases," replied Craig, absently.

"Just how does the venom act?"

"I believe it is generally accepted that there are two agents present in the secretion. One is a peptone and the other a globulin. One is neurotoxic, the other hemolytic. Not only is the general nervous system attacked instantly, but the coagulability of the blood is destroyed. One agent in the venom attacks the nerve cells; the other destroys the red corpuscles."

"You suspected something of this kind, then, when you first examined Stella Lamar?"

"Exactly! You see, the victim of a snake bite often is unable to move or speak. Doctor Blake observed that in the case of the stricken star. Her nerves were affected, resulting in paralysis of the muscles of the heart and lungs and giving us some symptoms of suffocation. Then the blood, as a result of the attack of the venom, is always left dark and liquid. That, too, I observed in the sample sent me from Tarrytown.

"The snake," Kennedy continued, "administers the poison by fangs more delicate than any hypodermic. Nature's apparatus is more precise than the finest appliances devised for the use of a surgeon by our instrument makers. The fangs are like needles with obliquely cut points and slit-like outlets. The poison glands correspond to the bulb of a syringe. They are, in reality, highly modified salivary glands. From them, when the serpent strikes, is ejected a pale straw-colored half-oleaginous fluid. You might swallow it with impunity. But once in the blood, through a cut or wound, it is deadly."

"There could be no snake in this case," I remarked. "The fangs of a serpent make two punctures, don't they; while here there was just the one scratch—"

"Of course there were no fangs when the deed was actually done," he rejoined, impatiently. "We've traced everything to the needle in the portieres and it is my belief that it was part of an all-glass hypodermic with a platinum-iridium point. It could hardly have been anything like the coarser syringe used by Werner, nor do I think it possible that the point of an ordinary needle would hold sufficient venom, since it would dry and form a coating like the incrustation on the inside of the ampulla McGroarty found."

"That was the venom?" I asked.

"Yes, I found it in the ampulla and in the stain on the portiere where the needle had pierced through."

"The towel, though—"

"Is something else. First thing in the morning we'll follow that up, as I promised you. Meanwhile let's concentrate on motives."

A long line of private cars and taxicabs outside Jacques' testified to the popularity of the restaurant. At the door stood a huge, bulking negro resplendent in the glaring finery of his uniform. It seemed to me that people literally were thronging into the place, for it was cleverly advertised as a center of night life.

Inside, the famous darky jazz band was in full swing. There was lilt and rhythm to the melody produced by the grinning blacks, and not a free arm or foot or shoulder or head of any of them but did not sway in time to their syncopated music.

We were shown to a table on a sort of gallery or mezzanine floor which extended around three sides of the interior. Below, in the center, was the space for dancing, surrounded by groups and pairs of diners. Stairs led to the balcony on both sides, as though the management expected none of their guests to resist the lure of the dance between courses. The band, I noticed, was at the farther end, on an elevated dais, so that the contortions of the various players could be seen above the heads of those on the floor.

We were at the rail so that we commanded a view of the entire place, a location I guessed had been maneuvered by Kennedy with a word to the head waiter. The only tables invisible to us were those directly beneath, but it would be a simple matter to cross around during any dance number to view them.

As we took our seats the lights were dimmed suddenly. I realized that we had arrived in the midst of the cabaret and that it was the turn of one of the performers. Kennedy, however, seemed to enjoy the entertainment, an example of his ability to gain recreation whenever and however he wished, to find relaxation under the oddest or most casual circumstances, out of anything from people passing on the street to an impromptu concert of a street band. In scanty garments, in the glare of a multi-colored spotlight, the girl danced a hybrid of every dance from the earliest Grecian bacchanal to the latest alleged Apache importation from Paris.

I have often wondered at Jacques' and places of the sort. The intermingling of eating and drinking and dancing was curious. What possible bearing this terpsichorean monstrosity might have upon the gastronomic inclinations of the audience it would have been difficult to fathom.

The lights flashed bright again and Kennedy gave our order. Meanwhile I glanced about at the people below us. There was no one in sight I knew until I leaned well over the rail, but upon doing that I felt little chills of excitement run from the top to the bottom of my spine, for I discovered in a very prominent situation at the very edge of the dance floor a party of four, of whom three very much concerned us. Lloyd Manton, back to the polished space behind him, was unmistakable in evening clothes. These bunched at his neck and revealed his habitual stoop as impartially as his business suits. Across from him, lounging upon the table likewise, but more immaculately and skillfully tailored, was Lawrence Millard. The writer, I noticed, flourished his cigarette holder, fully a foot in length, and emphasized his remarks to the girl on his right with a rather characteristic gesture made with the second finger of his left hand. The girl was Enid, quite mistress of herself in a gown little more than no gown; and the remarks were obviously confidential. The other girl, engrossed in Manton, seemed a dangerously youthful and self-conscious young lady. Her hair flamed Titian red and her neck, of which she displayed not half as much as Enid, gave her much concern.

"Kennedy! Look!" I reached over to attract his attention.

"Who's the second girl, I wonder?" He became as interested as I was.

With a blatant flourish of saxophone and cornet and traps the band began a jazzy fox-trot. Instantly there was a rush from the tables for the floor. Enid jumped to her feet, moving her bare shoulders in the rhythm of the music. Then Millard took firm hold of her and they wove their way into the crush. It seemed to me that the little star was the very incarnation of the dance. I envied her partner more than I dared admit to myself.

Manton and his companion rose also, but more leisurely. On her feet the girl did not seem so young, although the second impression may have been the result of the length of her skirt and the long slim, lines of her gown. We watched both couples through the number, then gave our attention to the food we had ordered. Another dance, a modified waltz, revealed Enid in the arms of Manton. I tried to determine from her actions if she felt any preference for the producer, or for Millard when again she took the floor with him. It was an idle effort, of course. The people surged out perhaps three or four times while we were at our meal. Each time the party below jumped up in response to the music. At our cigars, finally, I took to observing the other diners, wondering what we had gained by coming here.

Suddenly I realized that Kennedy was rising to greet some one approaching our table. Turning, rising also, I went through all the miseries of the bashful lover. It was Enid herself.

"I caught sight of you looking over the rail while I was dancing," she told Kennedy, accepting a chair pulled around by the waiter. "I knew you saw me. Also I glanced up and found that you were perfectly well aware of the location of our table. So"—engagingly—"unsociable creature! Why didn't you come down and say 'Hello!' or ask me for a dance?"

"Perhaps I intended to a little later."

"Yes!" she exclaimed, in mockery. "You see, since Mecca won't go to the pilgrim, the pilgrim has to come to Mecca."

"Did you ever hear of Mohammed and the mountain, Miss Faye?" Kennedy asked.

"Of course! That's the regular expression. But I agree with Barnum. As he said, some people can be original some of the time and some people can be original all of the time, and I propose to be original always, like a baby with molasses."

Kennedy laughed, for indeed she was irresistible. Then she turned to me, placing one of her warm little hands upon mine.

"And Jamie!" she purred. "Have you forgotten little Enid altogether? Won't—won't YOU come down and dance?"

"I—I can't!" I exploded, in agony. "I don't know how!" And I thought that I would never dare trust myself with her glistening shoulders clasped close to me, with her slim bare arm placed around my neck as I had watched it slip about the collar of Millard.

"Now that the pilgrim is at Mecca—" Kennedy suggested, interrupting cruelly, as I thought.

"Oh!" In an instant I sensed that I was forgotten, and I was hurt. "There's something which came out this afternoon at the studio," she began, "and I wonder if you know. Larry—that's Mr. Millard—assures me it is true, and—and I think you ought to hear about it. I—I want to assist all I can in solving the mystery of Stella Lamar's death, even though Stella's unfortunate end has meant my opportunity."

"What is it, Miss Faye?" Kennedy was studying her.

"It's about Jack Gordon. He's been trying to hold up the company for fifteen hundred a week, which would double his salary—perhaps you've heard that?"

Kennedy nodded, although it was news to him. "I've been thinking about Gordon," he murmured.

"Anyway," she went on, "it's gone around that he's desperately in need of money and that that is why he's so insistent upon the increase. It seems he owes everyone. In particular he owes Phelps some huge sums and old Phelps is on his tail, hollering and raising Ned. Phelps, you know, has uses for money himself just now. You had heard?"

Again Kennedy evaded a direct answer. "Money is fearfully tight, of course," he remarked, encouraging her to continue.

"Yes," she repeated, "Phelps is terribly hard up and after Gordon. And that's not all about our handsome leading man, Mr. Kennedy." She leaned forward. A certain intensity crept into her voice. She began to toy with his sleeve with the slender fingers of one hand, as though in that manner to compel his greater attention. "You know Stella Lamar really was in love with Jack Gordon. In fact she was daffy over him. And now I've found out that he was borrowing money from her, was taking nearly every cent she earned to sink in his speculations. Do you get that?" Enid's eyes snapped.

Most certainly I understood. I knew well the type of Stella. She had made many men give up to her motor cars, expensive furs, jewelry, all manner of presents. But in the end she had found one man to whom she in turn was willing to yield all. But what of him?

"In the last few weeks, they tell me, poor Stella disposed of many of her handsome presents from men like Manton and Phelps and others, all to get money to give to him. At the end she even raised money on her jewelry. I—I think you'll find it all in pawn now, if you'll investigate. I don't doubt but that poor Stella died without a penny to her name."

I was so surprised at this information that I failed to study Kennedy's face. I was completely jolted from my own rapt contemplation of the very soft curves of Enid's back. For here was a motive at last! Gordon was a possible suspect I had failed to take even halfway seriously. Yet the leading man was desperately pressed for money, had had a disgraceful fight with Phelps as we already knew; and not only owed huge sums to his fiancee as Enid now explained, but had quarreled with her just prior to her death, according to his own admission in the investigation at Tarrytown.

Suddenly the music struck up once more. Enid rose, adjusting the straps of her gown.

"There!" she exclaimed, smiling abruptly. "I thought you ought to know that, though I hate to peddle gossip. Now I must hurry back. I've been away long enough. But come down later and dance."

She swept off without further formality. An instant afterward we saw her in the clasp of Millard once again. We watched during the number and encore; then Kennedy called for the check.

"Let's go up to the apartment," he suggested. "I'd like to talk some of these things out with you. It will help me clarify my own impressions."

Underneath the balcony I noticed Kennedy turn for a last glance at Manton's party. I paused to look, also. Enid was leaning forward, talking to Millard earnestly, emphasizing what she had to say with characteristic movements of her head.

"She's pumping Millard for more information about Stella Lamar," I remarked.

Kennedy had no comment.

XVII

AN APPEAL

We strolled up Broadway, resisting the attraction of a garish new motion-picture palace at which Manton's previous release with Stella Lamar was now showing to capacity—much to the delight of the exhibitor who greatly complimented himself on his good fortune in being able to take advantage of the newspaper sensation over the affair.

On we walked, Kennedy mostly in silent deduction, I knew, until we came to the upper regions of the great thoroughfare, turned off, and headed toward our apartment on the Heights, not far from the university.

We had scarcely settled ourselves for a quiet hour in our quarters when the telephone rang. I answered. To my amazement I found that it was Marilyn Loring.

"Is Professor Kennedy in?" she asked.

"Yes, Miss Loring. Just a—"

"Never mind calling him to the phone, Mr. Jameson. I've been trying to find him all evening. He was not at the laboratory, although I waited over an hour. Just tell him that there's something I am very anxious to consult him about. Ask him if it will be all right for me to run up to see him just a few minutes."

I explained to Kennedy.

"Let her come along," he said, as surprised as I was. Then he added, humorously, "I seem to be father confessor to-night."

After sinking back in my seat in comfort once more I observed a quiet elation in Kennedy's manner. All at once it struck me what he was doing. The multitude of considerations in this case, the many cross leads to be followed, had confused me. But now I realized that, after all, this was only the approved Kennedy method, the mode of procedure which had never failed to produce results for him. Without allowing himself to be disturbed by the great number of people concerned, he had calmly started to pit them one against the other, encouraging each to talk about the rest, making a show of his apparent inaction and lack of haste so that they, in turn, would shake off the excitement immediately following the death of the girl and thereby reveal their normal selves to his keen observation.

Not five minutes passed before Marilyn was announced. Evidently she had been seeking us eagerly, for she had probably telephoned from a near-by pay station.

"Mr. Kennedy," she began, "I am going to find this very hard to say."

"Really," he assured her, "there is no reason why you should not repose your confidence in me. My only interest is to solve the mystery and to see that justice is satisfied. Beyond that nothing would give me greater happiness than to be of service to you."

"It's—it's about Merle Shirley—" she started, bravely. Then all at once she broke down. The strain of two days had been too much for her.

Kennedy lighted a fresh cigar, realizing that he could best aid her to recover her composure by making no effort to do so. For several moments she sobbed silently, a handkerchief at her eyes. Then she straightened, with a half smile, dabbing at the drops of moisture remaining. With her wet eyes and flushed cheeks she was revealed to me again as a very genuine girl, wholly unspoiled by her outward mask of sophistication. Furthermore, at this instant she was gloriously pretty.

"Again—why do you play vampire roles, Miss Loring?" I asked, as quickly as the thought flashed to me. "I think you'd be an ideal ingenue!"

"About a thousand people have told me that," she rejoined. As she replied her smile took full possession of her features. My idiotic repetition, entirely out of place, had served to restore her self-control to her. "No, the public won't stand for it. They've been trained to know me as a vamp, and a vamp I remain."

Facing Kennedy, she sobered. "Merle Shirley and I were engaged," she went on. "That you know. Then poor Stella made a fool of him. She didn't mean any harm, any real harm, but I don't think she knew how deep he feels or just what a fiery temper he has. Finally he found out that she was only playing with him. He was perfectly terrible. At first I thought he had killed her in a burst of passion. I really thought that."

"Yes?" Kennedy was interested. He needed no pretense.

"When I asked him point blank he said he didn't." A very wonderful light came into Marilyn Loring's eyes at this instant. "Whatever else he would do, Professor Kennedy, he wouldn't lie to me; that I know. He would tell me the truth because he knows I would shield him, no matter what the cost."

"You simply want to assure me of his innocence?" suggested Kennedy.

"No!" There was a touch of scorn to the little negative. "You don't believe him guilty; you didn't even when I did."

"Then—"

"But he knows something—something about the murder of Stella—and he won't tell me what it is. I—I'm afraid for him. He isn't sleeping at night, and I believe he's watching somebody at the studio, and I know—it's the WOMAN'S intuition, Professor"—she emphasized the word, and paused—"he's in danger. He's in some great threatening danger!"

"What do you wish me to do, Miss Loring?"

"I want you to protect him and"—slowly she colored, up and around and about her eyes as she always did, until she wasn't unlike an Indian maid—"and no one must know I've been up to see you."

Gravely Kennedy bowed her to the door, assuring her he would do all that lay in his power. When he returned I was ready for him.

"Now!" I exclaimed. "Now say it isn't Werner! Here is Merle Shirley watching some one at the studio. Isn't that likely to be the director? And if Shirley is watching Werner you have the explanation for the second intruder at Tarrytown last night. Shirley is big enough and strong enough to have given the deputy a nice swift tussle."

"A little tall, I'm afraid," Kennedy remarked.

"You can't go by the deputy's impressions. He didn't really remember much of anything. Certainly he was unobserving."

"Perhaps you're right, Walter." Kennedy smiled. "But how about Gordon?" he added. "There's genuine motive—money!"

"Or Shirley himself!" I attempted to be sarcastic. "There's genuine motive. Stella made a fool out of him."

"It wasn't a murder of passion," Kennedy reminded me. "No one in a white heat of rage would study up on snake venoms."

"If it were a slow-smoldering—"

"Shirley's anger wasn't that kind."

"But good heavens!" As usual I arrived nowhere in an argument with Kennedy. "Circumstantial evidence points to Werner almost altogether—"

"You've forgotten one point in your chain, Walter."

"What's that?"

"Whoever took the needle from the curtain last night scratched himself on it and left blood spots on the portieres, tiny ones, but real blood spots, nevertheless. That means the intruder inoculated himself with venom. I doubt that the poison was so dry as to be ineffectual. If it was Werner, how do you account for the fact that he is still alive?"

"Do you"—I guess my eyes went wide—"do you expect to dig up a dead man somewhere? Is there some one we suspect and haven't seen since yesterday?"

He didn't answer, preferring to tantalize me.

"How do you account for it yourself?" I demanded, somewhat hotly.

"Let's call it a day, Walter," he rejoined. "Let's go to bed!"

XVIII

THE ANTIVENIN

I slept late in the morning, so that Kennedy had to wake me. When we had finished breakfast he led the way to the laboratory, all without making any effort to satisfy my curiosity. There he started packing up the tubes and materials he had been studying in the case, rather than resuming his investigations.

"What's the idea?" I asked, finally, unable to contain myself any longer.

"You carry this package," he directed. "I'll take the other."

I obeyed, somewhat sulkily I'm afraid.

"You see," he added, as we left the building and hurried to the taxi stand near the campus, "the next problem is to identify the particular kind of venom that was used. Besides, I want to know the nature of the spots on the towel you found. They certainly were not of venom. I have my suspicions what they really are."

He paused while we selected a vehicle and made ourselves comfortable. "To save time," he went on, "I thought I'd just go over to the Castleton Institute. You know in their laboratories the famous Japanese investigator, Doctor Nagoya, has made some marvelous discoveries concerning the venom of snakes. It is his specialty, a matter to which he has practically devoted his life. Therefore I expect that he will be able to confirm certain suspicions of mine very quickly, or"—a shrug—"explode a theory which has slowly been taking form in the back of my head."

When we dismissed the taxi in front of the institute I realized that this would be my first visit to this institution so lavishly endowed by the multi-millionaire, Castleton, for the advancement of experimental science. Kennedy's card, sent in to Doctor Nagoya, brought that eminent investigator out personally to see us. He was the very finest type of Oriental savant, a member of the intellectual nobility of the strange Eastern land only recently made receptive to the civilization of the West. When he and Kennedy chatted together in low tones for a few moments it was hard for me to grasp that each belonged to a basic race strain fundamentally different from the other. East and West had met, upon the plane of modern science. The two were simply men of specialized knowledge, the Japanese pre-eminent in one field, Kennedy in another.

Carefully and thoroughly Kennedy and Nagoya went over the results which Kennedy had already obtained. After a moment Doctor Nagoya conducted us to his research room.

"Now let me show you," said the Oriental.

In a moment they were deep in the mysteries of an even more minute analysis than Kennedy had made before. I took a turn about the room, finding nothing more understandable than the study holding Kennedy's interest. Though I could not grasp it, curiosity kept me hovering close.

"You see"—Nagoya spoke as he finished the test he was making at the moment—"without a doubt it is crotalin, the venom of the rattlesnake, Crotalus horridus."

"There was no snake actually present," I hastened to explain, breaking in. Then at a glance from Kennedy I stopped, abashed, for all this had been made clear to the scientist.

"It is not necessary," Nagoya replied, turning to me with the politeness characteristic of the East. "Crotalin can be obtained now with fair ease. It is a drug used in a new treatment of epilepsy which is being tried out at many hospitals."

I nodded my thanks, not wanting to interrupt again.

Kennedy pressed on to the next point he wished established. "That was the spot on the portieres. Now the ampulla."

"Also crotalin." Doctor Nagoya spoke positively.

"How about this solution?" Kennedy took from my package the tube with the liquid made from the faint spots on the towel which I had found and which had been our first clue. "It is not crotalin."

The Japanese turned to his laboratory table.

Kennedy muttered some vague suggestions which were too technical for me but which seemed to enable Nagoya to eliminate a great deal of work. The test progressed rapidly. Finally the savant stepped back, regarding the solution with a very satisfied smile.

"It is," he explained, carefully, "some of the very anticrotalus venin which we have perfected right here in the institute."

Kennedy nodded. "I suspected as much." There was great elation in his manner. "You see, I had heard all about your wonderful work."

"Yes!" Nagoya waved his hand around at the wonderfully equipped room, only one detail in the many arrangements for medical research made possible by the generosity of Castleton. "Yes," he repeated, proud of his laboratory, as he well might be, "we have made a great deal of progress in the development of protective sera—antivenins, we call them."

"Are they distributed widely?" Kennedy asked, thoughtfully.

"All over the world. We are practically the only source of supply."

"How do you obtain the serum in quantity?"

"From horses treated with increasing doses of the snake venom."

A question struck me as I remembered the peculiar double action of the poison. "Can you tell me just how the antivenin counteracts the effects of the venom?" I inquired of the savant.

"Surely," he replied. "It neutralizes one of the two elements in the venom, the nervous poison, thus enabling the individual to devote all his vitality to overcoming the irritant poison. It is the nervous poison that is the chief death-dealing agent, producing paralysis of the heart and respiration. We advise all travelers to carry the protective serum if they are likely to be exposed to snake bites."

Kennedy picked up the tube containing the solution made from the towel spots. "This antivenin was your product, doctor?"

"Probably so," was the precise answer.

"Then the purchasers can be identified," I suggested.

"We have no record of ordinary purchasers," Nagoya explained, slowly.

Kennedy was keenly disappointed at that, and showed it. However, he thanked the scientist cordially, and we departed. Outside, he turned to me.

"Do you understand now why the night intruder at Tarrytown did not die—if he is one of our suspects—from the scratch of the needle?"

"You mean he had taken an injection of antivenin before—"

"Exactly! We are dealing with a criminal of diabolical cleverness. Not only did he make all his plans to kill Miss Lamar with the greatest possible care, but he prepared against accident to himself. He was taking no chances. He inoculated himself with a protective serum. The needle of the syringe he used for that purpose he wiped upon the towel you discovered in the washroom."

XIX

AROUND THE CIRCLE

"I'd like to have another talk with Millard about that Fortune Features affair," remarked Kennedy.

It was the third morning after the death of Stella Lamar, and I found him half through breakfast when I rose. About him were piled moving picture and theatrical publications, daily, weekly, and monthly. At the moment I caught him he had spread wide open the inner page of the Daily Metropolitan, a sheet devoted almost exclusively to sports and the amusement fields.

I went around to glance over his shoulder. He pointed to a small item under a heading of recent plans and changes.

FORTUNE FEATURES

> It is hinted to the Metropolitan Man-about-Broadway, by those in a position to know but who cannot yet be quoted, that Fortune Features is about to absorb a number of the largest competing companies. Rumors of great changes in the picture world have been current for some weeks, and this is the first reliable information to be given out. It is premature to give details of the new combination, or to mention names, but Fortune's strong backing in Wall Street will, we are assured, have a stabilizing influence at a critical time in the industry.

"Seems to be a lot of hot air," I said. "There isn't a name mentioned. Everything is 'by those in a position to know' and 'rumors of and 'it is premature to give details... or mention names'—Bah!"

Kennedy turned to places he had marked in several of the other periodicals and papers and I read them. Each was substantially to the effect of the note in the Metropolitan, although worded differently and generally printed as a news item.

"It's a feeler," Kennedy stated. "There's something back of it. When I caught the reference to Fortune Features in the Metropolitan, which I've been reading the past two days, I sent the boy out for every movie publication he could find. Result: half a dozen repetitions of the hint that Fortune is expanding. That means that it is deliberate publicity."

"You think this has something to do with the case?"

"I don't see the name of Manton mentioned once. Manton is a man who seeks the front page on every opportunity. You remember, of course, what Millard told us. Somehow I smell a rat. If nothing else develops for this morning, I want to find Millard and talk to him again. I believe Manton is up to something."

The sharp sound of our buzzer interrupted us. Because I was on my feet I went to the door. To my amazement I found it was Phelps who was our very early visitor.

"I hope you'll excuse this intrusion," he apologized to Kennedy, pushing by me with the rudeness which seemed inherent in the man. Then he recognized the sheet still spread out on the table. "I see you, too, have been reading the Metropolitan."

"Yes," Kennedy admitted, languidly. "There is nothing about Manton Pictures, though."

"Manton Pictures, hell!" In an instant Phelps exploded and the thin veneer of politeness was gone. With a shaking finger he pointed to the item which we had just been reading and discussing. "Did you read that! Did you see the reference to stabilizing the industry? STABILIZING! It ought to be spelled stable-izing, for they lead all the donkeys into stalls and tie them up and let them kick." He stopped momentarily for sheer inability to continue.

"I suppose you don't know Manton is behind this Fortune Features?"

"We were aware of the fact," Kennedy told him, quietly.

Phelps looked from one to the other of us keenly, as if he had thought to surprise us and had been disappointed. Nervously he began to pace the floor.

"Perhaps you know also that things haven't been going just right with Manton Pictures?"

Kennedy straightened. "When I asked you at Tarrytown, just two mornings ago, whether there was any trouble between Manton and yourself, you answered that there was not."

Phelps flushed. "I didn't want to air my financial difficulties with Manton. My—my answer was truthful, the way you meant your question. Manton and I have had no words, no quarrel, no disagreement of a personal nature."

"What is the trouble with Manton Pictures?"

"They are wasting money—throwing it right and left. That pay roll of theirs is preposterous. The waste itself is beyond belief—sometimes four and five cameras on a scene, retakes upon the slightest provocation, even sets rebuilt because some minor detail fails to suit the artistic eye of the director. Werner, supposed to watch all the companies, doesn't half know his business. In the making of a five-reel film they will overtake sometimes as much as eighty or a hundred thousand feet of negative in each of two cameras, when twenty thousand is enough overtake for anyone. That alone is five to ten thousand dollars for negative stock, almost fifteen with the sample print and developing. And the cost of stock, Mr. Kennedy, is the smallest item. All the extra length is long additional weeks of pay roll and overhead expense. I put an auditor and a film expert on the accounts of Stella Lamar's last picture. By their figures just sixty-three thousand dollars was absolutely thrown away."

Kennedy rose, folding the newspaper carefully while he collected his thoughts. "My dear Mr. Phelps," he stated, finally, "that is simply inefficiency. I doubt if it is anything criminal; certainly there is no connection with the death of Stella Lamar, my only interest in Manton Pictures."

Phelps was very grave. "There is every connection with the death of Stella Lamar!"

"What do you mean?"

"Mr. Kennedy, what I'm going to say to you I cannot substantiate in any court of law. Furthermore I'm laying myself open to action for libel, so I must not be quoted. But I want you to understand that Stella was inescapably wound up with all of Manton's financial schemes. His money maneuvers determined her social life, her friends—everything. She was then, as Enid Faye will be now, his come-on, his decoy. Manton has no scruples of any sort whatsoever. He is dishonest, tricky, a liar, and a cheat. If I could prove it I would tell him so, but he's too clever for me. I do know, however, that he pulled the strings which controlled every move Stella Lamar ever made. When she went to dinner with me it was because Manton wished her to do so. She was his right hand, his ears, almost his mouth. I have no doubt but that her death is the direct result of some business deal of his—something directly to do with his financial necessities."

Kennedy did not glance up. "Those are very serious assertions."

"It is a very serious matter. To show how unscrupulous Manton is, I can demonstrate that he is wrecking Manton Pictures deliberately. I've told you of the waste. Only the other day I came into the studio. Werner was putting up a great ballroom set. You saw it? No, that isn't the one I mean. I mean the first one. He had it all up; then some little thing didn't suit him. The next day I came in again. All struck—sloughed—every bit of it—and a new one started. 'Lloyd,' I said, 'just think a minute—that's my money!' What good did it do? He even began to alter the new set! He would only go on, encouraging Werner and the other directors to change their sets, to lose time in trying for foolish effects, anything at all to pad the expense.

"You think I am romancing, but you don't understand the film world," Phelps hurried on angrily. "Do you know that Enid Faye's contract is not with Manton Pictures but with Manton himself? That means he can take her away from me after he has made her a star with my money, at my expense. Why should he wreck Manton Pictures, you ask? Do you know that, bit by bit, on the pretext that he needed the funds for this that, or the other thing, Manton has sold out his entire interest in the company to me? It is all mine now. I tell you," complained Phelps, bitterly, "he couldn't seem to wreck the company fast enough. Why? Do you realize that there isn't room both for this older company and the new Fortune Features? Can you see that if Manton Pictures fails the Fortune company will be able to pick up the studio and all the equipment for a song? I'm the fall guy!

"And yet, Kennedy, all the efforts to wreck Manton Pictures would have failed, because 'The Black Terror' was too sure a success. In spite of all the expense, in spite of every effort to wreck it, that picture would have made half a million dollars. Stella's acting and Millard's story and script would have put it over. But now Millard's contract has expired and Manton has signed him for Fortune Features. Enid Faye will be made a star by 'The Black Terror,' but she is not now the drawing power to put it over big, as Stella would have done. I tell you, Kennedy, the death of Stella Lamar has completed the wreck of Manton Pictures!"

Kennedy jumped to his feet. There was a hard light in his eyes I had never seen before.

"Do I understand you, Phelps?" he snapped. "Are you accusing Manton of the cold-blooded murder of Stella Lamar to further various financial schemes?"

"Hardly!" Phelps blanched a bit, and I thought that a shudder swept over him. "I don't mean anything like that at all. What I mean is that Manton, in encouraging various sorts of dissension to wreck the company, inadvertently fanned the flames of passion of those about her, and it resulted in her death."

"Who killed her?"

"I don't know!" Grudgingly I admitted that this seemed open and frank.

"At Tarrytown," Kennedy went on, "I asked you if Stella Lamar was making any trouble, had threatened to quit Manton Pictures, and you said no. Is that still your answer?"

"For several months she had been up-stage. That was not because she wanted to make trouble, but because she had fallen in love. Manton found he couldn't handle her as he had previously."

"Do you suspect Manton of killing her himself?"

"I don't suspect anyone. That is an honest answer, Mr. Kennedy."

"What do you know about Fortune Features?"

The banker's eye fell on the newspaper again. "I know who this new Wall Street fellow is. I've got my scouts out working for me. It's Leigh—that's who it is. And I'm sore; I have a right to be."

Phelps was getting more and more heated, by the moment. "I tell you," he almost shouted, "this fake movie business is the modern gold-brick game, all right. Never again!"

I was amazed at the Machiavellian cleverness of Manton. Here he was, on one hand openly working with, yet secretly ruining, the Manton Pictures, while on the other hand he was covertly building up the competing Fortune Features.

Kennedy paced out into the little hall of our suite and back. He faced our visitor once more.

"Why did you come to see me this morning? At our last encounter, you may recall you said you wished you could throw me down the steps."

Phelps smiled ruefully. "That was a mistake. It was the way I felt, but—I'm sorry."

"Now—?"

Again the black clouds overshadowed the features of the financier. "Now I want you to bring out and prove the things I've told you." The malice showed in his voice plainly, for the first time. "I want it proved in court that Manton is a cheap crook. When you uncover the murderer of Stella Lamar you will find that the moral responsibility for her death traces right back to Lloyd Manton. I want him driven out of the business."

Kennedy's attitude changed. As he escorted Phelps to the door his tones were self-controlled. "Anything of the sort is beyond my province. My task is simply to find the person who killed the girl."

When the financier was gone I turned to Kennedy eagerly. "What do you think?" I asked.

"I think, more than ever, that we should investigate Fortune Features. Let's have a look at the telephone book."

There was no studio of the new corporation in New York, but we did find one listed in New Jersey, just across the river, at Fort Lee. We walked from the university down the hill and over to the ferry. On the other side a ten minutes' street-car ride took us to our destination.

Facing us was a huge barn-like structure set down in the midst of a little park. Inquiry for Manton brought no response whatever; rather, surprise that we should be asking for him here. However, I reflected that that was exactly what we ought to expect if Manton was working under cover. The girl at the telephone switchboard, smiling at Kennedy, had a suggestion.

"They're taking a storm exterior down in the meadow," she explained. "Perhaps he's down there, among the visitors—or perhaps there's someone who will be able to give you some information."

I glanced outdoors at the brightly shining sun. "A storm?" I repeated, incredulously.

"Yes," she smiled. "It might interest you to see it."

Following her directions, we started across country, leaving the studio building some distance behind and entering a broad expanse of meadow beyond a thin clump of trees. At the farther end we could see a large group of people and paraphernalia which, at the distance, we could not make out.

However, it was not long after we emerged from the trees that we perceived they were photographing squarely in our direction. Several began waving their arms wildly at us and shouting. Kennedy and I, understanding, turned and advanced, keeping well out of the camera lines, along the edge of the field.

"Hello!" a voice greeted us as we approached the group standing back and watching the action.

To my surprise it was Millard, with the spectators. I looked about for Manton but did not see him, nor anyone else we knew.

"It's a storm and cyclone," said Millard, his attention rather on what was going on than on us.

For the moment we said nothing.

The scene before us was indeed interesting. Half a dozen aeroplane engines and propellers had been set up outside the picture, and anchored securely in place. The wind from them was actually enough to knock a man down. Rain was furnished by hose playing water into the whirling blades, sending it driving into the scene with the fury of a tropical storm. Back of the propellers half a dozen men were frantically at work shoveling into them sand and dirt, creating an amazingly realistic cyclone.

We arrived in the midst of the cyclone scene, as the dust storm was ending and the torrential rain succeeded. For the storm, a miniature village had been constructed in break-away fashion, partially sawed through and tricked for the proper moment. Many objects were controlled by invisible wires, including an actual horse and buggy which seemed to be lifted bodily and carried away. Roofs flew off, walls crashed in, actors and actresses were knocked flat as some few of them failed to gain their cyclone cellars. Altogether, it was a storm of such efficiency as Nature herself could scarcely have furnished, and all staged with the streaming sunlight which made photography possible.

Pandemonium reigned. Cameras were grinding, directors were bawling through megaphones, all was calculated chaos. Yet it took only a glance to see that some marvelous effects were being caught here.

At the conclusion I recognized suddenly the little leading lady, It was the girl we had seen with Manton at Jacques' cabaret.

"That's the way to take a picture," exclaimed Millard. "Everything right—no expense spared. I came over to see it done. It's wonderful."

"Yes," was Kennedy's answer, "but it must be very costly."

"It is all of that," said Millard. "But what of it if the film makes a big clean-up? I wouldn't have missed this for anything. Werner never staged a spectacle like this in his life. Fortune Features are going to set a new mark in pictures."

"But can they keep it up? Have they the money?"

Millard shrugged his shoulders. "Manton Pictures can't—that's a cinch. Phelps has reached the end of his rope, I guess. I'm afraid the trouble with him was that he was thinking of too many things besides pictures."

There was no mistaking the meaning of the remark. Millard was still cut by Stella's desertion of him for the broker. I caught Kennedy's glance, but neither of us cared to refer to her.

"Where can I find Manton now?" Kennedy asked.

"Did you try his office at seven hundred and twenty-nine?" was Millard's suggestion.

"No; I wanted to see this place first."

"Well, you'll most likely find him there. I've got to go back to the city myself-some scenes of 'The Black Terror' to rewrite to fit Enid better. I'll motor you across the ferry and to the Subway."

At the Subway station, Millard left us and we proceeded to Manton's executive offices in a Seventh Avenue skyscraper, built for and devoted exclusively to the film business.

Manton's business suite was lavishly furnished, but not quite as ornate and garish as his apartment. The promoter himself welcomed us, for no matter how busy he was at any hour, he always seemed to have time to stop and chat.

"Well, how goes it?" He pushed over a box of expensive cigars. "Have you found out anything yet?"

"Had a visit from Phelps this morning." Kennedy plunged directly into the subject, watching the effect.

Manton did not betray anything except a quiet smile. "Poor old Phelps," he said. "I guess he's pretty uneasy. You know he has been speculating rather heavily in the market lately. There was a time when I thought Phelps had a bank roll in reserve. But it seems he has been playing the game on a shoestring, after all."

Manton casually flicked the ashes from his cigar into a highly polished cuspidor as he leaned over. "I happen to have learned that, to make his bluff good, he has been taking money from his brokerage business"—here he nodded sagely—"his customers' accounts you know. Leigh knows the inside of everybody's affairs in Wall Street. They say a quarter of a million is short, at least. To tell you the truth, poor Stella took a good deal of Phelps's money. Certainly his Manton Pictures holdings wouldn't leave him in the hole as deep as all that."

I reflected that this was quite the way of the world—first framing up something on a boob, then deprecating the ease with which he was trimmed.

Was it blackmail Stella had levied on Phelps, I wondered? Was she taking from him to give to Gordon? Had Stella broken him? Was she the real cause of the tangle in his affairs? And had Phelps in insane passion revenged himself on her?

In the conversation with Manton there was certainly no hint of answer to my queries. With all his ease, Manton was the true picture promoter. Seldom was he betrayed into a positive statement of his own. Always, when necessary, he gave as authority the name of some one else. But the effect was the same.

A hurried call of some sort took Manton away from us. Kennedy turned to me with a whimsical expression.

"Let's go!" he remarked.

"What do you make of it, offhand?" I asked, outside.

"We're going about in a circle," he remarked. "Strange group of people. Each apparently suspects the other."

"And, to cover himself, talks of the other fellow," I added.

Kennedy nodded, and we made our way toward the laboratory.

"I'll bet something happens before the day is over," I hazarded, for no reason in particular.

Kennedy shrugged.

As we went, I cast up in my mind the facts we had learned. The information from Manton was disconcerting, coming on top of what had already been revealed about the inner workings of his game. If Phelps had secretly "borrowed" from the trust accounts in his charge a quarter of a million or so, I saw that his situation must indeed be desperate. To what lengths he might go it was difficult to determine.

XX

THE BANQUET SCENE

For once I qualified as a prophet. We were hardly in our rooms when the telephone rang for Kennedy. It was District-Attorney Mackay, calling in from Tarrytown.

"My men have positive identification of one of the visitors to the Phelps home the night after the murder," he reported.

"Fine!" exclaimed Kennedy. "Who was it? How did you uncover his trail?"

"You remember that my deputy heard the sound of a departing automobile? Well, we have been questioning everyone. A citizen here, who returned home late at just about that hour, remembers seeing a taxicab tearing through the street at a reckless rate. He came in to see me this morning. He made a mental note of the license number at the time, and while nothing stuck with him but the last three figures, three sixes, he was sure that it was a Maroon taxi. We got busy and have located the driver who made the trip, from a stand at Thirty-third all the way out and back. On the return he dropped his fare at the man's apartment. The identification is positive."

"Who is it?" Kennedy became quite excited.

"Werner, the director."

"Werner!" in surprise. "What are you going to do?"

"Arrest him first—examine him afterward. I've sworn out the warrant already, and I'm going to start in by car just as soon as we hang up. I thought I'd phone you first in case you wanted to accompany me to the studio."

"We'll hurry there," Kennedy replied, "and meet you."

"Outside?"

"No, up on the floor."

"You'll be there fifteen minutes to half an hour ahead of me. I hope there is no way for anyone to tip him off so he can escape."

"We'll stop him if he attempts it."

"Good!"

The courtyard of the studio of Manton Pictures, Incorporated, was about the same as upon the occasions of our previous visits except that I detected a larger number of cars parked in the inclosure, including a number of very fine ones. Also, it seemed to me that there was a greater absence of life than usual, as though something of particular interest had taken everyone inside the buildings.

The gateman informed us that Werner was working the large studio. We made our way up through the structure containing the dressing rooms and found the proper door without difficulty. When we passed through under the big glass roof we grasped the reason for the lack of interest in the other departments about the quadrangle. Here everyone was gathered to watch the taking of the banquet scene for "The Black Terror." The huge set was illuminated brightly, and packed, thronged with people.

It was a marvelous set in many ways. To carry out the illusion of size and to aid in the deceptive additional length given by the mirrors at the farther end, Werner had decided against the usual one large table arranged horseshoe-like, but had substituted instead a great number of individual smaller tables, about which he had grouped the various guests. The placing of those nearest the mirrors had been so arranged as to give no double images, thus betraying the trick. The waiters, all the characters who walked about, were kept near the front toward the cameras for the same reason. It seemed as if the banquet hall was at least twice its actual size.

I saw that Millard had arrived ahead of us. Either the changing of the scenes in his script to fit Enid had not taken him very long or else the photographing of this particular bit of action had proved sufficiently fascinating to draw him away from his work. I wondered at first if he had come to the studio to use his office here, an infrequent happening, from Manton's account. Then I realized that he was in evening dress. Without doubt he planned to play a minor part in the banquet. His presence was no accident.

Then I picked out Manton himself from our point of observation in a quiet corner selected by Kennedy for that purpose. It was evident that the promoter had cleared up his business at the office rapidly since we had left him there to go to our quarters on the Heights and had departed immediately from the latter place so as to precede the District Attorney here.

Manton as well as Millard was in evening dress. A moment later I recognized Phelps, and he, too, wore his formal clothes. In an instant I grasped that Werner actually was saving money. Not only were these officials of the company present to help fill up the tables, but I was able now to pick out a number of the guests who were uneasy in their make-up and more or less out of place in full-dress attire. They certainly were not actors. One girl I definitely placed as the stenographer from Manton's waiting room at the studio; then other things caught my attention. I could not help but doubt the stories of waste told us by Phelps as I looked over the scene before me. The use of the mirrors to avoid building the full length of the floor did not seem to fit in with the theory that

Manton and Werner were making every effort to wreck the company deliberately.

I watched the financier for several moments, but did not detect anything from his manner except that he seemed to feel ill at ease and awkward in make-up. I picked out Millard again and this time found him talking with Enid Faye and Gordon. Immediately I sensed a dramatic conflict, carefully suppressed, but having too many of the outward indications to fool anyone. In fact, a child would have observed that Lawrence Millard and the leading man needed little urging to engage in a scuffle then and there. Though Stella Lamar was dead, this was the heritage she had left. Her touch had embittered two men beyond the point of reconciliation—the husband who had been, and the husband who was to be. Of the two, Millard had far the better control of himself, however.

After a brief word or so Gordon left them. At once I could see the relief in the expressions of both the others. Again I wondered just what might be between these two. It was an easy familiarity which might have been as casual as it seemed to be, no more, or which might have been a mask for something far deeper and more enduring, the schooled outer cloak of an inner perfect understanding.

Werner was by far the busiest of those waiting in the stifling heat beneath the glass roof. He was in evening dress, prepared to take his own place before the camera, and in straight make-up, so that he looked nothing like the slain millionaire, the part he had played in the opening scenes. I saw that he was a master in the art of make-up. I was sure that he was more nervous than usual. It struck me that he needed the stimulus of the drug he used, although later I knew that he must have felt, intuitively, the coming of events which followed close upon the attempt to photograph the action.

As more of the people hurried up from the offices and around from the manuscript and other departments, very conscious of their formal attire, and as the regular players changed and adjusted the make-ups of these amateurs, the banquet took on the proportions of a real affair.

The members of the cast were placed at the table in the foreground. Enid, Gordon, Marilyn, and a fourth man were assigned locations; after which Werner proceeded to fill the seats in the rear. With the exception of Millard and Phelps, none of the inexperienced people were allowed to face the camera. Manton, whose features were familiar through published interviews in many publicity campaigns, was placed to one side opposite Phelps. Millard was given charge of a group containing a number of giddy extra girls in somewhat diaphanous costume, and seemed to be in his element.

The tables themselves were prepared with perfect taste. I could see that real food was being used, in order to achieve a greater degree of realism, for a caterer had set up a buffet some distance out of the scene from which to serve the courses called for in the script. Many of the dishes were being kept hot, the steam curling from beneath the covers in appetizing wisps. The wine, supposed to be champagne, was sparkling apple juice of the best quality, and I don't doubt but that before the days of prohibition Werner would have insisted upon the real fizz water. In details such as these the director was showing no economy.

"All ready now?" Werner called, stepping back to a place at a table which he had reserved for himself. "All set? Remember the action of the script?"

Instantly the buzz of conversation died and everyone turned to him.

"No, no, no!" he exclaimed in vexation. "Don't go dead on your feet. This is a banquet. You are having a good time. It's not a funeral! You were all in just the right state of mind before, and you don't have to stop and gape to listen to me. Keep right on talking and laughing. My voice will carry and you can hear without getting out of your parts."

I turned to Kennedy, to see how the picture-making struck him. I saw that he was watching the two girls at the forward table closely and so I faced about to follow his glance. Marilyn's face was red with anger, while Enid, calm and rather malicious, was ignoring her to devote all attention to Gordon. The leading man, bored and irritated, made no effort to conceal a heavy scowl. In the momentary interval following Werner's instructions, Marilyn lost all control of herself.

"If you will pardon me, MISS Faye," she cried out in a voice which carried over to us and with cutting accent upon the "Miss," "I think that in this scene at least we should BOTH be facing the camera. If I understand the scene in the script at all it is intended to show the conflict between the two women over the one man seated between them. Jack Daring is to be swayed first by Stella Remsen, then by Zelda. At least this once I think the daughter of old Remsen and his ward are playing roles of equal importance."

For a moment I smiled, realizing that Marilyn was not going to let Enid "take the picture away" from her as we had seen the new star do in one of her first scenes with the leading man. Then I sobered, realizing that it was the outer reflection of the deep-running passion of these people. The cloud of Stella's death was over them still.

Enid responded, but in tones too low for us to hear. A new flush of red in Marilyn's face, however, demonstrated the power in the lash of the other girl's tongue. Werner hurried over to them, not masking his own irritation any too well. Without a word he began rearranging the table, moving it slightly so that while there was no great difference in its position he had yet made a show of satisfying Marilyn. In effect he pleased neither. The two pretty faces closest to the camera were a study in discontent.

"I don't wonder that moving-picture directors are nervous," Kennedy remarked. "Film manufacture must keep everyone under constant tension."

"What do you make of the feeling between the different people?" I asked. "Did you notice Millard and Gordon, and now Enid and Marilyn?"

"There's something under cover," he rejoined; "something behind all this. I get the impression that our suspects are watching one another, like as many hawks. At various times most of them have glanced over at us. They know we are here and are conscious they may be under suspicion. Therefore I particularly want to see how those two girls act when Mackay arrives to arrest Werner."

The director, stepping back to his place, took a megaphone from his assistant for use in the rehearsal.

"Now you must act just as though this were a real banquet," he shouted. "Try to forget that the Black Terror is lurking outside the window, that an attack is coming from him. Remember, when the shot is fired you must all leap up as though you meant it. Here! You—you—you—" designating certain extra girls, "faint when it happens. That's not until after the toast is proposed. I'll propose the toast from my table and it will be the cue for Shirley, outside. Now don't get ahead of the action. You amateurs, don't turn around to see if the camera is working. We'll go through the action up to the moment I propose the toast." The buzz of conversation rose slightly as though an effort was being put into the gayety. I glanced about at some of the people who were cast for only this one scene, wishing I could read lips, because I was sure many of them talked of matters wholly out of place in this setting. At the same time I kept an eye on the principals and upon Werner.

Finally the director was satisfied, after a second rehearsal.

"All right," he bellowed, throwing the megaphone from the scene. "Shoot!"

At the same instant he dropped to his place and apparently was a guest with no interest but in the food and wine before him.

At the cameras-there were three of them-the assistant director kept a careful watch of the general action. In actual time by the watch the whole was very short, a second measuring to sixteen pictures or a foot of film as I explained afterward to Kennedy. The entire scene perhaps ran one hundred or one hundred and fifty feet.

But on the screen, even to the spectators in the studio, the illusion in a scene of the kind would be the duration of half an hour or even more. This would be helped by close-ups of the individual action, especially by the byplay between the principals, taken later and inserted into the long shot by the film cutter.

I know I was carried away by a sense of reality. It seemed to me that waiters made endless trips to and fro, that here and there pretty girls broke into laughter constantly or that men leaned forward every other moment to make witty remarks; in fact I felt genuinely sorry I could not take part in the festivities. I knew that danger, in the person of the Black Terror as played by Shirley, lurked just out the window. I felt delicious anticipatory thrills of fear, so thoroughly was I in the spirit of the thing. Then I saw that Werner was about to propose the toast, about to give the cue for the big action.

"Watch him" whispered Kennedy. "He's an actor. He's taking that drink just as though he meant every drop of it."

Werner had raised his delicately stemmed glass as though to join his neighbor in some pledge when a new idea seemed to strike him. He leaped to his feet.

"Let's drink together! Let's drink to our hero and heroine of the evening!"

Other voices rose in acclamation. The wine had been poured lavishly.

Glasses clinked and we could hear laughter.

Suddenly at the window, back of everyone, appeared the evil, black-masked figure of Shirley, eyes glittering menacingly from their slits, two weapons glistening blue in his hands.

At the same moment there was a terrible groan, followed by a scream of agony. Werner staggered back, his left hand clutched at his breast. From his right hand the glass which he had drained fell to the canvas covered floor with an ominous dull crash.

This was not in the script! Practically everybody realized the fact, for the scene instantly was in an uproar. In the general consternation no one seemed to know just what to do.

Shirley was the first to act, the first to realize what had happened. Dropping his weapons, reaching the side of the stricken director in one leap, he supported him as he reeled drunkenly, then eased him to the floor. Behind us, before I could look to Kennedy to see what he would do, there was the gasp of a man out of breath from hurrying upstairs. I turned, startled. It was Mackay.

"Shall I make the collar?" he wheezed. At the same instant he saw the gathering crowd in the set. "What—what's happened?" he asked.

Kennedy had bounded forward only a few seconds after Shirley. As I pushed through after him, Mackay following, I discovered him kneeling at the side of Werner.

"Some one send for a doctor, quick," he commanded, taking charge of things as a matter of course. "Hurry!" he repeated. "He's gasping for air and it'll be too late in a minute."

Then he saw us. "Walter—Mackay"—he raised Werner's head—"push everyone back, please! Give him a chance to breathe!"

A thousand thoughts flashed through my head as politely but firmly I widened the space about Kennedy and the director. Was this a case of suicide? Had Werner known we were coming for him? Had he thought to bring about his own end in the most spectacular fashion possible? Was this the fancy of a drug-weakened brain?

Suddenly I realized that Werner was trying to speak. One of the camera men had helped Kennedy lift him to the top of a table, swept of its dishes and linen, so as to make it easier for him to breathe.

"Out in Tarrytown," he muttered, weakly, "that night—I suspected—and—saw—" His voice trailed off into nothingness. Even the motion of his lips was too feeble to follow.

In an instant I grasped the cruel injustice I had done this man in my mind. It was now that I remembered, in a flash, Kennedy's attitude and was glad that Kennedy had not suspected him.

"See!" I faced Mackay, speaking in quick, low tones so the others could not hear. "I—we—have been totally and absolutely wrong in suspecting Werner. Instead, it was he who has been playing our game—trying to confirm his own suspicions. I've been entirely wrong in my deductions from the discovery of his dope and needles."

"What do you mean, Jameson?" The district attorney had been taken completely off his feet by the unexpected developments. His eyes were rather dazed, his expression baffled. "What do you mean?"

"Why he was out at Tarrytown that night, all right, don't you see—but—but he was the second man, the man who watched!"

Mackay still seemed unable to comprehend.

"There were two men," I went on, excitedly; covering my own chagrin in my impatience at the little district attorney. "The one your deputy struggled with was short, rather than tall, and very strong. That's Werner! Can't you see it? Haven't you noticed how stockily and powerfully the director is built?"

"Werner must really have had some clue," murmured Mackay, dazed.

It left me wondering whether the stimulation of the dope might not have heightened Werner's imagination and urged him on in following something that our more sluggish minds had never even dreamed.

Meanwhile I saw that the doctor had arrived and that Kennedy had helped carry Werner to a dressing room where first aid could be given more conveniently. Now Kennedy hurried back into the studio, glancing quickly this way and that, as though to catch signs of confusion or guilt upon the faces of those about us.

I colored. Instead of making explanations to Mackay, explanations which could have waited, I might have used what faculties of observation I possessed to aid Kennedy while he was giving first consideration to the life of a man. As it was, I didn't know what had become of any of the various people upon our list of possible suspects. As far as I was concerned, any or every sign and clue to the attack upon Werner might have been removed or destroyed.

A sudden hush caused all of us to turn toward the door leading to the dressing rooms. It was the physician. He raised a hand for attention. His voice was low, but it carried to every corner of the studio:

"Mr. Werner is dead," he announced.

XXI

MERLE SHIRLEY OVERACTS

Appalled, I wondered who it was who had, to cover up one crime, committed another? Who had struck down an innocent man to save a guilty neck?

Kennedy hurried to the side of the physician and I followed.

"What symptoms did you observe?" asked Kennedy, quickly, seeking confirmation of his own first impressions.

"His mouth seemed dry and I should say he suffered from a quick prostration. There seemed to be a complete loss of power to swallow or speak. The pupils were dilated as though from paralysis of the eyes. Both pharynx and larynx were affected. There was respiration paralysis. It seemed also as though the cranial nerves were partially paralyzed. It was typically a condition due to some toxic substance which paralyzed and depressed certain areas of the body."

Kennedy nodded. "That fits in with a theory I have."

I thought quickly, then inquired; "Could it be the snake venom again?"

"No," Kennedy replied, shaking his head; "there's a difference in the symptoms and there is no mark on any exposed part of the body, as near as I could see in a superficial examination."

He turned to the physician. "Could you give me blood smears and some of the stomach contents, at once? Twice, now, some one has been stricken down before the very eyes of the actors. This thing has gone too far to trifle with or delay a moment."

The doctor hurried off toward the dressing room, anxious to help Kennedy, and as excited, I thought, as any of us. Next Kennedy faced me.

"Did you watch the people at all, Walter?"

"I—I was too upset by the suddenness of it," I stammered.

All seemed to have suspicion of some one else, and there was a general constraint, as though even the innocent feared to do or say something that might look or sound incriminating.

I turned. All were now watching every move we made, though just yet none ventured to follow us. It was as though they felt that to do so was like crossing a dead line. I wondered which one of them might be looking at us with inward trepidation—or perhaps satisfaction, if there had been any chance to remove anything incriminating.

Kennedy strode over toward the ill-fated set, Mackay and I at his heels. As we moved across the floor I noticed that everyone clustered as close as he dared, afraid, seemingly, of any action which might hinder the investigation, yet unwilling to miss any detail of Kennedy's method. In contrast with the clamor and racket of less than a half hour previously there was now a deathlike stillness beneath the arched ground-glass roof. The heat was more oppressive than ever before. In the faces and expressions of the awed witnesses of death's swift hand there was horror, and a growing fear. No one spoke, except in whispers. When anybody moved it was on tiptoe, cautiously. Millard's creation, "The Black Terror," could have inspired no dread greater than this.

Of the people we wished to study, Phelps caught our eyes the first. Dejected, crushed, utterly discouraged, he was slouched down in a chair just at the edge of the supposed banquet hall. I had no doubt of the nature of his thoughts. There was probably only the most perfunctory sympathy for the stricken director. Without question his mind ran to dollars. The dollar-angle to this tragedy was that the death of Werner was simply another step in the wrecking of Manton Pictures. Kennedy, I saw, hardly gave him a passing glance.

Manton we observed near the door. With the possible exception of Millard he seemed about the least concerned. The two, scenario writer and producer, had counterfeited the melodrama of life so often in their productions that even the second sinister chapter in this film mystery failed to penetrate their sang-froid. Inwardly they may have felt as deeply as any of the rest, but both maintained their outward composure.

On Manton's shoulders was the responsibility for the picture. I could see that he was nervous, irritable; yet, as various employees approached for their instructions in this emergency he never lost his grasp of affairs. In the vibrant quiet of this studio chamber, still under the shadow of tragedy, we witnessed as cold-blooded a bit of business generalship as has ever come to my knowledge. We overheard, because Manton's voice carried across to us in the stillness.

"Kauf!" The name I remembered as that of the technical, or art, director under Werner, responsible for the sets of "The Black Terror."

"Yes, Mr. Manton!" Kauf was a slim, stoop-shouldered man, gray, and a dynamo of energy in a quiet, subservient way. He ran to Manton's side.

"Remember once telling me you wanted to become a director, that you wanted to make pictures for me?"

"Yes, sir!"

"You are familiar with the script of 'The Black Terror,' aren't you? You know the people and how they work and you have sets lined up. How would you like to finish the direction?"

"But—but—" To the credit of the little man he dabbed at his eyes. I guess he had been fond of his immediate superior. "Mr.—Mr. Werner is d-dead—" he stammered.

"Of course!" Manton's voice rose slightly. "If Werner wasn't dead I wouldn't need another director at a moment's notice. Some one has to complete 'The Black Terror.' We have all these people on salary, and all the studio expense, and the release date's settled, so that we can't stop. It's your chance, Kauf! Do you want it?"

"Y-yes, sir!"

"Good! I'll double your salary, including all this week. Now can you finish this banquet set to-night, while you have the people—"

"To-night!" Kauf's eyes went wide, then he started to flush.

"Well, to-morrow, then! We simply can't lay off a day, Kauf!"

"All—all right, sir!"

It seemed to me that everyone in the place sensed the horror of this. Literally, actually, Werner's body could not be cold. Even the police, the medical examiner, had not had sufficient time to make the trip out for their investigation. Yet the director's successor had been appointed and told to hurry the production.

I glanced at Phelps. He raised his head slowly, his expression lifting at the thought that production was to continue without interruption. In another moment, however, there was a change in his face. His eyes sought Manton and hardened. His mouth tightened. Hate, a deep, unreasoning hate, settled into his features.

Kennedy, pausing just long enough to observe the promoter's appointment of Kauf to Werner's position, continued on toward the set. Now as I looked about I saw that Jack Gordon was missing, as well as Marilyn Loring. Presumably they had gone to their dressing rooms. All the other actors and actresses were waiting, ill at ease, wondering at the outcome of the tragedy.

Suddenly Kennedy stopped and I grasped that it was the peculiar actions of Merle Shirley which had halted him.

The heavy man was the only one of the company actually in the fabricated banquet hall itself. Clinging to him still were the grim flowing robes of the Black Terror. As though he were some old-fashioned tragedian, he was pacing up and down, hands behind his back, head bowed, eyes on the floor. More, he was mumbling to himself. It was evident, however, that it was neither a pose nor mental aberration. Shirley was searching for something, out in the open, without attempt at concealment, swearing softly at his lack of success.

Kennedy pushed forward. "Did you lose something, Mr. Shirley?"

"No!" The heavy man straightened. As he drew himself up in his sinister garb I thought again of the cheap actors of a day when moving pictures had yet to pre-empt the field of the lurid melodrama. It seemed to me that Merle Shirley was overacting, that it was impossible for him to be so wrought up over the slaying of a man who, after all, was only his director, certainly not a close nor an intimate relationship.

"Mr. Kennedy," he stated, ponderously, "there has been a second death, and at the hand which struck down Stella Lamar in Tarrytown. Somewhere in this banquet hall interior there is a clue to the murderer. I have kept a careful watch so that nothing might be disturbed."

"Do you suspect anyone?" Kennedy asked. Shirley glanced away and we knew he was lying. "No, not definitely."

"Who has been in the set since I left with the doctor?"

"No one except myself, that is"—Shirley wanted to make it clear—"no one has had any opportunity to hide or move or take or change a thing, because I have been right here all the time."

"I see! Thanks, and"—Kennedy seemed genuinely apologetic—"if you don't mind—I would prefer to make my investigation alone."

Shirley turned on his heel and made for his dressing room.

Meanwhile I had noticed a bit of by-play between Enid Faye and Lawrence Millard, the only others of our possible suspects about. Enid first had caught my eye because she seemed to be pleading with the writer, trying to hold him. I gathered from the look of disgust on Millard's face that he wanted to get Shirley out of the set before Kennedy should observe the heavy man's odd reaction to the tragedy. While I had never seen Millard and Shirley together, so as to establish in mind the state of their feelings toward each other, this would seem to indicate that they were friendly. Certainly Shirley was making a fool of himself. Enid acted, I guessed, so as to prevent Millard's interference, probably with the idea that Millard in some fashion might bring suspicion upon himself. It struck me that Enid had a wholesome respect for Kennedy.

At any rate, Millard watched the little scene between Kennedy and Shirley with a quizzical expression. As Shirley left he shrugged his shoulders, then he gave Enid's cheeks a playful pinch each and started out after the heavy man in leisurely fashion.

Just about the same moment Kennedy called me to his side.

"Walter," he pleaded, in a low voice, "will you hurry out to the dressing room where the doctor and I took Werner and get the blood smears and sample of the stomach contents? I don't want to leave this, because we must work fast and get all the data we need before the police arrive. With perhaps a hundred people to question they'll be apt to make a fine mess of everything. This is an outlying precinct where we'll draw the amateurs, you know."

I saw that Mackay was helping him and so I left cheerfully, making my way as fast as I could toward the door through which both Shirley and Millard had passed.

In the hallway of the building devoted to dressing rooms I found that I did not know which one contained Werner's body. This corridor was familiar. Here Kennedy and I had waited for Marilyn Loring and had witnessed the scene between Shirley and herself. Now I did not even remember the location of her room.

At last, on a chance, I tried a door softly. From within came whispered voices of deep intensity. About to close it quickly, I realized suddenly that I recognized the speakers in spite of the whispers. It was Marilyn and Shirley. They were together. Now I recollected the figured chintz which covered the wall and was to be seen through the crack made by the open door. It was her room. They had not heard my hand on the knob, nor the catch, did not know that anyone could eavesdrop.

"You see!" Her tones were the more vibrant "You waited!"

"I had to!"

"No! I advised you to act at once."

"I couldn't! I can't even now!"

"All right!" Her tone became bitter. "Go ahead, your own way. But you must count the cost. You may lose me again, Merle Shirley."

"How do you mean?"

Her answer, in the faintest of whispers, staggered me.

"If you have the blood of another man on your hands I'm through."

XXII

THE STEM

Though my hands trembled so that I could hardly control them, I managed to close the door softly and to back away down the hall without being discovered. My head was spinning and I was dizzy. With my own ears I had heard Marilyn Loring virtually betray the guilt of the man she loved and whom therefore she had tried to shield. "If you have the blood of another man on your hands—" What more could Kennedy want?

I started to run toward the studio. Then recollection of my errand stopped me. Kennedy wished the blood smears and stomach contents and was anxious to get them before the arrival of the police. At first I thought that all such evidence would be unnecessary now, after the dialogue I had overheard, but it struck me as an afterthought that it might be necessary still to prove Shirley's guilt to the satisfaction of a court and jury, and so I rushed to the next dressing room and to another, until I located the doctor and the body of the dead man.

With the little package for Kennedy safely in my pocket I hurried out again into the sweltering heat beneath the glass of the big studio, and to the side of Kennedy and Mackay in the banquet-hall set.

"You have a sample of each article of food now?" he was asking the district attorney. "You are sure you have missed nothing?"

"As far as possible I took my samples from the table where Werner sat," Mackay explained. "When the prop. boy gets here with an empty bottle and cork I'll have a sample of the wine. I think it's the wine," he added.

Kennedy turned to me. "You've got—"

"In my pocket!" I interrupted. Then, rather breathlessly, I repeated the conversation I had overheard.

"Good Lord!" Mackay flushed. "There it is! Shirley's the man, and I'll take him now, quick, without waiting for a warrant."

"See!" I ejaculated, to Kennedy. "He killed Stella because she made a fool of him and then, when Werner discovered that and followed him to Tarrytown the other night, it probably put him in a panic of fear, and so, to keep Werner from talking—"

"Easy, Walter! Not so fast! What you overheard is insufficient ground for Shirley's conviction, unless you could make him confess, and I doubt you could make him do that."

"Why?" This was Mackay.

"Because I don't think he's guilty. At least"—Kennedy, as always, was cautious in his statements, "not so far as anything we now know would indicate."

"But his anger at Stella," I protested, "and Marilyn's remark—"'

"Miss Lamar's death was the result of a cool, unfeeling plan, not pique or anger. The same cruel, careful brain executed this second crime."

Mackay, I saw, was three-quarters convinced by Kennedy. "How do you account for the dialogue Jameson overheard?" he asked.

"Miss Loring told us that Shirley suspected some one and was watching, and would not tell her or anyone else who it was. It seems most likely to me that it is the truth, Mackay. In that case her remark means that she believes his silence in a way is responsible for Werner's death."

"Oh! If Shirley had taken you into his confidence, for instance—?"

"I might possibly have succeeded in gaining sufficient evidence for an arrest, thus averting this tragedy. But it is only a theory of mine."

I scowled. It seemed to me that Kennedy was minimizing things in a way unusual for him. I wondered if he really thought the heavy man innocent.

"It's still my belief that Shirley is guilty," I asserted.

A sound of confusion from the courtyard beneath the heavy studio windows caught Kennedy's ear and ended the colloquy. From some of those near enough to look out we received the explanation. The police had arrived, fully three-quarters of an hour after Werner's death.

"I'll get the little bottle of wine, sure," Mackay murmured, picking up the food samples he had wrapped and crowding the bulky package into a pocket.

"I don't see why that would have been any easier to poison than the food," was my objection. "Everyone was looking."

"Very simple. The food was brought in quite late. Besides, it was dished out by the caterer before the eyes of forty or fifty people or more and there was no telling which plate would go to Werner's place. The drinks were poured last of all. I remember seeing the bubbles rise and wondering whether they would register at the distance."

Kennedy did not look at me. "Did it ever occur to you," he went on, casually, "that the glasses were all set out empty at the various places long before, and that there might easily have been a few drops of something, if it were colorless, placed in the bottom of Werner's glass, with scarcely a chance of its being discovered, especially by a man who had so much on his mind at the time as Werner had? He must have indicated where he would sit when he arranged the camera stands and the location of the tables."

I had not thought of that.

Kennedy frowned. "If only I could have located more of that broken glass!" As he faced me I could read his disappointment. "Walter, I've made a most careful search of his chair and the table and everything about the space where he dropped. The poison must have been in the wine, but there's not a tiny sliver of that glass left, nothing but a thousand bits ground into the canvas, too small to hold even a drop of the liquid. Just think, a dried stain of the wine, no matter how tiny, might have served me in a chemical analysis."

Very suddenly there was a low exclamation from Mackay. "Look! Quick! Some one must have kicked it way over here!"

Fully twenty feet from Werner's place in the glare of the lights was the hollow stem of a champagne glass, its base intact save for a narrow segment. In the stem still were a couple of drops of the wine, as if in a bulb or tube.

"Can it be the director's glass?" Mackay asked, handing it to Kennedy.

Kennedy slipped it into his pocket, fussing with his handkerchief so that the precious contents would not drip out. "I think so. I doubt whether any other glass was broken. Verify it quickly."

The police were entering now with Manton. Following them was the physician. Mackay and I ascertained readily that no other glass had been shattered, while Kennedy searched the floor for possible signs that the stem was part of a glass broken where we had found it. Unquestionably we had a sample of the actual wine quaffed by the unfortunate Werner. Elated we strolled to a corner so as to give the police full charge.

"They'll waste time questioning everyone," Kennedy remarked. "I have the real evidence." He tapped his pocket.

The few moments that he had had to himself had been ample for him to obtain such evidence as was destroyed in so many cases by the time he was called upon the scene.

A point occurred to me. "You don't think the poison was planted later during the excitement?"

"Hardly! Our criminal is too clever to take a long chance. In such a case we would know it was some one near Werner and also there would be too many people watching. Foolhardiness is not boldness."

I took to observing the methods of the police, which were highly efficient, but only in the minuteness of the examination of witnesses and in the care with which they recorded names and facts and made sure that no one had slipped away to avoid the notoriety.

The actors and actresses who had stood rather in awe of Kennedy, both here and in Kennedy's investigation at Tarrytown, developed nimble tongues in their answers to the city detectives. The result was a perfect maze of conflicting versions of Werner's cry and fall. In fact, one scene shifter insisted that Shirley, as the Black Terror, had reached Werner's side and had struck him before the cry, while an extra girl with a faint lisp described with sobering accuracy the flight of a mysterious missile through the air. I realized then why Kennedy had made no effort to question them. Under the excitement of the scene, the glamour of the lights, the sense of illusion, and the stifling heat, it would have been strange for any of the people to have retained correct impressions of the event.

The police sergeant knew Kennedy by reputation and approached him after a visit to the dead man's body with the doctor. His glance, including Mackay and myself, was frankly triumphant.

"Well," he exclaimed, "I don't suppose it occurred to any of you SCIENTIFIC guys to search the fellow, now did it?"

Kennedy smiled, in good humor. "Searching a man isn't always the scientific method. You won't find the word 'frisk' in any scientific dictionary."

"No?" The police officer's eyes twinkled. There was enough of the Irish in him to enjoy an encounter of this kind. "Maybe not, but you might find things in a chap's pocket which is better." With a flourish he produced a hypodermic syringe, the duplicate of the one I had appropriated, and a tiny bottle. "The man's a dope," he added.

"I knew that," replied Kennedy. "I examined his arm, where he usually took his shots, and found no fresh mark of the needle."

"That doesn't prove anything. Wait until the medical examiner gets here. He'll find the fellow's heart all shot full of hop, or something. I guess it isn't so complicated, after all. He was a hop fiend, all right."

"Still, there's nothing to indicate that he was a suicide."

"Not suicide; accident-overdose," was the sergeant's reply.

"How could he have died from an overdose of the drug, when he hasn't taken any recently?"

"Well"—unabashed—"then he croaked because he hadn't had a shot—the same thing. Heart failure, either way. Excited, and all, you know, making the scene. Maybe he forgot to use the needle at that."

"Perhaps you're right." Kennedy shrugged calmly. What was the use of disputing the matter?

I started to protest against the detective's hypothesis. The idea of any drug addict ever forgetting to take his stimulant was too preposterous. But Kennedy checked me. All were now keenly listening to the argument. Better, perhaps, to let some one think that nothing was suspected than to disclose the cards in Craig's hand. I saw that he wished to get away and had not spoken seriously. He turned to Mackay.

"Walter and I will have to hurry to the laboratory. Would you like to come along?"

"You bet I would!" The district attorney showed his delight. "I was just going to ask if I might do so. There's nothing for me in Tarrytown to-day and this is out of my jurisdiction."

As we turned away the police sergeant saw us and called across the floor, not quite concealing a touch of professional jealousy.

"The three of you were here at the time, weren't you?"

"No," Kennedy answered. "Mr. Jameson and myself."

"Well, you two, then! You're witnesses and I'll ask you to hold yourself in readiness to appear at the hearing."

I thought that the policeman was particularly delighted at his position to issue orders to Kennedy, and I was angered. Again Craig held me in check!

"We'll be glad to tell anything we know," he replied, then added a little fling, a bit of sarcasm which almost went over the other's head. "That is," he amended, "as eye-witnesses!"

XXIII

BOTULIN TOXIN

Mackay drove us to the laboratory in his little car and it was dark and we were dinnerless when we arrived. Knowing Kennedy's habits, I sent out for sandwiches and started in to make strong coffee upon an electric percolator. The aroma tingled in my nostrils, reminding me that I was genuinely hungry. The district attorney, too, seemed more or less similarly disposed.

As for Kennedy, he was interested in nothing but the problem before him. He had been strangely quiet on the way, growing more and more impatient and nervous, as though the element of time had entered into the case, as though haste were suddenly imperative. Once the lights were on in the laboratory he hurried about his various preparations. The food samples he laid out, but he gave them no attention. The blood smears and stomach contents he put aside for future reference. His attack was upon the drop or two of liquid adhering to the stem of the broken champagne glass.

The entire chemical procedure seemed to be incomprehensible to Mackay and he was fascinated, so that he had considerable trouble at times keeping out of the way of Kennedy's elbow. Kennedy first washed the stem out carefully with a few drops of distilled water, then he studied the resulting solution. One after another he tried the things that occurred to him, making tests wholly unproductive of results. Slowly the laboratory table became littered completely with chemicals and apparatus of all sorts, a veritable arsenal of glass.

The sandwiches arrived, but Kennedy refused to drop his investigation for a moment. I did succeed in making him take a cup of strong coffee, and that was all. Over in a corner Mackay and I did full justice to the food, finishing the hot and welcome coffee and then refilling the percolator and starting it on the making of a second brew. The hours lengthened, and when Mackay grew tired of watching with intense admiration he joined me in the patient consumption of innumerable cigarettes.

Kennedy was filled with the joy of discovery. I noticed that he did not stop even for the solace of tobacco. It seemed to me that at times his nostrils dilated exactly like those of a hound on the scent. Finally he held up a test tube and turned to us.

"What is it?" I asked. "Some other poison as rare and little known as the snake venom?"

"No—something much more curious. In the stem of the glass I find the toxin of the Bacillus botulinus."

"Germs?" Mackay inquired.

Kennedy shook his head. "Not germs, but the pure toxin, the poison secreted by this bacillus."

"What does it do?" was my question.

"Well," thoughtfully, "botulism may be ranked easily among the most serious diseases known to medical science. It is hard to understand why it is not a great deal more common. It is one of the most dangerous kinds of food poisoning."

"Then the apple juice they used for the wine was bad, spoiled?"

"No, not that. Werner was the only one stricken. Somebody put the pure toxin in his glass. It was, as I suspected, deliberate murder, as in the case of Miss Lamar. Bacillus botulinus produces a toxin that is extremely virulent. Hardly more than a ten-thousandth of a cubic centimeter would kill a guinea pig. This was botulin itself, the pure toxin, an alkaloid just like that which is formed in meat and other food products in cases of botulism. The idea might also have been to make the death seem natural—due solely to bad food."

"Do you suppose it was used because it was quick and was colorless, so as not to be noticed in the glass?" I hazarded.

Kennedy paced up and down the laboratory several times in thought. "To me, Walter, this is another indication of the satanic cleverness of the unknown criminal in the case. First Miss Lamar is to be killed. For that purpose something was sought, probably, which could not be traced easily to the perpetrator. In snake venom an agent was employed which may be said to be almost ideal for the grim business of murder. It is extremely difficult to identify in its results, it is comparatively unknown, yet it is swift in action and to be obtained with fair ease.

"Differing from most poisons, it may be inflicted through a prick so slight as to be almost unnoticed by the victim. The scheme of fixing the needle in the curtain was so simple and yet so effective that the guilty person need never have feared its discovery under ordinary circumstances, or its association with the girl's death, if some one stumbled upon it accidentally. The idea of returning for the death-dealing point was only one of the many details of a precautionary measure upon which we have stumbled. Had I found it the next morning I would have been unable, in all probability, to identify it as belonging to or as obtained by any of our suspects.

"You must realize, Walter, that with all the scientific aids I have been able to bring to bear we possess almost no direct evidence. There are no fingerprints, no cigarette stubs, no array of personal, intimate clues of any sort to this criminal. These are the threads which lead the detective to his quarry in fiction and on the stage. Here we lack even the faintest description of the man, or woman if that is her sex. It is murder from a distance, planned with almost meticulous care, executed coolly and without feeling or scruple.

"After the death of Miss Lamar I was not so sure but that the selection of the snake venom was simply the inspiration of a perverted brain, the evolution of the detailed method of killing her—an outgrowth of someone's familiarity with studio life in general, with the script of 'The Black Terror' in particular. Now I realize that we are face to face with the studied handiwork of a skilled criminal. These two deaths may be his—or her—first departure into the realm of crime. But potentially we have a super-villain.

"I make that statement because of the manner of Werner's demise. It is evident that the director stumbled on a clue to the murderer. If my first hypothesis had been correct, if the use of snake venom and the unlucky thirteenth scene had been largely a matter of blind chance in the selection of poison and method, then we might have expected Werner to be struck down in some dark street, or perhaps decoyed to his death—at the best, inoculated with the same crotalin which had killed Miss Lamar.

"But let us analyze the method used in slaying the director. If he had been blackjacked there would be the clue of the weapon, always likely to turn up, the chance of witnesses, and also the likelihood in an extreme case that Werner might not die at once, but might talk and give a description of his assailant, or even survive. Much the same objections—from the criminal's standpoint—obtain in nearly all the accepted modes of killing a man. Even the use of venom a second time possesses the disadvantage of a certain alertness against the very thing on the part of the victim. Werner was a dope fiend, fully aware of the potency of a tiny skin puncture. I'll wager he was on constant guard against any sort of scratch.

"On the other hand, the few drops of toxin in the glass possessed every advantage from the unknown's standpoint. It was invisible, and as sure in its action as the venom. Also it was as rare and as difficult to trace. For, remember this. Botulism is food poisoning. If I had not found the stem of that glass it would be absolutely impossible to show that Werner died from anything on earth but bad food. That is why I do not even take time to analyze the stomach contents. That is why I say we are confronted by an archscoundrel of highest intelligence and downright cleverness. More"—Kennedy paused for emphasis—"I realize now the presence of a grim, invisible menace. It has just now been driven home to me. The botulin, with its deadly paralyzing power, sealed Werner's tongue even while he tried to tell me what he knew."

Mackay was tremendously impressed by Kennedy's explanation. "Does this mean," he asked, "that the guilty man or woman is some outsider? Those we have figured as possible suspects would hardly have this detailed knowledge of poisons."

"There are two possibilities," Kennedy answered. "The real person behind the two murders may have employed some one else to carry out the actual killing, a hypothesis I do not take seriously, or"—again he paused—"this may be a case of some one with intelligence starting out upon his career of crime intelligently by reading up on his subject. It is as simple to learn how to use crotalin or botulin toxin or any number of hundreds of deadly substances as it is to obtain the majority of them. In fact, if people generally understood the ease with which whole communities could be wiped out, and grasped that it could be done so as to leave virtually no clue to the author of the horror, they might not sleep as soundly at night as they do. The saving grace is that the average criminal is often clever, but almost never truly scientific. Unfortunately, we have to combat one who possesses the latter quality to a high degree."

"What is the invisible menace of which you spoke, Craig?" I inquired.

"The possibility of another murder before we can apprehend the guilty person or gain the evidence we need."

"Good heavens!" I imagine I blanched. "You mean—"

"Werner was struck down, apparently, for no reason but that he had guessed the identity of the villain. There is a second man in the company who has certain suspicions and is acting upon them. If he is on the right trail, by any chance—" Kennedy shrugged his shoulders soberly.

"Shirley?"

"Exactly! And there is still another possibility."

"What is that?"

"Here in this laboratory I have blood spots made on the portieres at the house of Phelps by the man who removed the needle, probably the unknown himself, possibly his—or her—agent. In any case it is a clue and—THE ONLY DIRECT AND INFALLIBLE CLUE IN EXISTENCE TO THE CRIMINAL! Also I have the evidence of the snake venom and of the botulin toxin here. Sooner or later the person who killed Werner because he suspected things will wake up to the fact that we possess tangible proof against him."

I grew pale. "You mean, then, that you may be attacked yourself? That even I—"

Kennedy smiled, unafraid. But from the expression in his eyes I knew that he took the thought of our possible danger very seriously.

XXIV

THE INVISIBLE MENACE

Mackay and I exchanged glances. Kennedy busied himself putting away some of the more important bits of evidence in the case, placing the tiny tubes of solution, the blood smears, and other items together in a cabinet at the farther corner of the laboratory. The vast bulk of his paraphernalia, the array of glass and chemicals and instruments, he left on the table for the morning. Then he faced us again, with a smile.

"Suppose you start up the percolator once more, Walter!" He took a cigar and lighted it from the match I struck. "I believe I've earned another cup of coffee," he added.

Mackay had been fidgeting considerably since Kennedy's explanation of the possible danger to Shirley, as well as to ourselves or even to others.

"Isn't there something we can do, Kennedy?" he exclaimed, suddenly. "Is it necessary to sit back and wait for this unknown to strike again?"

"Ordinarily," Kennedy replied, "on a case like this it has been my custom to permit the guilty parties to betray themselves, as they will do inevitably—especially when I call to my aid the recent discoveries of science for the detection and measurement of fine and almost imperceptible shades of emotion. But now that I realize the presence of this menace I shall become a detective of action; in fact, I shall not stop at any course to hurry matters. The very first thing in the morning I shall go to the studio and I want you and Jameson along. I"—his eyes twinkled; it was the excitement at the prospect—"I may need considerable help in getting the evidence I wish."

"Which is—?" It was I who interposed the question.

Kennedy blew a cloud of smoke. "There are three ways of tracing down a crime, aside from the police method of stool pigeons to betray the criminals and the detective bureau method of cross-examination under pressure, popularly known as the third degree."

"What are they?" Mackay asked, unaware that Kennedy needed little prompting once he felt inclined to talk out some matter puzzling him.

"One is the process of reasoning from the possible suspects to the act itself—in other words, putting the emphasis on the motive. A second is the reverse of the first, involving a study of the crime for clues and making deductions from the inevitable earmarks of the person for the purpose of discovering his identity. The third method, except for some investigations across the water, is distinctly my own, the scientific.

"In all sciences," Kennedy went on, warming to his subject, "progress is made by a careful tabulation of proved facts. The scientific method is the method of exact knowledge. Thus, in crime, those things are of value to us which by an infinite series of empiric observations have been established and have become incontrovertible. The familiar example, of course, is fingerprints. Nearly everyone knows that no two men have the same markings; that the same man displays a pattern which is unchanging from birth to the grave.

"No less certain is the fact that human blood differs from the blood of animals, that in faint variations the blood of no two people is alike, that the blood of any living thing, man or beast, is affected by various things—an infinite number almost—most of which are positively known to modern medical investigators.

"In this case my principal scientific clue is the blood left upon the portiere by the man who took the needle the night following the murder. Next in importance is the fact, demonstrated by me, that some one at the studio wiped a hypodermic on a towel after inoculating himself with antivenin. Of course I am presuming that this latter man inoculated himself and not some one else, because it is obvious. If necessary I can prove it later, however, by analyzing the trace of blood. That is not the point. The point is that whoever removed the needle pricked himself and yet did not die of the venom—unless it was a person not under our observation, an unlikely premise. Therefore, because of this last fact, and because again it is obvious, I expect to find that the same individual inoculated himself with antivenin and removed the needle from the portiere; and I expect to prove it beyond possibility of doubt by an analysis of his blood. A sample of the blood from this person will be identical with the spot on the portiere, and—much the easier test—will contain traces of the antitoxin.

"With that much accomplished, a little of the, well—third degree, will bring about a confession. It is circumstantial evidence of the strongest sort. Not only does a man take precautions against a given poison, but he is proved to be the one who removed the needle actually responsible for Miss Lamar's death.

"My handicap, however, is that I have no justifiable excuse for taking a sample of blood from each of the people we suspect, or feel we might suspect. For that reason I was waiting until one of the other detective methods should narrow the field of suspicion. Now that there is the menace of another attempt to take a life I am forced to act. To-morrow we will get samples of blood from everyone by artifice—or force!

"Meanwhile—" He hastened to continue, as though afraid we might interrupt to break his train of thought. "Meanwhile, to-night, let us see if it is possible to accomplish something by the deductive method.

"Already I have gone into an analysis starting from the nature of the crime and reasoning to the type of criminal responsible. The guilty man—or woman—is a person of high intelligence, added to genuine cleverness. But for the results accomplished in this laboratory we would be without a clue; our hands would be tied completely. Both Miss Lamar and Werner were killed by unusual poisons; deadly, and almost impossible to trace. There was a crowd of people about in each case; yet we have no witnesses. Now who, out of all our people with possible motives, are intelligent enough and clever enough to be guilty?"

Kennedy glanced first at me, then at Mackay.

"Manton? Phelps?" suggested the district attorney.

"The promoter," Kennedy rejoined, "is the typical man of the business world beneath the eccentricity of manner which seems to cling to everyone in the picture field. Ordinarily his type, thinking in millions of dollars and juggling nickel and dime admissions or other routine of commercial detail is apart from the finer subtle passions of life. When a business man commits murder he generally uses a pistol because he is sure it is efficient—he can see it work. The same applies to Phelps."

"Millard?" Mackay hesitated now to face the logic of Kennedy's keen mind. "He was Stella Lamar's husband!"

"Millard is a scenario writer and so apt to have a brain cluttered with all sorts of detail of crime and murder. At the same time an author is so used to counterfeiting emotion in his writings that he seldom takes things seriously. Life becomes a joke and Millard in particular is a butterfly, concerned more with the smiles of extra girls and the favor of Miss Faye than the fate of the woman whose divorce from him was not yet complete. A writer is the other extreme from the business man. The creator of stories is essentially inefficient because he tries to feel rather than reason. When an author commits murder he sets a stage for his own benefit. He is careful to avoid witnesses because they are inconvenient to dispose of. At the same time he wants the victim to understand thoroughly what is going to happen and so he is apt to accompany his crime with a speech worded very carefully indeed. Then he may start with an attempt to throttle a person and end up with a hatchet, or he may plan to use a razor and at the end brain his quarry with a chair. He lives too many lives to follow one through clearly—his own."

"How about Shirley?" I put in.

"At first glance Shirley and Gordon suggest themselves because both murders were highly spectacular, and the actor, above everything else, enjoys a big scene. After Werner's death, for instance, Shirley literally strutted up and down in that set. He was so full of the situation, so carried away by the drama of the occasion, that he failed utterly to realize how suspicious his conduct would seem to an observer. Unfortunately for our hypotheses, the use of venom and toxin is too cold-bloodedly efficient. The theatrical temperament must have emotion. An actor cruel and vicious enough to strike down two people as Miss Lamar and Werner were stricken, of sufficient dramatic make-up to conceive of the manner of their deaths, would want to see them writhe and suffer. He would select poisons equally rare and effective, but those more slow and painful in their operation. No, Walter, Shirley is not indicated by this method of reasoning. The arrangement of the scenes for the murders was simply another detail of efficiency, not due to a wish to be spectacular. The crowd about in each case has added greatly to the difficulty of investigation."

"Do you include Gordon in that?" Mackay asked.

"Yes, and in addition"—Kennedy smiled slightly—"I believe that Gordon is rather stupid. For one thing, he has had several fights in public, at the Goats Club and at the Midnight Fads and I suppose elsewhere. That is not the clever rogue. Furthermore, he had been speculating, not just now and then, but desperately, doggedly. Clever men speculate, but scientific men never. Our unknown criminal is both clever and intelligent."

"That brings you to the girls, then," Mackay remarked.

Kennedy's face clouded and I could see that he was troubled. "To be honest in this one particular method of deduction," he stated, "I must admit that both Miss Faye and Miss Loring are worthy of suspicion. The fact of their rise in the film world, the evidences of their popularity, is proof that they are clever. Miss Loring, in my few brief moments of contact with her on two occasions, showed a grasp of things and a quickness which indicate to me that she possesses a rare order of intelligence for a woman. As for Miss Faye"—again he hesitated—"one little act of hers demonstrated intelligence. When Shirley was standing guard in the set after Werner's death, and making a fool of himself, Millard evidently wanted to get over and speak to him, perhaps to tell him not to let me find him searching the scene as though his life depended upon it, perhaps something else. But Miss Faye stopped him. Unquestionably she saw that anyone taking an interest in the remains of the banquet just then would become an object of suspicion."

"Do you really suspect Marilyn or Enid?" I inquired.

"If this were half a generation ago I would say without hesitation that the crime was the handiwork of a man. But now the women are in everything. Young girls particularly—" He shrugged his shoulders.

Mackay had one more suggestion. "The camera men, the extras, the technical and studio staffs—they are not worthy of consideration, are they?"

Kennedy shook his head.

The odor of coffee struck my nostrils and I turned to find the percolator steaming. Kennedy leaned over, to take a whiff. Mackay rose. At that moment there was a sudden crash and the window-pane was shattered. Simultaneously a flash of light and a deafening explosion took place in the room, scattering broadcast tiny bits of glass from the laboratory table, splashing chemicals, many of them dangerous, over everything.

Kennedy hurried to the wreck of his paraphernalia. In an instant he held up a tiny bit of jagged metal.

"An explosive bullet!" he exclaimed. "An attempt to destroy my evidence!"

XXV

ITCHING SALVE

For once I rose with Kennedy. He preceded me to the laboratory after breakfast, however, leaving me to wait for Mackay. When the little district attorney arrived I noticed that he carried a package which looked as though it might contain a one-reel film can.

"The negative we took from the cameras at Tarrytown," he explained. "Also a print from each roll, ready to run. I've been holding this as evidence. Mr. Kennedy wanted me to bring it with me to-day."

"He's waiting for us at the laboratory," I remarked.

"He'll straighten everything up in a hurry, won't he?"

"Kennedy's the most high-handed individual I ever knew," I laughed, "if he sees a chance of getting his man." Then I became enthusiastic. "Often I've seen him gather a group of people in a room, perhaps without the faintest shred of legal right to do so, and there make the guilty person confess simply by marshaling the evidence, or maybe betray himself by some scientific device. It's wonderful, Mackay."

"Do you think he plans something of that kind this morning?"

I led the way to the door. "After what happened last night I know that Kennedy will resort to almost anything."

The district attorney fingered the package under his arm. "He might get everyone in the projection room then, and make them watch the actual photographic record of Stella's death—the scene where she scratched herself—"

"Let's hurry!" I interrupted.

When we entered the laboratory we found Kennedy vigorously fanning a towel which he had hung up to dry. I recognized it as the one I had discovered in the studio washroom immediately following the first murder.

"This will serve me better as bait than as evidence," he laughed. "I have impregnated it with a colorless chemical which will cling to the fibers and enable me to identify the most infinitesimal trace of it. We shall get up to the studio and start, well—I guess you could call it fishing for the guilty man." He fingered the folds, then jerked the towel down and flung it to me. "Here, Walter! It's dry enough. Now I want you to rub the contents of that tiny can of grease, open before you there, into the cloth."

He hurried over to wash his hands. I spread the towel out on the table and began to work in the stuff indicated by Kennedy. There was no odor and it seemed like some patent ointment in color. At first I was puzzled. Then, absently, I touched the back of one hand with the greasy fingers of the other and immediately an itching set up so annoying that I had to abandon my task.

Kennedy chuckled. "That's itching salve, Walter. The cuticle pads at your finger tips are too thick, but touch yourself anywhere else!—" He shrugged his shoulders. "You'd better use soap and water if you want any relief. Then you can start over again."

At the basin I thought I grasped his little plot.

"You're going to plant the towel," I asked, "so that the interested party will try to get hold of it?"

Evidently he thought it unnecessary to reply to me.

"Why couldn't you just put it somewhere without all the preparation," Mackay suggested, "and watch to see who came after it?"

"Because our criminal's too clever," Kennedy rejoined. "Our only chance to get it stolen is to make it very plain that it is not being watched. Whoever steals it, however, possibly will reveal himself on account of the itching salve. In any case I expect to be able to trace the towel to the thief, no matter what efforts are made to destroy it."

The towel was wrapped in a heavy bit of paper; then placed with a microscope and some other paraphernalia in a small battered traveling bag. Climbing into Mackay's little roadster, we soon were speeding toward the studio.

"Will you be able to help me, to stay with Jameson and myself all day?" Kennedy asked the district attorney, after perhaps a mile of silence.

"Surely! It's what I was hoping you'd allow me to do. I have no authority down here, though."

"I understand. But the police, or an outsider, might allow some of my plans to become known." He paused a moment in thought. "The film you brought in with you consists of the scenes on the rolls of negative in use at the time of Miss Lamar's collapse. It may or may not include the action where she scratched herself. Now I want the scenes up to thirteen put together in proper order, first as photographed by one camera, then as caught by the other. I'll arrange for the services of a cutter, and for the delivery to me of any other negative or positive overlooked by us when we had the two boxes sealed and given into your custody at Tarrytown. Will you superintend the assembly of the scenes, so that you can be sure nothing is taken out or omitted?"

"Of course! I want to do anything I can."

Upon arrival at the studio we detected this time all the signs of a complete demoralization. The death of Werner, the fact that he had been stricken down during the taking of a scene and on the very stage, had served to bring the tragedy home to the people. More, it was a second murder in four days, apparently by the same hand as the first. A sense of dread, a nameless, intangible fear, had taken form and found its way under the big blackened glass roofs and around and through the corridors, into the dressing rooms, and back even to the manufacturing and purely technical departments. The gateman eyed us with undisguised uneasiness as we drove through the archway into the yard. In that inclosure there were only two cars—Manton's, and one we later learned belonged to Phelps. The sole human being to enter our range of vision was an office boy. He skirted the side of the building as though the menace of death were in the air, or likely to strike out of the very heavens without warning.

We found Kauf in the large studio, obviously unhappy in the shoes of the unfortunate Werner. Probably from half-reasoned-out motives of efficiency in psychology the new director had made no attempt to resume work at once in the ill-fated banquet set, but had turned to the companion ballroom setting, since both had been prepared and made ready at the same time.

Kennedy explained our presence so early in the morning very neatly, I thought.

"I would appreciate it," he began, "if you could place a cutter at the disposal of Mr. Mackay. He has the scenes taken from the camera and sealed at the time of Miss Lamar's death. I would like to have any other film taken out there delivered to him and the whole joined in proper sequence. Then, Mr. Kauf, if you could arrange to have the same cutter take the film exposed yesterday when Mr. Werner—"

"You think you might be able to see something, to discover something on the screen?"

"Exactly!"

Kauf beamed. "Mr. Manton gave me orders to assist you in every way I could, or to put any of my people at your disposal. More than that, Mr. Kennedy, he anticipated you. He thought you might want to look at the scenes taken yesterday and he rushed the laboratory and the printing room. We'll be able to fix you up very quickly."

"Good!" Kennedy nodded to Mackay and the district attorney hurried off with Kauf. "Now, Walter!" he exclaimed, sobering.

I picked up the traveling bag and together we strolled toward the ballroom set. There most of the players were gathered already—in make-up and evening clothes of a fancier sort even than those demanded for the banquet. I saw that Kennedy singled out Marilyn.

"Good morning," she said, cheerfully, but with effort. It was obvious she had spent a nervous night. There were circles under her eyes ill concealed by the small quantity of cosmetic she used. Her hands, shifting constantly, displayed the loss of her usual poise. "You are out bright and early," she added.

"We've stumbled into a very important clue," Kennedy told her, with a show of giving her his confidence. "In that bag in Walter's hand is one of the studio towels. It contains a hint of the poison used to kill Miss Lamar and—of utmost consequence—it has provided me with an infallible clue to the identity of the murderer himself—or herself."

It seemed to me that Marilyn blanched. "Where—where did you find it?" she demanded, in a very awed voice.

"In one of the studio washrooms."

"It has been—it has been in the washroom ever since poor Stella's death?"

"No, not that! Jameson discovered it the same day but"—the very slight pause was perceptible to me; Kennedy hated to lie—"I haven't realized its importance until just this morning."

Enid Faye, seeing us from a distance, conquered her dislike of Marilyn sufficiently to join us. She was very erect and tense. Her eyes, wide and sober and searching, traveled from my face to Kennedy's and back. Then she dissembled, softening as she came close to me, laying a hand on my shoulder and allowing her skirt to brush my trousers.

"Tell me, Jamie," she whispered, her warm breath thrilling me through and through. "Has the wonderful Craig Kennedy discovered something?" It was not sarcasm, but assumed playfulness, masking a throbbing curiosity.

"I found a towel in one of the studio washrooms," I answered, "and Craig has demonstrated that it is a clue to the poison which killed Stella Lamar as well as to the person who did it."

Enid gasped. Then she drew herself up and her eyes narrowed. Now she faced Kennedy.

"How can the towel be a clue to the crime?" she protested. "Stella was—was murdered way out in Tarrytown! Mr. Jameson found the towel here!"

Kennedy shrugged his shoulders. "I cannot tell you that—just yet." He paused deliberately. "You see," he lied. "I have yet to make my analysis."

"But you know it's a clue to the—"

"That towel"—he raised his voice, as though in elation—"that towel will lead me to the murderer—infallibly!"

Merle Shirley had come up in time to hear most of the colloquy between Enid and Kennedy. At the last he flushed, clenching his fists.

"If you can prove who the murderer is, Mr. Kennedy," he exploded, "why don't you apprehend him before some one else meets the fate of Werner?"

"I can do nothing until I return to my laboratory this afternoon. I will not know the identity of the guilty person until I complete a chemical analysis."

One by one the various people possibly concerned in the two crimes joined the group. This morning all the faces were serious; most of them showed the marks of sleeplessness following the second murder. Kennedy walked away, but I saw that Jack Gordon hastened to question both the girls, ignoring their evident dislike for him. Among the others I recognized Watkins, the camera man, and his associate. Lawrence Millard came in and hastened to the side of Enid. As he drew her away to ask the cause of the gathering I wondered at his early presence. The scenario writer was typical of them all. The strange and unusual nature of the crimes, the evident relationship between them, had drawn the employees of Manton Pictures to the studio as a crowd of baseball fans collects before a public bulletin board. Not one of them but was afraid of missing some development in the case. In no instance could the interest of a particular individual be taken as an indication of guilt.

Phelps entered the studio from the door to the dressing rooms. Disdaining to join the other group, he approached us to ask the cause for the excitement. Kennedy explained, patiently, and I saw that Phelps looked at the black bag uneasily.

"I hope the guilty party is not a member of the company," he muttered.

"Why?" Kennedy's mouth tightened.

The financier grew red. "Because this picture has been crippled enough. First a new star; now a new director—if it wasn't so preposterous I'd believe that it was all part of a deliberate—" He stopped as if realizing suddenly the inadvisability of vague accusations.

"Don't you want justice done?" Kennedy inquired.

"Of course!" Phelps tugged at his collar uncomfortably. "Of course, Mr. Kennedy." Then he turned and hurried away, out of the studio.

Gordon and Millard detached themselves from the others, coming over.

"In which washroom was the towel found, Mr. Kennedy?" Gordon put the question as though he felt himself specially delegated to obtain this information.

I wondered how Kennedy would evade a direct answer. To my surprise he made no attempt at concealment.

"The one on the second floor of the office building."

Millard laughed, facing Gordon. "That puts it on myself—or the big boss!"

It struck me that the leading man was uneasy as he hurried back to the others. Millard, still smiling, turned to say something to us, but we were joined by Manton, entering from the other end of the big inclosure.

"Good morning," the promoter exclaimed, somewhat breathless. "I just learned you were here. Is—is there some new development. Is there something I can do?"

"I see you are not allowing anything to interfere with the making of the picture," Kennedy remarked. "All the people seem to be here bright and early."

A shadow crept into Manton's face. "It seems almost as cold-blooded as—as war," he admitted. "But I can't help myself, Mr. Kennedy. The company has no money and if we don't meet this release we're busted." All at once he lowered his voice eagerly. "Tell me, have you discovered something? Is there some clue to the guilty man?"

"He's found a towel," Millard put in, an expression of half amusement on his face as he faced the promoter. "In some way it's a clue to the identity of the murderer, an infallible clue, he says. He found it in the washroom by our offices. Since Werner is dead, that points the finger of suspicion at you or me."

Manton's jaw dropped. His expression became almost ludicrous, as if the thought that he could possibly be suspected himself was new to him. Millard's eyes sobered a bit at his superior's confusion.

"There's a door from the dressing rooms," Kennedy suggested. "Any of the actors or actresses could have used the place."

"Of course!" Manton grasped at the straw. "I had forgotten. There have been complaints to me about the players using that room."

"I have the towel with me, wrapped up in a paper in this grip," Kennedy went on. "It's so very valuable as a bit of evidence—I wonder if I could borrow a locker so as to keep it under lock and key until we're ready to return to the laboratory?"

"Sure! Of course!" Manton glanced about and saw the little knot of people still gathered in the set. "Millard! Go over and tell Kauf to get busy. He's losing time." Then he turned to us again. "Come on, Mr. Kennedy, we have some steel lockers out by the property room."

As we started across the floor I could see that Kennedy was framing a question with great care.

"Do you ever use snakes in films, Mr. Manton?" he asked.

"Why, no!" The promoter stopped in his surprise. "That is, not if we ever can help it. The censorship won't pass anything with snakes."

"You have used them, though?"

"Yes. Once we made a short-length special subject, nothing but snakes." Manton became enthusiastic. "It was a wonder, too; a pet film of mine. We made it with the direct co-operation and supervision of the greatest authority on poisonous snakes in the country, Doctor Nagoya of Castleton Institute."

XXVI

A CIGARETTE CASE

Kennedy's face betrayed only a remote interest. "Have you any copies of that particular film?"

"Just the negative, I believe."

"Could I have that for a few days?"

"Of course!" Manton seemed to wish to give us every possible amount of co-operation; yet this request puzzled him. "Would you care to go down to the negative vaults with me?"

Kennedy nodded.

First we stopped in a lengthy corridor in the rear building, where there were no great signs of life. Through a door I could see a long room filled with ornaments, pictures, furniture, rugs, and all the vast freak collections of a property room. Along the side of the hallway itself was a line of steel lockers of recent design.

Manton called out to an employee and he appeared after a long wait and unlocked one of them. At Kennedy's direction I put the traveling bag in the lower compartment, pocketing the key. Then we retraced our steps to broad steel stairs leading up and down. We descended to the basement and found ourselves in a high-ceilinged space immaculately clean and used generally for storage purposes.

"The film vaults," Manton explained, "are at the corner of the west wing. They have to be ventilated specially, on account of the high inflammability of the celluloid composition. Since the greatest fire risk, otherwise, is the laboratory and printing departments, and next to that the studios themselves with the scenery, the heat of the lights, the wires, etc., we have located them in the most distant corner of the quadrangle. The negative, you see, represents our actual invested capital to a considerable extent. The prints wear out and frequently large sections are destroyed and have to be reprinted. Then sometimes we can reissue old subjects. All in all we guard the negative with the care a bank would give actual funds in its vaults."

In our many visits to the Manton studios I had been struck by the scrupulous cleanliness of every part of the place. The impression of orderliness came back to me with redoubled force as we made our way around in the basement. Nothing seemed out of its proper position, although a vast amount of various material for picture making was stored here. We passed two projection rooms, one a miniature theater with quite a bit of comfort, the other small and bare for the use of directors and cutters.

Finally we saw the vaults ahead of us. The walls were concrete, matching the actual walls of the basement. There were two entrances and the doors were double, of heavy steel, arranged so that an air space would give protection in case of fire. At a roll-top desk, arranged for the use of the clerk in charge of the negatives and prints, was a young boy.

"Where's Wagnalls?" demanded Manton.

"He went out, sir," the boy replied, respectfully enough. "Said he would be right back and for me to watch and not to let anything get out."

The promoter led the way into the first room. Here on all four sides and in several rows down the center, like the racks in a public library, were shelves supporting stacks of square thin metal boxes or trays with handles and tightly fitting covers. Cards were secured to the front of each, by clamps, giving the name of the picture and the number under which the film was filed. I was surprised because I expected to find everything kept in ordinary round film cans.

"These are the negatives," Manton explained. He pulled out a box at random, opening it. "The negative is not all spliced together, the same length as the reels of positive, because the printing machines are equipped to take two-hundred-foot pieces at a time, or approximate fifths of a reel, the size of a roll of raw positive film stock. Then whenever there is a change in color, as from amber daylight to blue tint for night, the negative is broken because pieces of different coloring have to go through different baths, and that also determines the size of the rolls. The prints, or positives, in the other vaults, are in reel lengths and so are kept in the round boxes in which they are shipped."

Kennedy glanced about curiously. "The negative of that snake picture is here, you said?"

Manton went to a little desk where there was a card index. Thumbing through the records, he found the number and led us to the proper place in the rack. In the box were only two rolls of negative, both were large.

"This was a split reel," the promoter began. "It was approximately four hundred feet and we used it to fill out a short comedy, a release we had years ago, a reel the first part of which was educational and the last two-thirds or so a roaring slap-stick. We never made money on it.

"But this stuff was mighty good, Mr. Kennedy. We practically wrote a scenario for those reptiles. Doctor Nagoya was down himself and for the better part of a day it wasn't possible to get a woman in the studio, for fear a rattler or something might get loose."

"Were there rattlers in the film?"

"Altogether, I think. The little Jap was interesting, too. Between scenes he told us all about the reptiles, and how their poison—" Manton checked himself, confused. Was it because the thought of poison reminded him of the two deaths so close to him, or was it from some more potent twinge of conscience? "You'll see it all in the film," he finished, lamely.

"I may keep these for a little bit?" Kennedy asked.

"Of course! I can have the two rolls printed and developed and dry sometime this afternoon, if you wish."

"No, this will do very well."

Kennedy slipped a roll in each pocket, straining the cloth to get them in. Manton opened a book on the little table, making an entry of the delivery of the rolls and adding his own initials.

"I have to be very careful to avoid the loss of negative," he told us. "Nothing can be taken out of here except on my own personal order."

I thought that Manton was very frank and accommodating. Surely he had made no effort to conceal his knowledge of this film made with Doctor Nagoya, and he had even mentioned the poison of the rattlesnakes. Though it had confused him for a brief moment, that had not struck me as a very decisive indication of guilty knowledge. After all, no one knew of the use of crotalin to kill Stella Lamar except the murderer himself, and Kennedy and those of us in his confidence. The murderer might not guess that Kennedy had identified the venom. Yet if Manton were that man he had covered his feelings wonderfully in telling us about the film.

My thoughts strayed to the towel upstairs. Had an attempt been made yet to steal it from the locker? It seemed to me that we were losing too much time down here if we hoped to notice anyone with itching hands.

I realized that Kennedy had been very clever in including all our suspects in hearing at the time he revealed the importance of the clue. Of the original nine listed by Mackay, Werner was dead and Mrs. Manton had never entered the case. Enid we had assumed to be the mysterious woman in Millard's divorce, however, and the other six had all been upon the floor in contact with Kennedy. First there was Marilyn, the woman. Then the five men in order had displayed a lively interest in the towel—Shirley, Gordon, Millard, Phelps, and Manton.

Kennedy's voice roused me from my reverie.

"Does this door lead through to the other vaults, Mr. Manton?"

"Yes." The promoter straightened, after replacing the records of the negative. "I designed this system of storage myself and superintended every detail of construction. It is—" He checked himself with an exclamation, noticing that the door was open. With a flush of anger he slammed it shut.

"I should think the connecting doors would be kept shut all the time," Kennedy remarked. "In case of fire only one compartment would be a loss."

"That's the idea exactly! That's why I was on the point of swearing. The boys down here are getting lax and I'm going to make trouble." Manton turned back and called to the boy outside. "Where did you say Wagnalls went?"

"I don't know, sir! Sometimes he goes across to McCann's for a cup of coffee, or maybe he went up to the printing department."

Manton faced us once more. "If you'll excuse me just a moment I'm going to see who's responsible for this. Why," he sputtered, "if you hadn't called me around the rack I wouldn't have noticed that the door was open and then, if there had been a fire—I—I'll be right back!"

As Manton stormed off Kennedy smiled slightly, then nodded for me to follow. We passed through into the rooms for positive storage. These in turn had fireproof connecting doors, all of which were open. In each case Kennedy closed them. Eventually we emerged into the main part of the basement through the farther vault door. Nothing of a suspicious nature had caught our attention. I guessed that Kennedy simply had wished to cover the carelessness of the vault man in leaving the inner doors wide open.

At the entrance which had first admitted us to the negative room, however, Kennedy stooped suddenly. At the very moment he bent forward I caught the glint of something bright behind the heavy steel door, and in the shadow so that it had escaped us before. As he rose I leaned over. It was a cigarette case, a very handsome one with large initials engraved with deep skillful flourish.

"Who is 'J. G.'?" Kennedy asked.

I felt a quiver of excitement. "Jack Gordon, the leading man."

"What's an actor doing down in the film vaults?" he muttered.

Slipping the case into his pocket, he glanced about on the floor and something just within the negative room caught his eye. Once more he bent down. With a speculative expression he picked up the cork-tipped stub of a cigarette.

At this instant Manton returned, breathing hard as though his pursuit of the missing Wagnalls had been very determined. The butt in Kennedy's fingers attracted his attention at once.

"Did—did you find that here?" he demanded.

Kennedy pointed. "Right there on the floor."

"The devil!" Manton flushed red. "This is no place to smoke. By—by all the wives of Goodwin and all the stars of Griffith I'm going to start firing a few people!" he sputtered. "Here, sonny!" He jumped at the boy, frightening him. "Close all these doors and turn the combinations. Tell Wagnalls if he opens them before he sees me I'll commit battery on his nose."

Kennedy continued to hold the stub, and as Manton preceded us up the stairs he hung back, comparing it with the few cigarettes left in the case. Unquestionably they were of the same brand.

On the studio floor Mackay was waiting for us. Under his arm was a reel of film in a can. He clutched it almost fondly.

"All ready!" he remarked, to Kennedy.

Kennedy's face was unrevealing as he faced Manton. "This bit of film is valuable evidence also. I think perhaps it would be safer in that locker."

"Anything at all we can do to help," stated Manton, promptly. "Shall I show you the way again?"

I produced the key, handing it to Kennedy as the four of us arrived in the corridor by the property room. Kennedy slipped the bit of metal into the lock; then simulated surprise very well indeed.

"The lock is broken!" he exclaimed. "Some one has been here."

Apparently the traveling bag had been undisturbed as we took it out. Nevertheless, the paper containing the towel was gone.

"This is no joke, Mr. Kennedy," protested Manton, in indignation. "Where can I hire about a dozen good men to hang around and watch—and—and help you get to the bottom of this?"

Mackay, without releasing his grasp of the film, had been inspecting the broken lock.

"Look at the way this was done!" he murmured, almost in admiration. "This wasn't the work of any roughneck. It—it was a dainty job!"

XXVII

THE FILM FIRE

The bag lay open at my feet. The microscope and other paraphernalia brought by Kennedy were untouched. Taking the film from Mackay and placing the can in with the other things, Kennedy snapped the catch and turned to me as he straightened.

"I think our evidence is safest in plain sight, Walter. We'll carry it about with us."

Lloyd Manton seemed to be a genuinely unhappy individual. After some moments he excused himself, nervously anxious about the turn of affairs at the studio. Immediately I faced Kennedy and Mackay.

"Manton's the only one who knew just where we put the bag," I remarked. "When he left us in the basement he had plenty of time to run up and steal the towel and return."

"How about the itching salve?"

"In his hurry he might have left the towel in the paper, intending to destroy it later."

Kennedy frowned. "That's possible, Walter. I had not thought of that. Still"—he brightened—"I'm counting on human nature. I don't believe anyone guilty of the crime could have that towel in his possession, after the hints I have thrown out, without examining it so as to see what telltale mark or stain would be apt to betray his identity."

"You can see that Manton's the logical man?"

"It would be easy for anyone else to follow and observe us."

"Then—?"

"First of all we must keep an eye out for any person showing signs of the itching concoction. We must observe anyone with noticeably clean hands. Principally, however, another thing worries me."

"What's that, Mr. Kennedy?" asked Mackay.

"Walter and I found a cigarette case belonging to Jack Gordon in the basement; also a butt smoked three-quarters of the way down and left directly in the negative room. The fire doors between the different film vaults, which are arranged like the safety compartments in a ship, were all open. I want to know why Gordon was down there and—well, I seem to sense something wrong."

"Good heavens! Craig," I interposed. "You don't attach any importance to the fact that those doors were open!"

"Walter, in a case of real mystery the slightest derangement of matters of ordinary routine is a cause for suspicion."

I had no answer, and as we re-entered the studio I devoted my attention to the various people we had tabulated as possible suspects, noticing that Kennedy and Mackay did likewise.

Jack Gordon was in the ballroom scene in make-up. Kauf still was concerned with technical details of the set and lighting, and, although the cameras were set up, they were not in proper place, nor was either camera man in evidence. With Gordon was Enid. From a distance they seemed to be engaged in an argument of real magnitude. There was no mistaking the dislike on the part of each for the other.

Marilyn was the most uneasy of all of the principals. She was pacing up and down, glancing about in frank distress of mind. I looked at her hands and saw that she had crushed a tube of grease paint in her nervousness. Not only her fingers were soiled, but there were streaks on her arms where she had smeared herself unconsciously. As we watched she left the studio, hurrying out the door without a backward glance. Marilyn, at least, showed no indications of the salve, nor of painfully recent acquaintance with water.

Both Manton and Phelps were in evidence, decidedly so, I imagined, from, the viewpoint of poor Kauf. Manton, at the heels of his new director, was doing all he could to help. Phelps, following Manton about, seemed to be urging haste upon the promoter. The result was far from advantageous to picture making; it was concentrated distraction.

Millard was poring over the manuscript, perched upon a chair the wrong way so that its back would serve as a desk, engaged busily in making changes here and there in the pages with a pencil. Like any author, it was never too late for minor improvements and suggestions. I don't doubt but that if Manton had permitted it, Millard would have been quite apt to interrupt a scene in the taking in order to add some little touch occurring to him as his action sprang to life in the interpretation of players and director. At any rate, his hands seemed more clean than those of either Manton or Phelps, proving nothing because he was at a task not so apt to bring him into contact with dirt.

"Shirley is missing," observed the district attorney, in an undertone.

Kennedy faced me. "Give the bag to Mackay, Walter. While he keeps an eye on the people up here we'll pay a visit to Shirley's dressing room, and after that go down to the basement again. I can't account for it—intuition, perhaps—but I'm sure something's wrong."

The heavy man's dressing room, pointed out to us by some employee passing through the hall, was empty. I led the way into Marilyn's quarters, but again no one was about. In each case Kennedy made a quick visual search for the towel, without result. We did not dare linger and run the risk of giving away our trick; then, too, Kennedy was nervously anxious to look through the basement once more.

"I don't understand your suspicion of the state of affairs in the film vaults," I confessed.

"Why should Jack Gordon, the leading man, be down there?" he countered.

"That—that really is a cause for suspicion, isn't it."

"Now, Walter, think a bit!" We were crossing the yard, and so not apt to be overheard. "Granting that Gordon actually had been down there, why should the fact concern us? Manton explained that no negative or positive can be given out except upon order. There is nothing down there but film and so no other errand to bring the leading man to the vault except to get some scenes or pieces showing his own work, and that isn't likely."

"Unless," I interrupted, "Gordon is the guilty man and wanted to get the snake film before we did."

"How could that be? When we asked Manton about the Doctor Nagoya subject we went right down with him and procured it. I doubt anyone could have overheard us as we talked about it, in any case."

"Remember, Craig, we went to the locker first and it was some little time before that fellow came out to unlock it and give us the key. And when you questioned Manton we were passing right by all of them. Any one could have heard the mention of the snake film."

Kennedy frowned. "I believe you're right, Walter. Or it is possible that the guilty person believed that the scenes taken out at Tarrytown, or those taken when Werner died, revealed something and so would have to be stolen or destroyed, and that they were kept in the vault. It is even possible"—a gleam came into Kennedy's eyes—"it is even possible that the mind smart enough to reason out the damaging nature of the chemical analyses I was making, and clever enough to utilize an explosive bullet in an effort to destroy the fruits of my work, would also have the foresight to anticipate me and to realize that I might guess the existence of a film showing snakes and suggesting the use of venom."

"It's damning to Gordon, all right," I said.

"On the contrary, Walter." Kennedy lowered his voice as we entered the building across the quadrangle and descended stairs leading directly into the basement. "We have mentioned over and over again the cleverness of our unknown criminal. That man, or woman, never would drop a cigarette case with his or her initials and leave without it, nor smoke a cigarette in a place he, or she, was not supposed to be."

"What then?"

"It's a plant; a deliberate plant to throw suspicion upon Gordon."

"Why upon Gordon?"

"I don't know that, unless because Gordon is supposed to have the best possible motive for killing Miss Lamar—his money troubles—and so becomes the logical man to throw the guilt upon."

"As a matter of fact, Craig, why should the finding of that cigarette case be a cause for suspicion at all? That's what I didn't understand before."

"Ordinarily it wouldn't be. But those open inner doors, the absence of the man in charge—isn't it possible that we interrupted an attempt not only to search for the particular damaging pieces of film, but perhaps to destroy the whole? If some one acted between the time I asked Manton about the snake film and the moment we arrived in the basement to get it, that some one had to move very fast."

"In which case it might have been Gordon, after all. The cigarette stub may have been thrown in lighted to start a fire. He may not have had time to pick up the case, not knowing just where he dropped it."

Kennedy shrugged his shoulders. "It all shows the futility of trying to arrive at a conclusion without definite facts. That is where science is superior to deduction."

"It's all a maze to me just now," I agreed.

We made our way to the vaults in silence, and, to our surprise, found that they were closed and that even the boy was gone now. The cellar, as a whole, probably for the purpose of fire protection on a larger scale, was divided into sections corresponding to the units of the buildings above, and this time I noticed that the door through which we had arrived before was closed also. Had Manton taken fright in earnest at the possibility of fire, or had he given his employees a genuine scare?

We retraced our steps to the yard, and there the alert eye of Kennedy detected a slinking figure just as a man darted into the protection of a doorway. It was Shirley. Had he been watching us? Was he connected in some way with the vague mystery Kennedy seemed to sense in connection with the basement and the film vaults?

Kennedy led the way to the entrance where Shirley had disappeared. Here there was no sign of him; only steps leading up and down and the open door to a huge developing room. Returning to the yard, we caught a gesture from the chauffeur of a car standing near by and recognized McGroarty, the driver who had found the ampulla a few days previously.

"Excuse me, Mr. Kennedy," he apologized, as we approached. "I should have come to you instead of making you two walk over to me, but it's less suspicious this way."

"What do you mean?"

"You recognize me, McGroarty, the chauffeur as found the little bottle?"

Kennedy nodded.

"Well, I says to myself I ought to tell you, but I don't like to because it might be nothing, you know!"

"It might prove very valuable, McGroarty." Kennedy wanted to encourage him.

"Well, I've been sitting here for an hour, I guess. One of the other directors is going out to-day and his people are late and so here I am. Well, I don't like the way the heavy man Mr. Werner had—"

"Shirley? Merle Shirley?" I spoke up.

"That's him! Well, he's been, hanging and snooping around that building over there, where you just saw him, for twenty minutes or more. I guess he's gone in and out of that basement a dozen times. I says to myself, maybe he's up to something. You know how it is?"

Kennedy glanced at me significantly. Then he extended his hand to the chauffeur. "Again I thank you, McGroarty. As I said before, I won't forget you."

"Now what?" I asked, as we drew away.

"Shirley's dressing room, and the studio floor and Mackay."

As we rather expected, the heavy man's quarters were deserted. I thought that Kennedy would stop now to make a careful search, but he seemed anxious to compare notes with the district attorney.

"Nothing here," reported Mackay.

"Shirley?"

"Hasn't been a sign of him."

I looked about the moment we arrived under the big glass roof. "Marilyn Loring?" I inquired.

"She's been missing, too!" All at once Mackay grinned broadly. "You know, either there's no efficiency in making moving pictures at all, or these people have all gone more or less out of their heads as the result of the two tragedies. Look!" He pointed. "When you left me Phelps and Manton were stepping on each other's toes, trying to help that new director and about half driving him crazy; and now Millard seems to have figured out some new way of handling the action and he's over in the thick of it. It's worse than Bedlam, and better than a Chaplin comedy."

I was compelled to smile, although I knew that this was not uncommon in picture studios. Manton, Phelps, Millard, and Kauf were in the center of the group, all talking at once. Clustered about I saw Enid and Gordon, both camera men, and a miniature mob of extra people. But as I looked little Kauf seemed to come to the end of his patience. In an instant or two he demonstrated real generalship. Shutting up Manton and the banker and Millard with a grin, but with sharp words and a quick gesture which showed that he meant it, he called to the others gathered about, clearing the set of all but Enid and Gordon. He sent the camera men to their places; then confronted Phelps and Manton and the scenario writer once more. We could not hear his words, but could see that he was asserting himself, was forcing a decision so that he could proceed with his work.

This seemed uninteresting to me. I remembered my success in my visit to Werner's apartment, when I had essayed the role of detective.

"Listen, Kennedy!" I suggested. "Suppose I go out by myself and see if I can locate Shirley or Marilyn. Everyone else is right here where you can—"

At that instant a deafening explosion shook the studio and every building about the quadrangle, the sound echoing and re-echoing with the sharpness of a terrific thunderclap.

Mixed with the reverberations, which were intensified by the high arch of the studio roof, were the screams of women and the frightened calls of men. Following immediately upon the first roar were the muffled sounds of additional explosions, persisting for a matter of ten to fifteen seconds.

With every detonation the floor beneath our feet trembled and rocked. Several flats of scenery stacked against a wall at our rear toppled forward and struck the floor with a resounding whack, not unlike some gigantic slap-stick. One entire side of the banquet set, luckily unoccupied, fell inward and I caught the sound as the dainty gold chairs and fragile tables snapped and were crushed as so much kindling wood.

Then—a fitting climax of destruction, withheld until this moment—there followed the terrifying snap of steel from above. An entire section of roof literally was popped from place, the result of false stresses in the beams created by the explosion. Upon the heads of the unlucky group in the center of the ballroom set came a perfect hailstorm of broken and shattered bits of heavy ground glass.

For an instant, an exceedingly brief instant, there was the illusion of silence. The next moment the factory siren rose to a shrill shriek, with a full head of steam behind it—the fire call!

Kennedy dashed over to the scene where those beneath the shower of glass lay, dazed and uncertain of the extent of their own injuries.

"Where are the first-aid kits?" he shouted. "Bring cotton and bandages, and—and telephone for a doctor, an ambulance!"

It seemed to me that Kennedy had never been so excited. Mackay and I, at his heels, and some of the others, unhurt, hurriedly helped the various victims to their feet.

Then we realized that by some miracle, some freak of fate, no one had been hurt seriously. Already a property boy was at Kennedy's side with a huge box marked prominently with the red cross. Inside was everything necessary and Kennedy started to bind up the wounds with all the skill of a professional physician.

"Mackay," he whispered, "hurry and get me some envelopes, or some sheets of paper, anything—quick!" And to me, before I could grasp the reason for that puzzling request: "Don't let anyone slip away, Walter. No matter what happens, I must bind up these wounds myself."

A few moments later I understood what Kennedy was up to. As he finished with each victim he took some bit of cotton or gauze with which he had wiped their cuts, enough blood to serve him in chemical analysis, and handed it to Mackay. The district attorney, very unobtrusively, slipped each sample into a separate envelope, sealing it, and marking it with a hieroglyph which he would be able to identify later. In this fashion Kennedy secured blood smears of Manton and Phelps, Millard and Kauf and Enid, Gordon, the two camera men, and a scene shifter. I smiled to myself.

Meanwhile a bitter, acrid odor penetrated through the windows and to every part of the structure, the odor of burning film, an odor one never forgets to fear. All those uninjured in the explosions had rushed out to see the fire, or else to escape from any further danger, the moment they recovered their wits. Manton, only cut at the wrist, and impatient as Kennedy cleaned, dusted, and bound the wound, was the first to receive attention.

"The vaults!" he called, to the men who seemed disposed to linger about. "For God's sake get busy!" The next instant he was gone himself.

Enid was cut on the head. Tears streamed from her eyes as she clung to Kennedy's coat, trembling. "Will it make a scar?" she sobbed. "Will I be unable to act before the camera any more?"

He reassured her. In the case of Millard, who had several bad scalp wounds, he advised a trip to a doctor, but the scenario writer laughed. Phelps was yellow. It seemed to me that he whimpered a bit. Gordon was disposed to swear cheerfully, although a point of glass had penetrated deep in his shoulder and another piece had gashed him across the forehead.

Finally Kennedy was through. He packed the little envelopes in the bag, still in the possession of Mackay, and added the two rolls of film from his pocket. Then, for the first time, he locked it.

As he straightened, his eyes narrowed.

"Now for Shirley," he muttered.

"And Marilyn," I added.

XXVIII

THE PHOSPHORUS BOMB

We rushed out into the courtyard, Kennedy in the lead, Mackay trailing with the bag. Here there were dense clouds of fine white suffocating smoke mixed with steam, and signs of the utmost confusion on every hand. Because Manton, fortunately, had trained the studio staff through frequent fire drills, there was a semblance of order among the men actually engaged in fighting the spread of the blaze. Any attempt to extinguish the conflagration in the vault itself was hopeless, however, and so the workers contented themselves with pouring water into the basement on either side, to keep the building and perhaps the other vaults cool, and with maintaining a constant stream of chemical mixture from a special apparatus down the ventilating system into and upon the smoldering film.

The studio fire equipment seemed to be very complete. There was water at high pressure from a tank elevated some twenty to thirty feet above the uppermost roof of the quadrangle. In addition Manton had invested in the chemical engine and also in sand carts, because water aids rather than retards the combustion of film itself. I noticed that the promoter was in direct charge of the fire-fighters, and that he moved about with a zeal and a recklessness which ended for once and all in my mind the suspicion that Phelps might be correct and that Manton sought to wreck this company for the sake of Fortune Features.

In an amazingly quick space of time the thing was over. When the city apparatus arrived, after a run of nearly three miles, there was nothing for them to do. The chief sought out Manton, to accompany him upon an inspection of the damage and to make sure that the fire was out. The promoter first beckoned to Kennedy.

"This is unquestionably of incendiary origin," he explained to the chief. "I want Mr. Kennedy to see everything before it is disturbed, so that no clue may be lost or destroyed."

The fire officer brightened. "Craig Kennedy?" he inquired. "Gee! there must be some connection between the blaze and the murder of Stella Lamar and her director. I've been reading about it every day in the papers."

"Mr. Jameson of the Star," Kennedy said, presenting me.

We found we could not enter the basement immediately adjoining the vaults—that is, directly from the courtyard—because it seemed advisable to keep a stream of water playing down the steps, and a resulting cloud of steam blocked us. Manton explained that we could get through from the next cellar if it was not too hot, and so we hurried toward another entrance.

Mackay, who had remained behind to protect the bag from the heat, joined us there.

"I've put the bag in charge of that chauffeur, McGroarty, and armed him with my automatic," he explained. He paused to wipe his eyes. The fumes from the film had distressed all of us. "Shirley and Marilyn Loring are both missing still," he added. "I've been asking everyone about them. No one has seen them."

The fire chief looked up. "Everyone is out? You are sure everybody is safe?"

"I had Wagnalls at my elbow with a hose," Manton replied. "I saw the boy around, also. No one else had any business down there and the vaults were closed and the cellar shut off."

The door leading from the adjoining basement was hot yet, but not so that we were unable to handle it. However, the catch had stuck and it took considerable effort to force it in. As we did so a cloud of acrid vapor and steam drove us back.

Then Kennedy seemed to detect something in the slowly clearing atmosphere. He rushed ahead without hesitation. The fire chief followed. In another instant I was able to see also.

The form of a woman, dimly outlined in the vapor, struggled to lift the prone figure of a man. After one effort she collapsed upon him. I dashed forward, as did Mackay and Manton. Two of them carried the girl out to the air; the other three of us brought her unconscious companion. It was Marilyn and Shirley.

The little actress was revived easily, but Shirley required the combined efforts of Kennedy and the chief, and it was evident that he had escaped death from suffocation only by the narrowest of margins. How either had survived seemed a mystery. Their clothes were wet, their faces and hands blackened, eyebrows and lashes scorched by the heat. But for the water poured into the basement neither would have been alive. They had been prisoners during the entire conflagration, the burning vault holding them at one end of the basement, the door in the partition resisting their efforts to open it.

"Thank heaven he's alive!" were Marilyn's first words.

"How did you get in the cellar?" Kennedy spoke sternly.

"I thought he might be there." Now that the reaction was setting in, the girl was faint and she controlled herself with difficulty. "I was looking for him and as soon as I heard the first explosion I ran down the steps into the film-vault entrance—I was right near there—and I found him, stunned. I started to lift him, but there were other explosions almost before I got to his side. The flames shot out through the cracks in the vault door and I—I couldn't drag him to the steps; I had to pull him back where you found us." She began to tremble. "It—it was terrible!"

"Was there anyone else about, anyone but Mr. Shirley?"

"No. I—I remember I wondered about the vault man."

"What was Mr. Shirley down there for, Miss Loring?"

"He"—she hesitated—"he said he had seen some one hanging around and—and he didn't want to report anything until he was sure. He—he thought he could accomplish more by himself, although I told him he was—was wrong."

"Whom did he see hanging around?"

"He wouldn't tell me."

Shirley was too weak to question and the girl too unstrung to stand further interrogation. In response to Manton's call several people came up and willingly helped the two toward the comfort of their dressing rooms.

At the fire chief's suggestion the stream of water into the basement was cut off. Manton led the way, choking, eyes watering, to the front of the vaults. Feverishly he felt the steel doors and the walls. There was no mistaking the conclusion. The negative vault was hot, the others cold.

"The devil!" Manton exclaimed. A deep poignancy in his voice made the expression childishly inadequate. "Why couldn't it have been the prints!" Suddenly he began to sob. "That's the finish. Not one of our subjects can ever be worked again. It's a loss of half a million dollars."

"If you have positives," Kennedy asked, "can't you make new negatives?"

"Dupes?" Manton looked up in scorn. "Did you ever see a print from a dupe negative? It's terrible. Looks like some one left it out in the wet overnight."

"How about the 'Black Terror'?" I inquired.

"All of that's in the safe in the printing room; that and the two current five reelers of the other companies. We won't lose our releases, but"—again there was a catch in his voice—"we could have cleared thousands and thousands of dollars on reissues. All—all of Stella's negative is gone, too!" To my amazement he began to cry, without attempt at concealment. It was something new to me in the way of moving-picture temperament. "First they kill her and now—now they destroy the photographic record which would have let her live for those who loved her. The"—his voice trailed away to the merest whisper as he seemed to collapse against the hot smoked wall—"the devil!"

The fire chief took charge of the job of breaking into the vault. First Wagnalls attempted to open the combination of the farther door, but the heat had put the tumblers out of commission. Returning to the entrance of the negative vault itself, the thin steel, manufactured for fire rather than burglar protection, was punctured and the bolts driven back. A cloud of noxious fumes greeted the workers and delayed them, but they persisted. Finally the door fell out with a crash and men were set to fanning fresh air into the interior while a piece of chemical apparatus was held in readiness for any further outbreak of the conflagration.

Manton regained control of himself in time to be one of the first to enter. Mackay held back, but the fire chief, the promoter, Kennedy, and myself fashioned impromptu gasmasks of wet handkerchiefs and braved the hot atmosphere inside the room.

The damage was irremediable. The steel frames of the racks, the cheaper metal of the boxes, the residue of the burning film, all constituted a hideous, shapeless mass clinging against the sides and in the corners and about the floor. Only one section of the room retained the slightest suggestion of its original condition. The little table and the boxes of negative records, the edges of the racks which had stood at either side, showed something of their former shape and purpose. This was directly beneath the ventilating opening. Here the chemical mixture pumped in to extinguish the fire had preserved them to that extent.

All at once Kennedy nudged the fire chief. "Put out your torch!" he directed, sharply.

In the darkness there slowly appeared here and there on the walls a ghostly bluish glow persisting in spite of the coating of soot on everything.

Kennedy's keen eye had caught the hint of it while the electric torch had been flashed into some corner and away for a moment.

"Radium!" I exclaimed, entirely without thought.

Kennedy laughed. "Hardly! But it is phosphorus, without question."

"What do you make of that?" The fire chief was curious.

"Let's get out!" was Kennedy's reply.

Indeed, it was almost impossible for us to keep our eyes open, because of the smarting, and, more, the odor was nauseating. A guard was posted and in the courtyard, disregarding the curious crowd about, Kennedy asked for Wagnalls and began to question him.

"When did you close the vaults?"

"About two hours before the fire. Mr. Manton sent for me."

"Was there anything suspicious at that time?"

"No, sir! I went through each room myself and fixed the doors. That's why the fire was confined to the negatives."

"Have you any idea why the doors were open when we went through?"

"No, sir! I left them shut and the boy I put there while I went over to McCann's said no one was near. He"—Wagnalls hesitated. "Once he went to sleep when I left him there. Perhaps he dozed off again."

"Why did you leave? Why go over to McCann's in business hours?"

"We'd worked until after midnight the night before. I had to open up early and so I figured I'd have my breakfast in the usual morning slack time—when nothing's doing."

"I see!" Kennedy studied the ground for several moments. "Do you suppose anyone could have left a package in there—a bomb, in other words?"

Wagnalls's eyes widened, but he shook his head. "I'd notice it, sir! If I do say it, I'm neat. I generally notice if a can has been touched. They don't often fool me."

"Well, has any regular stuff been brought to you to put away; anything which might have hidden an explosive?"

Again Wagnalls shook his head. "I put nothing away or give nothing out except on written order from Mr. Manton. Anything coming in is negative and it's in rolls, and I rehandle them because they're put away in the flat boxes. I'd know in a minute if a roll was phony."

"You're sure nothing special—"

"Holy Jehoshaphat!" interrupted Wagnalls. "I'd forgotten!" He faced Manton. "Remember that can of undeveloped stuff, a two-hundred roll?" He turned to Kennedy, explaining. "When negative's undeveloped we keep it in taped cans. Take off the tape and you spoil it—the light, you know. Mr. Manton sent down this can with a regular order, marking on it that some one had to come to watch it being developed—in about a week. Of course I didn't open the can or look in it. I put it up on top of a rack."

"When was this?"

"About four days ago—the day Miss Lamar was killed."

The expression on Manton's face was ghastly. "I didn't send down any can to you, Wagnalls," he insisted.

"It was your writing, sir!"

Kennedy rose. "What did you do with orders like that, such as the one you claim came with the can of undeveloped negative?"

"Put them on the spindle on that table in the vault."

"Wet your handkerchief and come show me."

When they returned Kennedy had the spindle in his hand, the charred papers still in place. This was one of the items preserved in part by the chemical spray through the ventilating opening above.

"Can you point out which one it is?" Kennedy asked.

"Let's see!" Wagnalls scratched his head. "Next to the top," he replied, in a moment. "Miss Lamar's death upset everything. Only one order came down after that."

With extreme care Kennedy took his knife and lifted the ashy flakes of the top order. "Get me some collodion, somebody!" he exclaimed.

Wagnalls jumped up and hurried off.

The fire chief leaned forward. "Do you think, Mr. Kennedy, that the little can he told you about started the fire?"

"I'm sure of it, although I'll never be able to prove it."

"How did it work?"

"Well, I imagine a small roll of very dry film was put in to occupy a part of the space. Film is exceedingly inflammable, especially when old and brittle. In composition it is practically guncotton and so a high explosive. In this recent war, I remember, the Germans drained the neutral countries of film subjects until we woke up to what they were doing, while in this country scrap film commanded an amazing price and went directly into the manufacture of explosives. Then I figure that a quantity of wet phosphorus was added, to fill the can, and that then the can was taped. The tape, of course, is not moisture proof entirely. With the dampness from within it would soften, might possibly fall off. In a relatively short time the phosphorus would dry and burn. Immediately the film in the can would ignite. As happened, it blew up, a minor explosion, but enough to scatter phosphorus everywhere. That, in the fume-laden air of the vault—there are always fumes in spite of the best ventilation system made—caused the first big blast and started all the damage."

Mackay had rejoined us in time to hear the explanation. "Ingenious," he murmured. "As ingenious as the methods used to murder the girl and her director."

Breathless, Wagnalls returned with the collodion. We watched curiously as Kennedy poured it over the charred remains of the second order on the spindle. It seemed almost inconceivable that the remnants of the charred paper would even support the weight of the liquid, yet Kennedy used it with care, and slowly the collodion hardened before us, creating a tough transparent coating which held the tiny fibers of the slip together. At the same time the action of the collodion made the letters on the order faintly visible and readable.

"A little-known bank trick!" Kennedy told us.

Then he held the slip up to the light and the words were plain. Wagnalls had been correct. The order from Manton was unmistakable. The can was to be kept in the negative vault for a week without being opened, until a certain party unnamed was to come to watch the development of the film.

The promoter wet his lips, uneasily. "I—I never wrote that! It—it's my writing, all right, and my signature, but it's a forgery!"

XXIX

MICROSCOPIC EVIDENCE

Kennedy made some efforts to preserve the forged order which he had restored with the collodion, but I could see that he placed no great importance upon its possession. Gradually the yard of the studio had cleared of the employees, who had returned to their various tasks. Under the direction of one stout individual who seemed to possess authority the fire apparatus had been replaced in a portable steel garage arranged for the purpose in a farther corner, and now several men were engaged in cleaning up the dirt and litter caused in the excitement.

Except in the basement there were few signs of the blaze. Manton accompanied the fire chief to his car, then hurried up into the building without further notice of us. Mackay went to McGroarty's machine to claim the traveling bag containing our evidence. Kennedy and I started for the dressing rooms.

"I want to get blood smears of Shirley and Marilyn," he confided in a low voice. "I shall have to think of some pretext."

Neither of the two we sought were in their quarters and so we continued on into the studio. Here we found Kauf at work; at least he was engaged in a desperate attempt to get something out of his people.

"Ye gods, Gordon!" we heard him exclaim, as we made our way through the debris of the banquet set to the ballroom now dazzlingly bright under the lights. "What if you do have to wear a bandage around your head? It's a masked ball, isn't it? You've got a monk's cowl over everything but your features, haven't you?"

It struck me that the faces had never been more ghastly, although my reason convinced me it was simply the usual effect of the Cooper-Hewitt tubes. But there was no question but that the explosion had given everyone a bad fright, that not an actress or actor but would have preferred to have been nearly anywhere else but under the heat of the glass roof, now a constant reminder of the accident because of the gaping hole directly above them.

Marilyn was in the center of the revelers in the set, already in costume. Shirley I saw close to the camera men, standing uneasily on shaky legs, shielding his eyes with one hand while he clung to a massive sideboard for support with the other. He had not yet donned his carnival clothes, nor essayed to put on a make-up.

Enid Faye, the only one in sight whose spirits seemed to have rallied at all, was offering him comfort of a sort.

"You'll get by, all right, Merle, if you can keep on your pins, and I'll say you deserve credit for trying it. There's"—she stepped back a bit to study him—"there's just one thing. Your eyes show the result of all that smoke and vapor—no color or luster at all. I—I wonder if belladonna wouldn't brighten them up a bit and—well, get you by, for to-day?"

"I'll go out and get some at lunch." He smiled weakly. "I'll try anything once."

"That's the spirit!" She patted him on the shoulder, then danced on into the center of the set, stopping to direct some barbed remark at Marilyn.

Kauf took his megaphone to call his people around him. There seemed to be a certain essential competence about the little man, now that Manton and Phelps and Millard were not about to bother him. While we watched he succeeded in photographing one of the full shots of the general action or atmosphere of the dance. Then he hurried to the side of Shirley, to see if the heavy man felt equal to the task of resuming his make-up once more.

I found the time dragging heavy on my hands and I wished that Kennedy would return to the laboratory or decide upon some definite action. Though I racked my brain, I failed to think of a device whereby Kennedy could get blood smears of Shirley or Marilyn without their knowledge. Once more my reflections veered around to the matter of the stolen towel and I wondered if that had been wasted effort on Kennedy's part; if the fire had thrown out his carefully arranged plans to trap whoever took it.

Suddenly I realized that Kennedy was following a very definite procedure, that his seeming indifference, his apparent idle curiosity concerning the scene taking, masked a settled purpose. When Phelps entered he approached him casually and turned to him with skilled nonchalance, holding up a finger.

"Will you lend me a pocket knife for a moment?" he asked, "to get a hang-nail?"

Phelps produced one, rather grudgingly. Kennedy promptly went over to the window, as though seeking better light. Thereafter he avoided Phelps. Soon the banker had forgotten the incident.

Some time later Manton rushed in from the office. Kennedy maneuvered his way to the promoter's side and waited his chance to borrow that man's pocket knife under conditions when Manton would be the least apt to remember it. Then he made his way around to Mackay and I saw that both the acquisitions went into little envelopes of the sort used to take the blood smears after the explosion and falling glass.

Kennedy now seemed rather elated. Millard entered and he borrowed the scenario writer's knife in exactly the same fashion as the others. No one of the three men noticed his loss. I thought it lucky that all three carried the article, and tried to guess how far Kennedy intended to carry this little scheme.

Kauf's announcement of lunch gave me my answer. It seemed that there would be just half an hour and that the entire cast was expected to make shift at McCann's rather than attempt to go to any better place at a greater distance. Immediately Kennedy turned to me.

"Hurry, Walter! Twenty minutes' quick work and then it's the laboratory and the solution of this mystery."

With Mackay and the bag we stole to the dressing rooms, waiting until sure that everyone was downstairs. In Enid's chamber Kennedy glanced about carefully but swiftly. When nothing caught his attention he picked up her finger-nail file, gingerly, from the blunt end, slipping it into one of the little envelopes which Mackay held open. Thereupon the district attorney put his identifying mark upon the outside and we went to the next room.

It proved to be Gordon's. The general search was barren of result, but the dressing table yielded another finger-nail file, handled in the same manner as before. Then we entered Marilyn's room and left with the file from her dressing stand. In Shirley's quarters, the last we visited, we were in greater luck, however. While Kennedy and Mackay abstracted the usual file, I discovered some bits of tissue paper used in shaving. There was caked soap left to dry just as it had been wiped from the razor. More, there was a blood stain of fair proportions.

"Here's your smear, Kennedy," I exclaimed.

"Good! Fine!" He faced Mackay. "Now I lack just one thing, a sample of the blood of Miss Loring."

"Is that all?" The district attorney brightened. "Let me try to get it!
I—I'll manage it in some way!"

"All right!" Kennedy took the bag. "Explain your marks so I'll know—" He stopped suddenly. "No, don't tell me anything. I'll make my chemical analyses and microscopic examinations without knowing the identity in the case either of the blood samples or the finger-nail files. If I obtain results by both methods, and they agree, I'll return armed with double-barreled evidence. Meanwhile, Mackay, you get a smear from Miss Loring and follow us to the laboratory. I'll coax McGroarty to drive us down, so you'll have your car and you can bring us back."

The district attorney nodded. "Me for McCann's," he muttered. "That's where she went to eat." He rushed off eagerly.

Kennedy had no difficulty persuading McGroarty to put his particular studio car at our disposal without an order from Manton or from the director who had called him. In a very brief space of time we were at the laboratory.

"You expect to find the blood of one of those people showing traces of the antivenin?" I grasped Kennedy's method of procedure, but wanted to make sure I understood it correctly. Already I was blocking out the detailed article for the Star, the big scoop which that paper should have as a result of my close association with Kennedy on the case. "One of those samples should correspond, I suppose, to the trace of blood on the portieres?"

"Exactly!" He answered me rather absently, being concerned in setting out the apparatus he would need for a hasty series of tests.

"Will the antivenin show in the blood after four, perhaps five days?"

"I should say so, Walter. If it does not, by any chance, I will be able to identify the blood, but that is much more involved and tedious—a great deal more actual work."

"I've got it straight, then. Now—" I paced up and down several times. "The finger-nail files should show a trace of the itching salve? Is that correct, Craig?"

For a moment he didn't answer, as his mind was upon his paraphernalia. Then he straightened. "Hardly, Walter! The salve is soluble in water. What I shall find, if anything, is some of the fibers of the towel. You see, a person's finger nails are great little collectors of bits of foreign matter, and anyone handling that rag is sure to show some infinitesimal trace for a long while afterward. If the person stealing the towel filed or cleaned his nails there will be evidence of the fibers on his pocket knife or finger-nail file. I impregnated the towel with that chemical so that I would be able to identify the fibers positively."

"The use of the itching salve was unnecessary?"

A quizzical smile crept across Kennedy's face. "Did you think I expected some one to go walking around the studio scratching his hands? Did you imagine I thought the guilty party would betray his or her identity in such childish fashion, after all the cleverness displayed in the crimes themselves?"

"But you were insistent that I rub in the—"

"To force them to wash their hands after touching the towel, Walter."

"Oh!" I felt rather chagrined. "Wouldn't some pigment, some color, have served the purpose better?"

"No, because anyone would have understood that and would have taken the proper measures to remove all traces. But the itching salve served two purposes. It was misleading, because obviously a trap upon reflection, and so it would distract attention from the impregnated fibers, my real scheme. Then it was the best device of all I could think of, for it set up a local irritation of the sort most calculated to make a person clean his finger nails. The average man and woman is not very neat, Walter. I was not sure but a scientific prodding was necessary to transfer my evidence to some object I could borrow and examine under a microscope."

Meanwhile Kennedy's long fingers were busy at the preliminary operations in his tests. He turned away and I asked no more questions, not wishing to delay him.

I noticed that first he examined the blood samples under the microscope. Afterward he employed a spectroscope. But none of the operations took any great amount of time, since he seemed to anticipate his results.

Mackay burst in upon us, very elated, and produced a handkerchief with a bit of blood upon it.

"I scratched her deliberately with the sharp point of my ring," he chuckled. "I found her in the restaurant and the seat beside her was empty. I—I talked about everything under the sun and I guess she thinks I'm a clumsy boob! Anyhow she cried out when I did it, and got red in the face for a moment; but she suspects nothing."

Kennedy cut the spot from the handkerchief, put it in an envelope, and turned back to his table. I drew Mackay into the corner.

As the minutes sped by and Craig worked in absorbed concentration,
Mackay grew more and more impatient to get back to the studio.

"Did you find anything?" repeated Mackay, for the tenth time.

With a gesture of annoyance, Kennedy reached out for the nail files.

"This is a grave matter," he frowned. "I must check it up—and double check it—then I'm going back to the studio to triple check it. Let me see what the nail files reveal. It will be a bare ten minutes more."

Insisting that we remain back in the corner, he spread out the four nail files and the open blades of the three pocket knives, setting each upon the envelope which identified it.

The next quarter of an hour seemed interminable. Finally Kennedy started replacing the files and the pocket knives in their envelopes, his face still wearing the inscrutable frown. Next he packed the blood samples and other evidence in the traveling bag once more.

Mackay was bursting with impatience, but Craig still refused to betray his suspicions.

"I must get back there—quick," he hastened. "I want everybody in the projection room. In court, a jury might not grasp the infallibility of the methods I've used. There would be a great deal of medical and expert testimony required—and you know, Mackay, what that means."

"Is it a man—or a woman you suspect?" persisted the district attorney. "Three of the men had pocket knives and—"

Kennedy led the way to the door without answering, and Mackay cut short his hopeless quizzing as Craig nodded to me to carry the bag.

XXX

THE BALLROOM SCENE

Sounds of music caught our ears as we entered the studio courtyard of Manton Pictures. Carrying the bag with its indisputable proof of some person's guilt, we made our way through the familiar corridor by the dressing rooms, out under the roof of the so-called large studio. There a scene of gayety confronted us, in sharp contrast with the gloomy atmosphere of the rest of the establishment.

Kauf, however, had thoroughly demonstrated his genius as a director. To counteract the depression caused by all the recent melodramatic and tragic happenings, he had brought in an eight-piece orchestra, establishing the men in the set itself so as to get full photographic value from their jazz antics. Where Werner and Manton had dispensed with music, in a desperate effort at economy, Kauf had realized that money saved in that way was lost through time wasted with dispirited people. It was a lesson learned long before by other companies. In other studios I had seen music employed in the making of soberly dramatic scenes, solely as an aid to the actors, enabling them to get into the atmosphere of their work more quickly and naturally.

Under the lights the entire set sparkled with a tawdry garishness apt to fool those uninitiated into the secrets of photography. On the screen, colors which now seemed dull and flat would take on a soft richness and a delicacy characteristic of the society in which Kauf's characters were supposed to move. Obviously fragile scenery would seem as heavy and substantial as the walls and beams of the finest old mansion. Even the inferior materials in the gowns of most of the girls would photograph as well as the most expensive silk; in fact, by long experience, many of the extra girls had learned to counterfeit the latest fashions at a cost ridiculous by comparison.

Kennedy approached Kauf, then returned to us.

"He asks us to wait until he gets this one big scene. It's the climax of the picture, really, the unmasking of the 'Black Terror.' If we interrupt now he loses the result of half a day of preparation."

"He may lose more than that!" muttered Mackay; and I wondered just whom the district attorney suspected.

"Is everyone here?" I asked. "All seven?"

Gordon and Shirley, of the men, and Marilyn and Enid, of course, were out on the floor of the supposed ballroom. Gordon I recognized because I remembered that he was to wear the garb of a monk. Marilyn was easily picked out, although the vivacity she assumed seemed unnatural now that we knew her as well as we did. Her costume was a glorious Yama Yama creation, of a faint yellow which would photograph dazzling white, revealing trim stockinged ankles and slender bare arms, framing face and eyes dancing with merriment and maliciousness. Unquestionably she was the prettiest girl beneath the arcs, never to be suspected as the woman who had braved the terrors of a film fire to rescue the man she loved. Enid was stately and serene in the gown of Marie Antoinette. In the bright glare her features took on a round innocence and she was as successful in portraying sweetness as Marilyn was in the simulation of the mocking evil of the vampire.

Shirley interested me the most, however. I wondered if Kennedy still eliminated him in guessing at the identity of the criminal. I called to mind the heavy man's presence in the basement at the time of the explosion and McGroarty's information that he had been hanging about that part of the studio for some time previously. Some one had planted a cigarette case and stub to implicate Gordon, according to Kennedy's theory. Shirley certainly had had opportunity to steal the towel from the locker as well as to point suspicion toward the leading man.

In the midst of my reverie Shirley approached and passed us. He was in the garb of Mephisto. Like the others, he had not yet masked his face. A peculiar brightness in his eyes struck me and I nudged Kennedy.

"Belladonna," Kennedy explained when he was beyond earshot.

"Oh!" I remembered. "Enid told him to use it."

"What?"

I repeated the conversation as near as I could reconstruct it.

"H-m! That's a new cure for smoke-burned eyes; no cure at all."

I was unable to get any more out of Kennedy, however.

Manton I detected in the background with Phelps. The two men were arguing, as always, and it was evident that the banker was accomplishing nothing by this constant hanging about the studio. Where previously my sympathy had been with Phelps entirely, now I realized that the promoter had won me. Indeed, Manton's interest in all the affairs of picture making at this plant had been far too sincere and earnest to permit the belief that he was seeking to wreck the company or to double-cross his backer.

Millard entered the studio as I glanced about for him. He handed some sheets to Kauf, then turned to leave. I attracted Kennedy's attention.

"You don't want Millard to get away," I whispered.

Kennedy sent Mackay to stop him. The author accompanied the district attorney willingly.

"Yes, Mr. Kennedy?"

"As soon as this scene is over we're going down to the projection room; everyone concerned in the death of Miss Lamar and of Mr. Werner."

The scenario writer looked up quickly. "Do you—do you know who it is?" he asked, soberly.

"Not exactly, but I will identify the guilty person just as soon as we are assembled down in front of the screen."

Shirley had left the studio floor, apparently to go to his dressing room. Now I noticed that he returned and passed close just in time to hear Millard's question and Kennedy's answer. His eyes dilated. As he turned away his face fell. He went on into the set, but his legs seemed to wabble beneath him. I was sure it was more than the weakness resulting from his experience in the fire.

Kauf's voice, through the megaphone, echoed suddenly from wall to wall, reverberating beneath the roof.

"All ready! Everyone in the set! Masks on! Take your places!"

At a signal the orchestra struck up and the couples started to dance. It was a wonderfully colorful scene and I saw that Kauf proposed to rehearse it thoroughly, doing it over and over without the cameras until every detail reached a practiced perfection. In this I was certain he achieved results superior to Werner's slap, dash, and bang.

Then came the call for action.

"Camera!" Kauf began to bob up and down. "Into it, everybody!"

For fascination and charm this far exceeded the banquet scene which we had witnessed in the taking previously. The music was surprisingly good, so that it was impossible for the people not to get into the swing, and the result was a riotous swirling of gracefully dancing pairs; the girls, selected for their beauty, flashing half-revealed faces toward the camera, displaying eyes which twinkled through their masks in mockery at a wholly ineffectual attempt at concealment.

Enid maintained her stately carriage, but made full use of the dazzling whiteness of her teeth. Early she permitted the attentions of the cowled monk whom she knew to be her lover. Marilyn was everywhere, making mischief the best she could. Shirley stalked about in his satanic red, which would photograph black and appear even more somber on the screen.

Of course the whole was not photographed in a continuous strip from one camera position. I saw that Kauf made several long shots to catch the general atmosphere. Then he made close-up scenes of all the principals and of some of the best appearing extras. At one time he ordered a panorama effect, in which the cameras "panned," swept from one side to the other, giving a succession of faces at close range.

Finally everything was ready for the climax. Shirley had been playing a sort of Jekyll and Hyde role in which he was at once the young lawyer friend of Enid and the Black Terror. Unmasked and cornered at this function of a society terrified by the dread unknown menace, he was to make the transformation directly before the eyes of everyone, using the mythical drug which changed him from a young man of good appearance and family to the being who was a very incarnation of evil.

For once Kauf did not rehearse the scene. Shirley was obviously weakened from his experience and the director wished to spare him. All the details were shouted out through the megaphone, however, and I grasped that the action of this part of the dance was familiar to everyone; it was the big scene of the story toward which all other events had built.

Then came the familiar order. "Camera!"

At the start of this episode the orchestra was playing and the dancers were in motion. Suddenly Gordon, as the hero, strode up to Shirley and unmasked him with a few bitter words which later would be flashed upon the screen in a spoken title. Instantly a crowd gathered about, but in such a way as not to obstruct the camera view.

Cornered, seeing that flight was impossible unless he became the Black Terror and possessed the strength and fearlessness of that strange other self, Shirley drew a little vial from his breast pocket and drank the contents. Evidently he knew his Mansfield well. Slowly he began to act out the change in his appearance which corresponded with the assumption of control by the evil within. His body writhed, went through contortions which were horrible yet fascinating. It was almost as though a new fearful being was created within sight of the onlookers. Not only was the face altered, but the man's stature seemed to shrink, to lose actual inches. I thought it a wonderful exhibition.

The very next instant there came a groan from Shirley, something which at once indicated pain and realization and fear. He lost all control of himself and in a moment pitched forward upon the floor, sputtering and clutching at the empty air. Another cry broke from between his lips, a ghastly contracted shriek as treble as though from the throat of a woman.

This was no part of the story, no skillful bit of acting! It was real! Even before I had grasped the full significance of the happening Kennedy had dashed forward. The cameras still were grinding and they caught him as he kneeled at the side of the stricken man. Hardly a second afterward Mackay and I followed and were at Kennedy's side. Kauf and the others, their faces weirdly ashen, clustered about in fright.

A third time the invisible hand had struck at a member of the company. "The Black Terror," with all the horror written into that story, contained nothing as fearful as the menace to the people engaged in its production.

Shirley's skin was cold and clammy, his face almost rigid. While conscious, he was helpless. Kennedy found the little vial and examined it.

"Atropin!" he ejaculated. "Walter!" He turned to me. "Get some physostigmin, quick! Have Mackay drive you! It's—it's life or death! Here—I'll write it down! Physostigmin!"

As I raced madly out and down the stairs, Mackay at my heels, I heard a woman's scream. Marilyn! Did she think him dead?

Once in the car, headed for the nearest drug store, grasping wildly at the side or at the back of the seat every few moments as the district attorney skidded around curves and literally hurdled obstacles, I remembered a forgotten fact.

Atropin! That was belladonna, simply another name for the drug. Shirley had procured the stuff for use in his eyes. Nevertheless, he had been aware, undoubtedly, of its deadly nature. Passing by Kennedy and the rest of us, he had overheard Kennedy state that the murderer would be identified as soon as all could be assembled in the projection room. The heavy man had not cared to face justice in so prosaic a manner. With the same sense of the melodramatic which had led him to slay Stella Lamar in the taking of a scene, Werner in the photographing of another, he had preferred suicide and had selected the most spectacular moment possible for his last upon earth.

Yes, Shirley was guilty. Rather than wait the slow processes of legal justice he had attempted suicide. Now we raced to save his life, to preserve it for a more fitting end in the electric chair.

XXXI

PHYSOSTIGMIN

The first drug store we found was unable to supply us. At a second we had better luck. All in all, we were back at the Manton Pictures plant in a relatively few minutes, a remarkable bit of driving on the part of the district attorney.

Shirley was still in the set. Kennedy at once administered the physostigmin, I thought with an air of great relief.

"This is one of the rare cases in which two drugs, both highly poisonous, are definitely antagonistic," he explained. "Each, therefore, is an antidote for the other when properly administered."

Marilyn was chafing Shirley's cold hands, tears resting shamelessly upon her lids, a look of deep inexpressible fear in her expression.

"Will—will you be able to save him, Professor?" she asked, not once, but a dozen different times.

None of the rest of us spoke. We waited anxiously for the first signs of hope, the first indication that the heavy man's life might be preserved. It was wholly a question whether the physostigmin had been given to him quickly enough.

Kennedy straightened finally, and we knew that the crisis was over. Marilyn broke down completely and had to be supported to a chair. Strong, willing arms lifted Shirley to take him to his dressing room.

At that moment Kennedy stood up, raising his voice so as to demand the attention of everyone, taking charge of matters through sheer force of personality.

"I have come here this afternoon," he began, "to apprehend the man or woman responsible for the death of Miss Lamar and Mr. Werner, for the fire in the negative vault, and now for this attempt upon the life of Mr. Shirley."

Not a sound was evident as he paused, no movement save a vague, uneasy shifting of position on the part of some of those who had been on the point of leaving.

"I have indisputable evidence of the guilty person's identity, but, nevertheless, for reasons which I will explain to you I have not yet completed my identification. To do so it is necessary that certain photographed scenes be projected on the screen and that certain other matters be made perfectly clear. I am very anxious, you see, to eliminate the slightest possibility of error.

"Mr. Mackay here"—Kennedy smiled, very slightly—"is the district attorney with jurisdiction at Tarrytown. At my request, since yesterday—or, to be exact, since the death of Mr. Werner warned us that no time could be lost—he has carried a 'John Doe' warrant. Immediately following my identification of the guilty person he—or she—will be placed under arrest. The charge will be the murder of Stella Lamar by the use of poison in a manner which I will explain to you. The trial will take place at White Plains, the county seat of Westchester County, where the murder occurred. Mr. Mackay informs me that the courts there are not crowded; in fact, he personally has been able to devote most of his time to this case. Therefore the trial will be speedy and I am sure that the cold-blooded methods used by this criminal will guarantee a quick sentence and an early trip to the electric chair at Ossining. Now"—suddenly grim—"if everyone will go down to the projection room, the larger one, we will bring matters to their proper conclusion."

I imagined that Kennedy's speech was calculated to spread a little wholesome fear among the people we had considered suspects. In any case that was the result, for an outsider, from the expressions upon the various faces, might have concluded that several of them were guilty. Each seemed to start off across the studio floor reluctantly, as though afraid to obey Kennedy, yet unable to resist the fascination of witnessing the identification of the criminal, as though feeling that he or she individually might be accused, and yet unwilling to seek safety at the expense of missing Kennedy's revelation of his methods and explanation of their result.

I drew him aside as quickly as I could.

"Craig," I started, eagerly, "isn't this all unnecessary? Can't you see that Shirley is the guilty man? If you will hurry into his room with paper and pencil and get his confession before he recovers from his fright and regains his assurance—"

"What on earth, Walter!" Kennedy interrupted me with a look of surprise which I did not miss even in my excitement. "What are you driving at, anyway?"

"Why, Shirley is the criminal. He—"

"Nonsense! Wasn't an attempt made to kill him just now? Wasn't it evident that he was considered as dangerous to the unknown as Werner, the director? Hasn't he been eliminated from our calculations as surely as the man slain yesterday?"

"No!" I flushed. "Not at all, Craig! This was not an attempt at murder. There were none of the criminal's earmarks noticeable at Tarrytown or in the banquet scene."

"How do you mean, Walter?" For once Kennedy regarded me seriously.

"Why, you pointed out yourself that this unknown was exceptionally clever. The attempt on Shirley, if it were an attempt, was not clever at all."

"Why?"

"Why?" I was a little sarcastic, because I was sure of myself. "Because the poison was atropin—belladonna. That is common. I've read of any number of crimes where that was used. Do you think for a moment that the mind which figured out how to use snake venom, and botulin toxin, would descend to anything as ordinary as all this?"

"Well, if it was not an attempt at murder, what was it?"

"Suicide! It's as plain as the nose on your face. Shirley was passing us as we were standing with Millard and as you told Millard we all were to go to the projection room to identify the criminal. Therefore Shirley knew he was at the end of his rope. With the theatrical temperament, he took the poison just as he finished playing his last great scene. It—it was a sort of swan song."

"Quite a theory, Walter!" Now I knew Kennedy was unimpressed. "But, where did he get the belladonna?"

"For his eyes. After the smoke smart."

"The drug is of no use against such inflammation."

"No, but it served to brighten his eyes. Enid suggested it to him and he went out and got it. It helped him play his scenes. It gave him the glittering expression he needed in his characterization."

Again Kennedy seemed to grasp my view. He hesitated for several moments. Finally he looked up.

"If Shirley is the criminal, and if he is above using as common a drug as atropin for killing another man, then—then why isn't he above using it upon himself?"

That struck me as easy to answer. "Because if he is killing himself it is not necessary for him to cover his tracks, or to do it cleverly, and besides"—it was my big point—"he probably didn't decide to try to do it until he overheard us and realized the menace. At that time he had the belladonna in his pocket. He did not have an opportunity to procure anything else."

Kennedy grinned. "You're all wrong, Walter, and I'll show you where your reasoning is faulty. In the first place if this criminal was the type to commit suicide at the moment he thought he was about to be caught he would be the type who would reflect upon that idea beforehand. As his crimes show a great deal of previous preparation, so we may assume that he would prepare for suicide, or rather for the possibility that he might wish to attempt it. Therefore he would have something better for that purpose than atropin."

I shook my head, but Kennedy continued.

"As a matter of fact, the use of that drug is not less clever than the use of the venom or the toxin; it is more so. Stop and think a minute! The snake venom was employed in the case of Miss Lamar's death because it offered about the least possible chance of leaving telltale clues behind. The snake poison could be inflicted with a tiny scratch, and in such a way that an outcry from the girl would never be noticed. Nothing but my pocket lens caught the scratch; only the great care I used in my examination put us on the trail at all.

"Now remember how Werner met his death. The toxin gave every symptom of food poisoning. Except that we discovered the broken stem of the wineglass we would never have been able to prove the tragedy anything but accident. Very possibly we have Shirley to thank for the fact that our one clue there was not removed or destroyed.

"In both cases the selection of the poison was suited to the conditions. Therefore, if an attempt was made to kill Shirley—and of the fact I am sure—we might expect that the agent likewise would be one least apt to create suspicion. There are no portieres, no opportunity for the use of another venom; and besides, that has lost its novelty, and so its value. Similarly there is no use of food or wine in the scene, precluding something else along the toxin order.

"Our unknown realizes that the safest place to commit murder is where there is a crowd. He has followed that principle consistently. In the case of the heavy man, who has a bit of business before the camera where he drinks the contents of a little bottle, the very cleverest thing is to use belladonna, because Shirley has employed it for his eyes, and because"—maliciously, almost—"it leads immediately to the hypothesis of suicide."

"Ye gods, Craig!" A sudden thought struck me and rather terrified me. "Do you suppose Enid Faye suggested the use of the drug to Shirley as part of the scheme to kill him? Is she—"

"I prefer," Kennedy interrupted—"I prefer to suppose that the guilty person overheard her, or perhaps saw him buy it or learned in some other way that he was going to use it."

Completely taken up with this new line of thought, I failed to question Kennedy further, and it was just as well because most of the people were on their way down to the projection room, not only those we wished present, but practically everyone of sufficient importance about the studio to feel that he could intrude.

Kennedy turned to Mackay, who had taken no part in our discussion, although an interested listener. "You have the bag and all the evidence?"

"Yes!" Mackay picked it up. "Watkins, the camera man, watched it for me while Jameson and I went after that drug."

Kennedy stooped down quickly, but it was locked and had not been tampered with.

In the corridor by the dressing rooms we met Kauf, and Kennedy stopped him.

"How long would it take to make a print from the scene where Shirley took the poison?"

"We could have it ready in half an hour, in a case of grim necessity."

"Half an hour?" I exclaimed at that, in disbelief. "You couldn't begin to dry the negative in that time, Kauf."

He glanced at me tolerantly. "We make what is called a wet print; that is, we print from the negative while it is still wet and so we only have the positive to dry. Then we put it on drums in a forced draught of hot air. The result is not very good, but it's a fine thing sometimes to get a picture of a parade or some accident in a theater right after it happens."

"Will you do it for me, Kauf?" Kennedy broke in, impatiently. "This is a case of grim necessity," he added.

Kauf hurried off and we made our way across the yard to the stairs leading down into the basement and to the projection room specified by Kennedy. Here Manton was waiting, uneasy, flushed, his face gathered in a frown and his hands clenching and unclenching in his nervousness.

"Do you—do you know who it is?" he demanded.

"Not yet," Kennedy replied. "First I must marshal all my evidence."

"Who—who do you want present in the projection room?"

"Mr. Phelps, Mr. Millard, and—yourself, Mr. Manton. Miss Loring and Miss Faye. Mr. Gordon. Anyone else who wishes, if there is room."

"Phelps, Millard, Gordon, and the two girls are inside already."

"Good! We will start at once."

Manton turned, to lead the way in. At that moment there was a call from the yard. We stopped, looking up. It was Shirley.

"Wait just a minute," he cried. He was so weak that the two extra men who were helping him virtually supported his weight. On his face was a look of desperate determination. "I—I must see this too!" he gasped.

XXXII

CAMERA EVIDENCE

Coming in from the bright light of open day, the projection room seemed a gloomy, forbidding place, certainly well calculated to break down the reserve of perhaps the cleverest criminal ever pitting his skill against the science of Craig Kennedy.

It was a small room, long and not so wide, with a comparatively low ceiling. In order to obviate eye strain the walls were painted somberly and there were no light colors in evidence except for a nearly square patch of white at the farther end, the screen upon which the pictures were projected. The illumination was very dim. This was so that there would be no great contrast between the light reflected from the images cast upon the screen during pictures and the illumination in the room itself between reels; again designed to prevent strain upon the eyes of the employees whose work was the constant examination of film in various stages of its assembly.

The chairs were fastened to the floor, arranged in tiny crescents and placed so as not to interfere with the throw of the pictures from behind. The projection machines themselves, two in number in order to provide continuous projection by alternating the reels and so threading one machine while running the other, were in a fireproof booth or separate room, connected with the tiny auditorium only by slits in the wall and a sort of porthole through which the operator could talk or take his instructions.

Directly beneath the openings to the booth were a table equipped with a shaded lamp, a stand for manuscripts, and a signal button. Here the film cutters and editors sat, watching the subject upon which they worked and making notes for changes, for bits of superfluous action to be cut out, or for titles or spoken inserts to be moved. At a signal the operator could be instructed to stop at any point, or to start, or to wind back and run some given piece over again. The lights in the room were controlled from within the booth and also by a switch just at the side of the door. A telephone on the table offered a connection with any part of the studio or with the city exchanges, so that an official of the company could be reached while viewing a picture.

As we entered I tried to study the different faces, but found it a hopeless task on account of the poor light. Kennedy took his place at the little table, switching on the little shaded lamp and motioning for Mackay to set the traveling bag so he could open it and view the contents. Then Mackay took post at the door, a hand in his pocket, and I realized that the district attorney clasped a weapon beneath the cover of his clothing, and was prepared for trouble. I moved over to be ready to help Kennedy if necessary. As Kennedy took his key, unlocking the bag, it would have been possible to have heard the slightest movement of a hand or foot, the faintest gasp of breath, so tense was the silence.

First Kennedy took out the various rolls of film. Looking up, he caught the face of the operator at the opening in the wall and handed them to him one by one.

"Here are two sections of the opening of the story, scenes one to thirteen of 'The Black Terror' put together in order, but without subtitles. One is printed from the negative of the head camera man, Watkins. The other is exactly the same action as taken by the other photographer. We will run both, but wait for my signal between each piece. Understand?"

"Yes, sir!"

"Now I am giving you two rolls which contain prints of the negative from both cameras of the action at the moment of Werner's death. Those are to be projected in the same way when I give you the signal. Following that there will be two very short pieces which show the attempt upon the life of Mr. Shirley. They are being rushed through the laboratory at this moment and will be brought to you by the time we are ready for them. Finally"—Kennedy paused and as he took the rolls of negative of the snake film I could see that he hesitated to allow them out of his hands even for a few moments—"here is some negative which will be my little climax. It—it is very valuable indeed, so please be careful."

"You—you want to project the NEGATIVE?" queried the operator.

"Yes. They tell me it can be done, even with negative as old and brittle as this, if you are careful."

"I'll be careful, sir! You punch the button there once to stop and two to go. I'll be ready in a moment." As he spoke he disappeared and soon we heard the unmistakable hiss of the arcs in his machines.

Kennedy stooped and from the bag produced the little envelopes with the pocket knives and nail files, the set of envelopes with the samples of blood, the piece of silk he had cut from the portiere at Tarrytown, the tiny bits he had cut from the towel found by me in the washroom of this studio, and a microscope—the last, I guessed, for effect.

Around in the semidarkness I could see the faces as necks were craned to watch us. Kennedy's deliberateness, his air of certainty, must have struck terror home to some one person in the little audience. Often Kennedy depended upon hidden scientific instruments to catch the faint outward signs of the emotions of his people in a seance of this sort, to allow the comparison of their reactions in the course of his review of the evidence, to give him what amounted to a very sure proof of the one person's guilt. The very absence of some such preparation indicated to me the extent of his confidence.

At length he began his little lecture, for all the world as though this were one of his classes at the University, as though there were at stake some matter of chemical reaction.

"I need not tell you, ladies and gentlemen, that this is a highly scientific age in which we live." His tones were leisurely, businesslike, cool. "Your own profession, the moving picture, with all its detail of photography and electricity, its blending of art and drama and mechanics, is indicative of that, but"—a pause for emphasis—"it is of my own profession I wish to talk just now, the detection and prevention of crime.

"Criminals as a whole were probably the very first class of society to realize the full benefit of modern science. Banks and business institutions, the various detective and police forces, all grades and walks of life have been put to it to keep abreast of the development of scientific crime. So true has this been that it is a matter of common belief with many people that the hand of the law may be defied with impunity, that justice may be cheated with absolute certainty, just so long as a guilty man or woman is sufficiently clever and sufficiently careful.

"Fortunately, the real truth is quite the reverse. Science has extended itself in many dimensions of space. With the use of a microscope, for instance, a whole new world is opened up to the trained detective.

"Everyone knows now that the examination of hands and fingers is an infallible aid in the identification of criminals and in the proof of the presence of a suspect at the scene of a crime—I refer to fingerprints, of course. But fingerprints are only one small detail in this department of investigation. Our criminals know that gloves must be worn, or any smooth surface wiped so as to remove the prints. In that way they believe they cheat the microscope or the pocket lens.

"As a matter of fact few people have thought of another way of gaining evidence from the finger tips, but it is a method possible to the scientist, and is not only practicable but exceedingly effective. In time it will be recognized by all specialists in crime. Now I refer to the deposits under the finger nail.

"Indeed, it is surprising how many things find their way under the nail and into the corners of the cuticle." Kennedy indicated the files and pocket knives visible in the shaded square of light before him. "The value of examining finger-nail deposits becomes evident when we realize that everyone carries away in that fashion a sample of every bit of material he handles. To touch a piece of cloth, even lightly, will result in the catching of a few of its fibers. Similarly, the finger nails will deposit either a small or large portion of their accumulation upon such things as the knife blades or files used to clean them; and there identification still is possible. Nothing in the world is too infinitesimal for use as evidence beneath the microscope.

"In classifying these accumulations"—Kennedy paused and the silence in the little room was death-like—"we may say that there are some which are legitimate and some which are not. It is the latter which concern us now. The first day we were here at the studio, just four days ago now, and immediately following the murder of Miss Lamar, Mr. Jameson discovered a towel in the washroom on the second floor of the office building. On that towel there were spots of Chinese yellow, make-up, as though it had been used to wipe a face or hands by some actor or actress. Those spots were unimportant. There were others, however, of an entirely different nature, together with the mark of blood and a stain which showed that a hypodermic needle had been cleaned upon the towel before it was thrown in the basket."

Kennedy leaned forward. His eyes traveled from face to face. "That towel was a dangerous clue." Now there was a new grim element in his voice. "That towel alone has given me the evidence on which I shall obtain a conviction in this case. To-day I let it be known that it was in my possession and the guilty man or woman understood at once the value it would be to me. In order to gain additional clues I purposely gave the impression that I had yet to analyze either the spots or the trace of blood. I wanted the towel stolen, and for that purpose I placed the bag containing it in a locker and left the locker unguarded. I coated the towel with a substance which would cause discomfort and alarm—itching salve—not with the idea that anyone would be foolish enough to go about scratching before my eyes, but with the idea of making that person believe that such was my purpose and with the idea of driving him—or her—to washing his hands at once and, more, with the idea of forcing him or scaring him into cleaning his fingernails.

"I succeeded. On one of these files or knife blades I have found and identified the fibers of that towel. I do not yet know the person, but I know the mark placed by Mackay on the outside of the little envelope, and when I tell Mackay the mark he will name the guilty person."

"Mr. Kennedy!" Manton spoke up, impulsively, "every towel in the studio is the same. I bought them all at the same time. The fibers would all be alike. You have named seven people to me, including myself, as possibly guilty of these—these murders. Your conclusions may be very unjust—and may lead to a serious miscarriage of justice."

Kennedy was unperturbed. "This particular towel, in addition to the itching salve, was thoroughly impregnated with a colorless chemical which changed the composition of the fibers in a way easily distinguishing them from the others under the microscope. Do you see, Mr. Manton?"

The promoter had no more to say.

"Now what connection has the towel with the case? Simply this!" Kennedy picked up one of the tiny pieces he had cut out of it. "The poison used to kill Miss Lamar was snake venom." He paused while a little murmur went through his audience, the first sound I had detected. "These spots on the towel are antivenin. The venom itself is exceedingly dangerous to handle. The guilty man—or woman—took no chances, but inoculated himself with antivenin, protection against any chance action of the poison. The marks on the towel are the marks made by the needle used by that person in taking the inoculation.

"If you will follow me closely you will understand the significance of this. Miss Lamar was killed by the scratch of a needle secreted in the portieres through which she came, playing the scene in Mr. Phelps's library. That I will prove to you when I show you the film. The night following her death some one broke into the room there at Tarrytown and removed the needle. In removing the needle that person scratched himself, or herself. On the portieres I found some tiny spots of blood." Kennedy paused to hold up the bit of heavy silk. "I analyzed them and found that the blood serum had changed in character very subtly. I demonstrated that the blood of the person who took the needle contained antivenin, and if necessary I can prove the blood to come from the same individual who wiped the needle on the towel in the studio."

Kennedy pressed the button before him, twice. "Now I want you to see, actually see Miss Lamar meet her death."

The lights went out, then the picture flashed on the screen before us, revealing the gloom and mystery of the opening scene of "The Black Terror." We saw the play of the flashlight, finally the fingers and next the arm of Stella as she parted the curtains. In the close-up we witnessed the repetition of her appearance, since the film was simply spliced together, not "matched" or trimmed. Following came all the action down to the point where she collapsed over the figure of Werner on the floor. Before the camera man stopped, Manton rushed in and was photographed bending over her.

Kennedy's voice was dramatically tense, for not one of us but had been profoundly affected by the reproduction of the tragedy.

"Did you notice the terror in her face when she cried out? Was that terror, really? If you were watching, you would have detected a slight flinch as she brushed her arm up against the silk. For just a moment she was not acting. It was pain, not pretended terror, which made her scream. The devilish feature to this whole plot was the care taken to cover just that thing-her inevitable exclamation. Now watch closely as I signal the operator to run the same action from the other camera. Notice the gradual effect of the poison, how she forces herself to keep going without realization of the fact that death is at hand, how she collapses finally through sheer inability to maintain her control of herself a moment longer."

During the running of the second piece the tense silence in the room was ghastly. Who was the guilty person? Who possessed such amazing callousness that an exhibition of this sort brought no outcry?

"Now"—Kennedy glanced around in the dim light, switched on between the running of the different strips—"I'm going to project the banquet scenes and show you the manner of Werner's death."

Scene after scene of the banquet flashed before us. Here the cutter had not been sure just what Kennedy wanted and had spliced up everything. We saw the marvelous direction of Werner, who little realized that it was to be his last few moments on earth, and we grasped the beauty and illusion of the set caused by the mirrors and the man's skill in placing his people. Yet there was not a sound, because we knew that this was a tragedy, a grim episode in which there was no human justification whatever.

Werner rose at his place. He proposed his toast. He drank the contents of his glass. Then, his expression changed to wonderment and from that to fear and realization, and he dropped to the floor.

Kennedy's voice, interrupting, seemed to me to come from a great distance, so powerfully was I affected by the bit of film.

"The poison used to kill Mr. Werner was botulin toxin, selected because its effects could not be diagnosed as anything other than ordinary food poisoning. When we look at the print from the second camera's negative you will notice how quickly it acted. It was the pure toxin, placed in his glass before the wine was poured."

Once more the unfortunate director's death was reproduced before us.

"Struck down," exclaimed Craig, "as though by some invisible lightning bolt, without mercy, without a chance, without the slightest bit of compunction! Why? I'll tell you. Because he suspected, in fact knew, who the guilty person was. Because he followed that person out to Tarrytown the night the needle was removed from the portieres. Because he was a menace to that person's life!"

Kennedy turned to the operator. "Have those other scenes come down?"

"Yes, sir!"

"All right!" Kennedy faced the rest of us again. "There was, or rather is, another person who suspects the identity of the criminal. To-day an attempt was made upon the life of Shirley. Shirley will not tell whom he suspects because he has no definite proof, yet for the mere fact that he suspects he narrowly escaped the fate of Stella Lamar and Werner." Kennedy pressed the button. "Witness the effort to kill the man playing the part of the Black Terror."

The print was terribly bad, in appearance almost a "dupe," due to the speed with which it had been made. Nevertheless the two very brief scenes rushed through for this showing were more absorbingly thrilling, more graphic than anything ever to be seen even in a news reel at a movie theater.

"Notice!" Kennedy exclaimed. "He puts his hand in one pocket, he fumbles, hesitates, then finds the bottle in the other. Whoever put the poison in the vial replaced it in the wrong pocket. The film shows that very clearly. The camera proves that it was not an attempt at suicide. Yet the poison used was belladonna, selected because this victim had purchased some and because it would seem sure, therefore, that he had committed suicide."

We sat in silence, listening, horrified.

"There is still another matter," Kennedy went on, after a moment. "The fire in the negative vault this morning was incendiary. I have proved to the satisfaction of several of us that a bomb was constructed of wet phosphorus and old film and placed in the vault by trickery four days ago, the same day Stella Lamar was killed. Through a miscalculation the phosphorus was slow in drying and the fire did not occur until to-day. Thanks to that fact I have in my possession a bit of negative which the murderer very likely wished to have destroyed; in fact, I believe its destruction to be the motive in planning the fire in the vault." He faced the operator. "Ready to run the negative?"

"Yes, sir!"

Kennedy pressed the button and when the projection machine threw its picture upon the screen I saw something such as I had never imagined before. Everything was black which should have been white and everything white which should have been black. The two extremes shaded into each other in weird fashion. In fact it was uncanny to watch a negative projected and I followed, fascinated.

"This is a film made with the co-operation of Doctor Nagoya of the Castleton Institute and I am told by Mr. Manton that it is one of the finest snake pictures ever made." Kennedy spoke fast, so that we would get the full benefit of his explanation and so that it would not be necessary to subject the negative to the wear and tear of the sprocket wheels in the projection machine again. "I am running this for you to show you the action of the rattlesnake, whose venom was used to kill Miss Lamar, and to give you an idea of the source of the murderer's knowledge of snake poison."

At this moment Doctor Nagoya, whom I could barely recognize in the inverted photography, seized one of the rattlers. It was a close-up and we could see the reptile dart out its forked tongue, seeking to get at the hands of the Japanese, locked firmly about its neck. Then another man walked into the picture, holding a jar. At once the snake struck at the glass. As it did so it was possible to see drops of the venom projected into the jar.

Other details followed and there were views of other sorts and breeds of snakes, from the poisonous to the most harmless. The principal scene, however, had been the one showing the venom.

"Lights up!"

The operator threw the switch again, stopping the film and at the same time lighting the projection room. Kennedy stepped forward and turned to face us.

"There was this negative in the vaults." He spoke rapidly. "It bore a certain name on the film, as editor. Some one knew that proof of the possession of this knowledge of snakes might prove a powerful link in the chain against him. If that had been a positive instead of a negative, you would have recognized Doctor Nagoya's 'assistant.' There was a double motive in blowing that vault—to destroy the company and to protect himself. In fact, all the rest of the negative was destroyed. Only by chance I saved this piece—the very one that he wanted to destroy."

Everyone waited breathlessly for Kennedy's next move. Suddenly Kennedy flushed. I could see that he became genuinely angry.

"In this room," he exclaimed, "there sits the most unscrupulous, cold-blooded, inhuman being I have ever known. Yet he maintains silence, believing still that he can defy the scientific evidence of his crimes. I have not yet mentioned, however, the real proof of his guilt."

Kennedy picked up one of the little envelopes, one which contained a blood smear. "During the explosion this morning a number of you were cut by falling glass. You will remember that I bound up your cuts, carefully cleansing each one and wiping away the blood. That gave me a sample of the blood of everyone but Miss Loring and Mr. Shirley. Subsequently, without their knowledge, I obtained a sample from each of them. Thus I have a specimen from everyone concerned, or possibly concerned in the murders."

He glanced about, but even now there was no telltale revelation.

"I have analyzed these and one shows that the person from whom I obtained the sample has been inoculated with antivenin. The mark on the envelope is the same as the mark on the envelope containing the towel fibers, a double proof. Furthermore, I am prepared to show that it is the same blood as the blood upon the portiere." He faced me. All at once his voice carried the sharpness of a whip. "Walter, relieve Mackay at the door and take his weapon. Let no one out. Mackay, come here!"

An instant later the district attorney leaned over. He glanced at the mark indicated by Kennedy, then whispered a name. The next instant Kennedy rose. "I thought so," he muttered.

Raising his voice, he addressed all of us.

"Here is a man who thought crime so long that he believed he could get away with—murder! Not only did he commit a second murder and plan a third to cover the first, but he planted evidence against nearly all of you. He dropped the ampulla in McGroarty's car to implicate any one of four people. He coolly stole a cigarette case to put it where it would be found after the film fire and clinch suspicion.

"For all this, what justification has he had? Jealousy, jealousy of the narrowest, most primitive, sort actuated him. Not only was he willing to kill Stella Lamar, but he sought to destroy every foot of negative in which she had appeared. He was jealous of her success, greater than his, jealous of her interest in other men, greater than her interest in him. Her divorce was maneuvered directly by him simply because he thought it would hurt and humiliate her, and for no other reason.

"When nothing seemed to stop her, on her upward climb, when he realized that she was as ambitious as he was and that her position in the picture world alone interested her, he sought by devious means, by subtle schemes, by spreading dissatisfaction and encouraging dissension, to wreck the company which had made her. At the end—he killed her—waiting craftily until she was at the very climax of her finest piece of work, the opening scenes of 'The Black Terror.'"

There was bitterness in Kennedy's tones. "Before, I would not believe that a man—"

Suddenly the projection room was plunged into darkness. Some one had pushed the wall switch close by me. I backed into the doorway, raising my weapon to resist any attempt to escape.

Almost at the same instant there were the sounds of a struggle. Kennedy had dashed forward in the darkness, sure of the position of his man, unafraid.

A scream I recognized from the throat of Enid. I groped for the switch, but the operator in the booth anticipated me. In the first burst of illumination I saw that Kennedy had forced his antagonist back over the front row of chairs. Almost I heard the crack of the man's spine.

I caught a glimpse of the man's face and gasped at the murderous rage as he struggled and strove to break Kennedy's iron grip.

Enid was the first at Kennedy's side. With an expression I failed to analyze until long afterward she sought to claw at the murderer's unprotected features, twitching now in impotent fury.

"You wrote that note for her to meet you at the tearoom," Kennedy muttered, eyes narrowing grimly, "knowing she would be dead before that time. You protected yourself against the poisoned needle in the portieres—but—your own blood convicts you—Millard!"

THE END

Notes

DATE:

Notes

DATE: ....

Notes

DATE: ....

Notes

DATE:

Notes

DATE: ....

Notes

DATE: ....

Notes

DATE: ....

Notes

DATE:

Notes

DATE:

Notes

DATE:

Notes

DATE:

Notes

DATE: ....

Notes

DATE:

Notes

DATE: ....

Notes

DATE: ....

Notes

DATE: ....

Notes

DATE: ....

Notes

DATE: ....

Notes

DATE: ....

Notes

DATE: ....

Printed in Great Britain
by Amazon

38032931R00123